Eyes Wide O...

By Lucy Felthouse

Text Copyright 2019 © Lucy Felthouse.

All Rights Reserved.

With the exception of quotes used in reviews, this book may not be reproduced or used in whole or in part by any means existing without written permission from the aforementioned author.

Warning: The unauthorised reproduction or distribution of this copyrighted work is illegal. No part of this book may be scanned, uploaded or distributed via the Internet or any other means, electronic or print, without the author's written permission.

This book is a work of fiction and any resemblance to persons, living or dead is purely coincidental. The characters are productions of the author's imagination and used fictitiously.

Table of Contents

Chapter One

Chapter Two

Chapter Three

Chapter Four

Chapter Five

Chapter Six

Chapter Seven

Chapter Eight

Chapter Nine

Chapter Ten

Chapter Eleven

Chapter Twelve

Chapter Thirteen

Chapter Fourteen

Chapter Fifteen

Chapter Sixteen

Chapter Seventeen

Chapter Eighteen

Chapter Nineteen

Chapter Twenty

Chapter Twenty-one

Chapter Twenty-two

Chapter Twenty-three

Chapter Twenty-four

Chapter Twenty-five

Chapter Twenty-six

Chapter Twenty-seven

Chapter Twenty-eight

Chapter Twenty-nine

Chapter Thirty

Chapter Thirty-one

Epilogue

About the Author

If You Enjoyed Eyes Wide Open

Chapter One

Fiona Gillespie wiped a damp cloth half-heartedly over the surface of the bar. It was a pointless exercise. The pub's fittings and fixtures were so old that no amount of scrubbing would remove the grime that had been ingrained in the wood over the decades. That and the next time she served one of the old drunks who frequented the place, it'd just get beer spilled on it again.

Glancing at her surroundings in distaste, Fiona stifled a derisive snort when she caught sight of the swinging pub sign through the window. It had never really registered before, but *The Royal Oak?* There was nothing remotely royal about the pub in London's East End where she worked. If an actual royal—even a minor one—so much as stepped foot across the threshold, they'd run screaming in the other direction. A shame, really, as a chance to try to woo Prince Harry would not go amiss. She was sure those mischievous eyes and smile hid a multitude of sexy sins. His grandmother would *not* approve. And besides, he was spoken for now.

Abandoning her cloth with a sigh, she reached for a newspaper one of the patrons had left behind. There was hardly anyone in, as usual, so no glasses to collect, tables to wipe, or bowls of nuts to refill. A flick through the paper was her only source of entertainment. Or at least the only thing to stop her going completely out of her mind with boredom.

It wasn't quite where she'd seen herself when she'd decided to take a chance and move to London after graduating from university. But while she figured out her next career move—or *any* career move—this would have to do. It served a purpose—paying her a paltry wage, just enough to cover the rent and bills on her scummy flat, and food. There really wasn't much left after that, so her social life mainly consisted of vegging in front of the TV with her flatmates.

They'd club together their miniscule amount of disposable income to buy some cheap, supermarket own-brand lager and swap stories, either about their pasts or about how their current situation was just temporary—just a stepping stone on their way to success, to high-flying, ridiculously well-paid jobs in the banking world, the publishing industry, in PR, advertising, acting, production, tourism… The list went on.

Fiona was absolutely determined to get a foot on the career ladder. She'd rather scurry back home to her parents in Birmingham with her tail between her legs than stay in this dump for much longer. The only trouble was, the others at least knew what they were aiming for, which particular ladder they were trying to grab hold of. She'd graduated with a first class honours in creative writing and didn't have a clue what to do with the damn degree now she had it.

Nobody got approached just for having a degree in creative writing, then were given a ton of money and told to sit down and write a book. It simply didn't work like that—more was the pity. Even the world's most famous and successful writers had had to start somewhere. And she wasn't sure fiction writing was the way to go, anyway.

A cough, accompanied by a whiff of stale smoke and booze,

alerted her to the presence of a customer.

Fixing a smile on her face, she turned to him and said politely, "What can I get you?"

A white-haired, grizzled old guy with yellowing teeth—the teeth he still had, anyway—squinted at her. "Pint, if you're not too busy reading the bleeding newspaper."

Holding the smile so firmly in place it hurt her now-gritted teeth, she took the proffered glass and filled it. After placing it back on the bar, she picked up the money that had been left. The exact right amount. This guy bought enough pints to know. She murmured her thanks as she deposited the money in the till, but she needn't have bothered. The grumpy old sod was already halfway back to his table, precious beer in hand.

She rolled her eyes. Then, after double checking there was nothing that needed doing, shifted her attention back to the newspaper, figuring it was better than wondering about a career she couldn't even imagine.

As it happened, the paper wasn't all that engaging. It was several days out of date, so she knew about all the big news pieces already, and the weather and TV listings were now obsolete. But her interest was piqued when she reached the jobs section. She'd never looked in this particular publication for jobs before, thinking the online searches she did on various websites were more targeted, more relevant. But then, how could you target a role you didn't even know you wanted?

Skimming through the ads, she immediately dismissed many of them. She had no wish—or the qualifications—to drive an HGV, look after sick or old people, cold call, sell advertising, work in retail or become a model. But amongst all that was something interesting. Something that maybe, just maybe, she could do.

She wasn't entirely sure what being a PR assistant entailed, but it sounded like a very posh job title, and she could sure as hell tick the box of the phrase in the ad that had caught her eye in the first place. *We're looking for someone with creative writing skills.*

As she read through the information again, excitement bubbled in her stomach. The role was at a top London hotel—in Mayfair, no less—offered live-in accommodation, a generous starting salary, access to all the hotel's amenities and, best of all, career progression. It was clear they wouldn't employ just anybody and, if Fiona was honest with herself, they were probably looking for someone with more experience than her—which wasn't difficult—but she had to give it a go. She had nothing to lose. If she didn't get it, then she'd have gained some valuable interview experience—if she even got that far, that was—and if she did, well, then she'd have well and truly grabbed the bottom rung of the career ladder she'd been striving for.

It was only on her third read-through, when she was mentally picking out key words and phrases she could use to help tailor her CV to the role and to write a spectacular covering letter, that she noticed the closing date for applications.

For fuck's sake! How typical was that? The only job advert she'd seen since arriving in the capital that had got her genuinely fired up, and she'd missed the bloody date by one day. One. Single. Day.

Barely stopping herself from screwing up the page and throwing it across the room in a fit of temper, Fiona stepped away and took a long drink from the pint of Coke she had stashed behind the bar. Just as she replaced the glass, another customer came up—one of the few she actually liked.

"Hello, Bob," she said pleasantly, her smile genuine this time. "How are you?"

"Fine and dandy thanks, love. And yourself?"

She shrugged. "Yeah, I'm all right, thanks."

Bob narrowed his eyes. "Well, that didn't sound very convincing. Want to tell me about it while you're pouring my pint?"

Unable to help the grin that took over her face, Fiona replied, "Subtle, Bob, very subtle. Being nice on the surface, but underneath it all you're really saying, 'Hurry up and pour my drink, wench!'"

Clutching a hand to his chest, Bob widened his eyes and shaped his lips into a perfect 'o' shape. "What, me?" After a beat, his expression morphed into a good-natured grin to rival her own. "What can I say? I am a nice guy, but I like my beer. Seriously, though, tell me what's wrong."

As she slotted the pint glass into place beneath the pump and began filling it, she found herself wanting to tell him. She wasn't in the habit of chatting with the customers, and they weren't the sort who wanted to prop up the bar all day and regale her with their life stories—thank God. She was more accustomed to pouring pints, handing over packets of crisps and pork scratchings, taking money, and giving change with nothing more than basic manners and a smile.

But what harm could it do? She didn't know the guy beyond these four walls, didn't know what he did for a living—though by the looks of him he was getting close to retirement age. Maybe he could help, give her some advice? And even if he blabbed to her boss, the pub landlord, Cyril, it wouldn't matter. He probably wouldn't care either way. Bar staff were ten a penny—he'd have the role filled within a day.

Plus, underneath all that gruff, abrupt bluster, she had an inkling that Cyril was actually human—and smart. He'd have known from day one of taking her on—from the moment he interviewed her, even—that she wasn't in the job for the long haul. And as long as he had someone at least vaguely competent behind the bar, it didn't make the slightest difference to him.

Fiona jerked her head in the direction of the newspaper. "Just found a great job in that crummy old newspaper."

"Why's that a problem?" he replied with a frown.

She slid his pint onto the bar, then wrinkled her nose. "Emphasis on *old*. It's a fantastic bloody role, but the closing date for applications was yesterday. I'm gutted. I've been treading water a bit since I've been in London because I didn't know what direction I wanted to go, career-wise, and that could have set me on the perfect path. Reckon I'd have been good at it, too."

Bob handed over the money, then took a sip of his beer and swallowed it. After a moment, a thoughtful expression on his face, he said, "Wouldn't hurt to send your application anyway, would it? I'm guessing you can send it by email? Send it today and explain you only just saw the advertisement and know the closing date has passed, but you're so interested in the role, you thought you'd apply anyway. Who knows? Maybe they'll be impressed by your enthusiasm and put you in the running. For what it's worth, I reckon you should try. You've got nothing to lose."

"Yeah." She ran a hand through her hair. Then she punched numbers into the till, opened it, put Bob's cash in the drawer and retrieved his change. "I was thinking the same thing myself about the job before I realised I'd missed the closing date. I think I will. After all, if I don't apply, I won't even be in with a chance. And even the tiniest of chances is better than nothing!"

"Better than working here, too."

Passing over his change, she said, "How do you know? You don't even know what the job's for."

"Doesn't matter. It's got to be better than here. Besides, I've always thought you were too good for this place. Too damn smart to be pulling pints—though you've got that down to a fine art, I must say." He took another sip and winked at her over the rim of the glass. "Still," he added, "if you do end up getting that job, or any other, I will be sad to see you go. Brighten up the place, pretty girl like you does. Anyway, let me know how you get on. Good luck!"

With another broad grin and a wink, Bob stuffed the coins into his pocket and sauntered over to take a seat by the window.

She watched him for a moment or two, pondering what he'd said. Then, her mind made up, she grabbed the newspaper and tore out the advert before folding it carefully and putting it in her pocket. There were only a couple more hours of her shift to go. As soon as she got home, she'd dust off her creative writing skills, tart up her

CV, craft an awesome covering letter and ping them over on an email.

The Portmannow Hotel wouldn't know what had hit it.

Chapter Two

Fiona spent the next few days in a blur of working, doing her share of chores in the flat—which this week included shopping and cooking—and catching some sleep when she could. She also spent an inordinate amount of time checking her emails, hoping for a reply from The Portmannow Hotel.

When it came, just three days after sending the application—which to her felt like three weeks—she was too scared to open it. She was so sure it was going to be a very polite *thanks, but no thanks* that she let out a squeak and quickly shut her laptop lid.

One of her flatmates, Gary, glanced at her from the other easy chair in their shared living room and raised an enquiring eyebrow. "What are you squeaking at, Fi? It sounded like you just squashed a mouse in your laptop."

As heat bloomed in her cheeks, she shook her head and tried to adopt a nonchalant tone. "Oh, it's nothing."

Now both of Gary's eyebrows inched towards his hairline. "Really? I'm not convinced, 'cause usually you're as cool as a cucumber. Come on. What's got you all het up?"

She sighed. This was the exact reason she hadn't told anyone—except Bob—about the job application. Her flatmates would undoubtedly have been supportive, but rejection was bad enough without the humiliation of them knowing about it too. Then coming out with the usual "oh, there'll be other jobs" or "you're too good for them anyway" or even "well, it's their loss".

"I applied for a job."

"Uh, yeah? Isn't that kind of the point of being here?"

"Well, yes, but this one's special. Or it was, anyway. It's a PR role at a swish Mayfair hotel. I saw the ad in a newspaper a few days ago. Trouble is, I'd already missed the closing date for applications by the time I saw the ad, but I sent my CV and a covering letter anyway."

"Good for you. But I'm still failing to see the problem."

"Well, they've emailed me." She crept her hands across the laptop and gripped its edges, as though it would spring open by itself if she didn't.

"So read it!"

"I can't! They're bound to have said no. I was late sending in an application, and I've no experience."

Gary shook his head, unfolded his lanky frame from the chair and came to perch on the arm of Fiona's. "They may also have said yes, but you'll never find out while you've got your frigging laptop in a death grip. Come on. Open it up. Or give it here and I'll read it for you."

"No!" She cradled the machine to her chest, then reluctantly placed it back on her lap. "All right… I'll look. But if it's a no, can we just move on and forget about it, please? No sympathy. Just go back to what we were doing before this conversation even started? And please don't mention it to the others, either."

He held his hands up in supplication. "You have my word."

Nodding slowly, Fiona carefully lifted the laptop lid and waited for the screen to flicker back to life. After a second or two, her inbox reappeared, now with that particular unread email sitting at the top, seeming to scream at her to open it.

Taking a deep breath, she did just that. It took all her effort not to squeeze her eyes shut as the words filled the screen. She felt the heat from Gary's body as he leaned in closer to read it, too, but she forced herself to ignore him and focus on the message.

Dear Ms. Gillespie,

Thank you for your recent application for the PR assistant's role at The Portmannow Hotel. Having read your covering letter and CV, we would very much like to invite you to attend an interview at our premises. Are you available at 2.30 p.m. on Wednesday?

We look forward to hearing from you.

Kind Regards,

Jane Cresswell

Human Resources Department, The Portmannow Hotel

Gary reacted before her brain had even processed what she'd just read. "Wow, that's fantastic, Fiona. Well done! See? There must have been something in your CV or letter they liked, because despite you missing the deadline, they still want to see you."

"Th-they want to see me." She blinked dazedly. Then it suddenly hit her. "Holy fuck, *they want to see me!*"

"Yes! Come on. Pull yourself together, woman, and email them back, letting them know you'll be there on Wednesday." He nudged her in the ribs with his elbow, grinning.

As she playfully nudged him back, she was aware her own face had broken out into an enormous smile too, but she tried to rein in her excitement. Just because she had an interview didn't mean she had the job. Not even close. A job like that, at a place like that, with those benefits and career prospects, was incredibly desirable. She'd have a ton of competition—and tough competition, at that. But it was all good interview experience and, there was that sentiment again—she had nothing to lose.

Dear Ms. Cresswell,

Thank you for your email. I would be delighted to attend an interview with you at 2.30 p.m. on Wednesday. Thank you for the opportunity.

Kind Regards,

Fiona Gillespie

"Does that sound all right?" She turned the laptop so Gary could read her reply more easily.

After a moment he replied, "Yep, looks great to me. Enthusiastic but not desperate, polite and professional. Damn, you really know how to work that degree of yours, don't you, gorgeous? I think I'm gonna have to get you to have a look at my CV."

"Let me just send this, and I'd be happy to." After reading the email through one more time, just to make sure she hadn't made a silly mistake or a typo, she gritted her teeth and hit send. Okay, it was gone. She was officially going for an interview for a job—a brilliant job! One that could launch an exciting and lucrative career—

Shaking her head to rid herself of all the thoughts bubbling around in her mind, she looked up at Gary. "I mean it, you know. I could do with something to distract me now, I'm so bloody excited. Do you want to email me your CV and I'll go through it with you? I'm sure there are some improvements that can be made."

"Yeah, sure. Hang on. I'll grab my iPad. Shall we celebrate with a cup of tea?"

"Oh yes, good idea. Go on. You get your iPad and email me the file. I'll make the tea."

***

Fiona stepped carefully from the Tube car and scurried over to the wall to avoid being pushed and shoved by the rushing crowds. She'd deliberately left plenty of time to get from her dump of a flat in Leytonstone to Mayfair, determined not to arrive at The Portmannow Hotel sweaty, stressed and flustered.

After emerging from Bond Street Station, she stood out of the way of the throngs as she retrieved the map she'd printed out to get her from here into the heart of Mayfair. It wasn't an area she knew, aside from having done some shopping—mostly window shopping, but also a smidge of the real kind on Oxford Street, Bond Street and Piccadilly—and admired the luxury hotels on Park Lane. It was barely a ten-minute walk to the hotel, nestled in a spot between Grosvenor and Berkeley Squares, and she still had fifty minutes until her interview—ample time to get there, have a little look at the adjacent buildings and get a feel for the area, then head inside and announce herself.

Tracing the route with her finger as she memorised it, Fiona nodded, then put the piece of paper back into her handbag.

Right. Time to get this show on the road.

She looked up and around, as well as ahead, as she walked, admiring the beautiful, regal-looking buildings, exclusive boutiques and restaurants and garages selling high-end luxury and sports cars. It was like a complete other world, particularly when compared to the grimy, run-down area of the city she'd just come from.

God, what would the interviewers—she assumed there'd be more than one—make of her, a recent graduate with a broad Brummy accent? Yes, she'd made a serious effort with her appearance. She wore a beautiful outfit she'd splashed out on when arriving in London, seeing it as an investment in her career, in her future, but she couldn't hide who she was—just a regular girl from the Midlands. How was she supposed to fit in with the other staff, never mind the clientele, who would all be filthy rich and speak in posh, upper-class British accents?

Pausing on the opposite side of the square from the hotel, she chastised herself for being so ridiculous. For one, they knew perfectly well where she was from. It was there on her CV in black and white. Secondly, the very idea that all the hotel staff and clientele would sound the same was ludicrous. Both the employees and the patrons would come from all over the world. It was bound to be a veritable melting pot of appearances, backgrounds, voices and accents. One slim, blonde Brummy was not going to stand out, not even a little bit.

Her silly ideas knocked on the head, Fiona moved across the square, drinking in the lavish sights before her. Damn, she hadn't even crossed the threshold yet and already she was impressed. The square was quiet—especially by London standards—since it was well off the beaten tourist trail, and it was full of beautiful red-bricked buildings with white stone window frames, balconies and porticos.

The hotel itself was the epitome of style from pavement to rooftop, in the same red and white as the surrounding buildings, with elegant railings at the very top, suggesting a roof garden. Maybe even a pool, though she felt that was unlikely, given they were in England, not Ecuador. But then again, maybe it was a heated swimming pool.

Smiling, she stood in the shade of a large tree with an artistic-looking fountain built around it, and watched as a sleek, gunmetal-grey Mercedes purred its way up to the front doors. It had barely stopped when a smartly-attired attendant zipped over and opened the rear car door. Following a gesture, another attendant scurried around to the other side and opened that door, too.

Fiona shouldn't have been surprised, not really, but her mouth dropped open as she realised just who was getting out of the car. After glancing around to make sure no one was paying any attention to her, she watched the world-famous footballer and his equally famous wife emerge from the vehicle. They came together at the base of the steps up to the entrance, where the wife took her husband's arm and they entered the hotel, without a second thought for the luggage they'd left in the car.

They didn't need to give it a thought, Fiona realised, as the hotel staff had it well under control. The designer luggage was placed carefully onto a trolley and taken inside. It would no doubt be whizzed up to the penthouse suite in a service elevator and be in the room before its owners, maybe even with snappily-dressed, highly-efficient housekeeping staff unpacking it for them.

Fiona shook her head, glad she'd allowed herself this extra time in order to simply *observe*. Only now had it really sunk in precisely what a lavish world she was about to enter. Yes, this place was cosmopolitan, but they'd still expect the very highest standards from their staff—even those who didn't have regular contact with the clientele. She'd have to tread carefully, do her very best to impress, show she was keen to learn, determined to get it perfect. Let them know she was a good choice for the role.

This was an amazing opportunity, and she wanted to give herself the best chance at success.

Chapter Three

Fiona opened her bag and pulled out the bottle of water she had stashed in there. Holding it away from her body—she didn't want to end up with splash marks on her gorgeous clothes—she twisted off the cap and took several long swallows of the cool liquid. It probably wouldn't stop her throat going dry with nerves once she got inside the interview room, but at least she wouldn't get dehydrated.

She replaced the bottle, then whipped out her compact mirror and did a quick check of her makeup, which was fine. Finally, knowing she didn't have any more time to waste, she tugged at her clothes to make sure they were straight and crease-free, and walked towards the hotel.

One of the door attendants she'd seen buzzing around the Mercedes was there, and he moved to open the door for her, giving a polite nod.

"Thank you," she said, flashing him a warm smile and passing through into the lobby.

The first impression that hit her was one of space. *Damn,* this was just the reception area and it was cavernous. And yet it was far from sparse. Off to the left side was what appeared to be a sitting area, which was probably also used for informal meetings. It was carpeted in a lush dark purple, with round, very stylish, light wood tables and comfortable-looking black leather chairs.

To her right were a couple of elevators and a large archway, which, according to the sign over it, led to the spa and gym facilities. She suspected it was situated just inside the main doors because it was open to non-guests too.

The flooring was marble, and large potted plants and trees were dotted around, drawing her gaze to the beautiful wooden panelling on the walls, and the paintings hung at what she suspected were far from random intervals. The whole place had an authentic, old-fashioned feel to it, but more like it had been decorated to look that way, rather than because the décor had been like that for decades. It all appeared fresh and immaculate, and she didn't envy the no doubt huge team of people employed to keep it that way.

Finally, she turned her attention to the reception desk. It was set in an alcove, with a wooden surface that matched the wall panelling and had stunning flower arrangements perched at each end. There was still plenty of room between, however, and no less than three pretty receptionists waited there to deal with guests—or should she say two pretty ones and one handsome one, since there were two women and a man.

Pulling in a deep breath and straightening her posture, she moved from where she'd been loitering off to one side of the main doors and walked to the desk—aware how easy it would be to tumble off her shoes on the smooth surface beneath her feet. It was the sort of place where people would rush to her aid and make sure she was okay, rather than laugh their arses off, but still, that was *not* the kind of first impression she wanted to make. Plus, she wasn't sure her ego could take the humiliation.

"Hello," the nearest receptionist, a redhead, said as Fiona approached. "Welcome to The Portmannow Hotel. How can I help you?"

She'd obviously clocked that Fiona didn't have any luggage or a bellboy hovering nearby, which was why she'd not asked if she was checking in. Smiling, Fiona replied, "Hello. I'm here for an interview. My name is Fiona Gillespie."

"Oh right. Just bear with me a moment, Ms. Gillespie, I'll let them know you're here." She picked up the telephone receiver nearest to her and punched in a number. After a beat, she spoke. "Hello, it's Isa from Reception. I'm just calling to let you know Fiona Gillespie is here for her interview." A pause, then, "Yes, of course. No problem. Thank you."

Putting the phone down, she smiled at Fiona and said, "Do you want to go and take a seat in the area over there? Someone will come and get you shortly."

"Great, thanks."

"You're welcome. And good luck!"

"Thank you."

Isa's smile seemed genuine. Fiona returned it warmly, then made for the area with the comfy leather chairs. Choosing one near to the edge, so she was easy to spot when someone came to collect her, she tugged at the hem of her skirt a little before settling down onto the cool material and subtly angling her body so she could see all around her.

A quick glance at the stylish clock on the wall opposite her, with its huge face and roman numerals, told her she still had fifteen minutes left before her interview. She could relax a little. She was here. She was ready. All she had to do was get up when someone arrived, put one foot in front of the other until she reached the interview room, then do her best to wow them. Broken down into small chunks like that, the whole thing didn't seem nearly so daunting.

Determined to try to take her mind off her nerves, she looked around some more. She hadn't been able to see it from the door, due to the angle—which was likely deliberate—but from her new vantage point, she could sneak a glimpse into the restaurant. One of the restaurants, anyway. This one was probably the more casual one, for want of a better word—one which allowed non-guests to book tables—though it'd still probably be well in advance—and was more suitable for daytime dining.

The super luxury restaurants were probably tucked away in more secluded corners of the building; not that the one she *could* see was exactly a greasy spoon, but still... Her research had told her the head chef had three Michelin stars—one of barely a handful of chefs in the country who did. So no matter which part of the hotel one ate in, a serious gastronomic delight was a given. She'd never been much of a foodie, but spending time in this place would be enough to change anyone's mind, she was sure.

Immaculately-dressed staff whizzed back and forth between the tables, delivering food and drinks, taking away empty plates, swapping cutlery, bringing new linens... The tasks were myriad, and endless, and they were all performed with quiet efficiency. By the looks of it, patrons would have water carafes and coffee cups refilled before they even realised they were empty. Nobody, not even the pickiest, most awkward diva-ish folk could find this place anything but utterly amazing.

What's more, the members of staff looked happy, too. There was a difference between smiling because it was what was expected of you and was polite, and smiling because you actually enjoyed your job and wanted to be there. The door attendant, the receptionists and the whizzing waiters and waitresses in the restaurant all appeared to be in the latter group. Of course, they could just be very good at faking it, but Fiona doubted it. The warmth behind Isa's smile and her tone of voice when she'd wished her luck had been real.

Well, so much for distracting herself and trying to keep the nerves at bay. Yes, her observations had given her some interesting insights into the place, its staff and the way it was run, but they had also driven home for her just how much she wanted this role. She hoped like hell the aching need she now had in her stomach would aid her performance in the interview, because she knew if she didn't get the job, the ache would turn into a big, heavy ball that would sit in her tummy and make her life very unpleasant.

"Ms. Gillespie?"

The voice startled her out of her thoughts, and a gasp escaped her lips before she could prevent it. She smiled and rose from the seat, turning to face the owner of the voice. "Hello. I'm so sorry I didn't see you there. You startled me. I'm Fiona." She held out her hand.

The woman, a tall, curvaceous brunette maybe ten years her senior, took her hand and they shook. "Sorry," she said, smiling. "I didn't mean to make you jump. I'm Sophia Lowrey, PR Manager. It's lovely to meet you."

"Oh, I'm sorry, I thought you were Ms. Cresswell."

Sophia shook her head. "No. She's in the interview room, making a few notes on the last applicant. We'll both be interviewing you."

"I see. Okay, great. Sorry. It's lovely to meet you, too. I'm sorry, I'm a little nervous." *Bloody hell, Fiona, stop saying sorry!*

The older woman smiled again, then held out her arm to indicate that Fiona should walk with her. "Don't worry. You'll be fine. Just be yourself. That's all we ask."

Even if 'myself' is a penniless graduate with no experience whatsoever in PR? You'd be better off sticking me behind the bar. Though, even there I'd be no good—not much call for champagne and cocktails at The Royal Oak, but I pull a mean pint.

Instead, she smiled back, picked up her bag and followed Sophia out of the lobby, past the elevators and through a discreet door tucked into the far corner of the space. Once through the door, Fiona could immediately see why someone came to fetch the interviewees—giving directions to someone who'd never set foot in the building before would be a recipe for disaster. It was like a labyrinth—albeit an incredibly clean, stylish one.

That really showed what standards The Portmannow Hotel strove for. Even the areas not open to the public were awe-inspiring. As she was half a pace behind Sophia, Fiona allowed herself to drink in the lavishness around her—the beautiful paintings, stunning sculptures, the fact that the carpet was so deep it felt a little like quicksand. The glimpses she caught out of a couple of windows they passed were impressive, too. It seemed there was a central courtyard nestled amongst the stately walls, and it housed a gorgeous haven of greenery.

As if sensing her curiosity, Sophia said over her shoulder, "Once your interview's concluded, Ms. Gillespie, I'll give you a tour of the building. You're the last person we're seeing today, so I can take you myself."

"Wow, that would be wonderful. Thank you. This place is beautiful." She meant every word, but also couldn't help thinking it was a little cruel to show each applicant around the place, knowing only one of them would get the job. It was a bit like *look at what you could have won.*

But, on the other hand, for the person who *was* lucky enough to land the position, every glimpse would be worth its weight in gold, because she was sure whoever it was would spend their first day—probably their first week, actually—getting lost. She'd been paying attention to where they'd been going, and yet she found herself hoping she'd be escorted back to the lobby when she was done. Otherwise, she'd still be wandering these corridors days later, trying to find her way out.

After what felt like a couple of miles, Sophia stopped at a door marked *PR & Marketing Suite.*

Bloody hell, even the behind-the-scenes places have posh names. Suite? Not department, but suite!

"Okay," Sophia said, resting her hand on the door handle and half-turning to Fiona, "we're here. Just remember what I said. Be yourself. And please try to relax. Neither of us bites."

With a shy smile, Fiona nodded. "I will. Thanks."

They passed through the doorway into a reception-type area, where a girl around her age sat behind a desk, clicking away on her keyboard. Sophia nodded politely to her, then led Fiona through another door into a huge, open-plan office, with a handful of diligent staff working away on their various tasks. In one corner was a private office with glass walls.

Okay, kiddo. This is it. Knock 'em dead!

Chapter Four

Sophia entered the office without knocking, Fiona following close behind.

"Please take a seat, Ms. Gillespie. Can I get you a drink of anything before we start?" Sophia said.

"N-no, I'm fine. Thanks." As Sophia closed the door, Fiona moved to take a seat, smiling and nodding at the woman on the opposite side of the table—Jane Cresswell, she presumed. "Hello."

"Hello, Ms. Gillespie. Thank you so much for coming along."

"Thank you for asking me."

By now, Sophia had taken a seat, too. As the two women looked at notes and paperwork in front of them, Fiona got her water from her bag, as well as her notebook and pen. Placing the items on the table, she waited for the two women to begin the interview.

Glancing up, Jane said, "Okay, I think we're ready to start. Thank you again for coming, Ms. Gillespie. You've already met Sophia, obviously. I'm Jane Cresswell from Human Resources. Sophia is the PR Manager and would be your line manager, should you be successful."

Fiona smiled. "It's lovely to meet you. I'm very grateful for this opportunity, particularly since I sent my application in after the closing date."

"Yes…" Jane peered down at her notes, then back up with a smile. "You didn't see the advert until it was already too late, correct? But you applied anyway."

Making a huge effort not to pick up the pen and start

fidgeting with it, she remembered what Sophia had said about being herself. "I did. I was flicking through a newspaper that was a few days old and came across the advert. As soon as I saw it, I was really interested in the role, and it wasn't until I'd read through the information a couple of times that I realised the closing date for applications was the previous day. I was disappointed, but decided to apply anyway, just on the off-chance you might call me in. I'm really glad I did."

Now both women smiled, and Fiona, feeling more confident, smiled right back.

"So," Sophia said, taking the lead now, "why were you interested in this position?"

No sense in being anything but honest, here. "Well, I did my degree in creative writing, but didn't have a definite idea of what I wanted to do, career-wise. I moved to London a few months ago, as this is where most of the opportunities seem to be. Up until now, though, despite scouring websites, newspapers and magazines, I haven't seen anything that really called out to me. I just didn't know what I was looking for. But when I spotted the line in your ad about looking for someone with creative writing skills, my interest was definitely piqued. Then, when I got online and researched The Portmannow Hotel, I was totally enthused. It seems like an excellent hotel and chain to work for, and I'm very interested in the fact that there are career advancement opportunities."

She took a breath, then decided to pause her racing brain and mouth by having a quick drink. After a couple of sips of water, she continued, "Honestly, I don't know an awful lot about PR, but I do have the creative writing skills you're looking for, and I'm very keen to learn. I'm also incredibly interested in having a career, rather than just a job. And now I'm going to be quiet, because I'm waffling." Heat infused her face, and she took another big gulp of water, before flashing a sheepish smile at her interviewers.

Sophia's eyebrows were raised, but more in a surprised manner than a displeased one. She cleared her throat. "Not at all, Fiona. May I call you Fiona?" Fiona nodded, and she continued. "I asked you to be yourself, and you are. We appreciate that, particularly since your enthusiasm shines through so plainly. Your honesty is great, too. Now, let me tell you a little more about the company and your potential role within it."

***

By the time the interview finished, Fiona was wallowing in a bundle of different emotions—relief, excitement, worry, anticipation, hope…

She'd given many answers to Sophia and Jane's questions that she felt had been received favourably, but she also suspected she hadn't ticked all of their boxes. Her lack of experience let her down, but there was nothing she could do about that. Plus, they'd known she'd had no experience before they'd even called her in for an interview, so maybe it wasn't that much of an issue to them? She would just have to wait to find out.

First, before she was kicked out of the lap of luxury and had to head back to the relative squalor of home, Sophia had promised to give her a tour of the building.

After gathering up her things, shaking hands with Jane and thanking her for her time, Fiona followed Sophia back into the rabbit warren. She hoped it wouldn't be her last time passing through these corridors.

"Ready?" Sophia said, smiling. "I'll have to stick with the highlights, I'm afraid, otherwise this tour could take hours, maybe days."

"Of course. I appreciate you taking the time, I know you're very busy."

Waving a dismissive hand, the woman replied, "It's not a problem. As I said, you were the last interviewee of the day, and I'd already cleared my to-do list anyway. If anything urgent comes up, Becky—the department's PA—will just phone my mobile."

"Fair enough." *Bloody hell—the department has its own PA?*

"Okay, let's go." She began walking down the corridor, pointing out offices as she passed. "As you've probably already worked out, this is where most of the offices are—PR & Marketing—the departments work very closely together, which is why we share the space—HR, Accounting, Security, Quality Assurance, Dining, Entertainment… The spa offices aren't here, though, and nor is the general manager's office. He's got a space up on the top floor, and the spas are managed from a suite adjacent to the private facilities."

"Ah yes, you mentioned spas, plural, earlier."

"I did. That's because, although we're a very exclusive hotel, we do also offer some facilities to non-guests. Namely one of the spas—which you'll have seen the entrance to in the lobby—and one of the restaurants, also just off the lobby. Other than those two areas, though, everything else is reserved for those staying with us—and for discretionary staff use. It means we get to offer the best of both worlds—a taster for those who perhaps don't have the time or opportunity to stay with us, but also keeping our residents happy by having areas open only to them."

"Makes sense. So, what would you say are the highlights, then? To me, it's all pretty spectacular."

Flashing Fiona a smile, Sophia said, "I know what you mean. I've been here since the hotel opened, and although I'm used to it, I'm not blasé about it. I came from another five-star hotel in London to work here, and this place still impressed me. It continues to do so. I'm probably biased, but this place really is a cut above, and we don't rest on our laurels, either. There are always surveys and inspections going on to see if there's anything we could be doing better or something new we could introduce." She let out a laugh. "Now who's waffling? Anyway, to answer your question, the highlights—or at least, the ones I'm allowed to show you—are the residents-only spa, one of the top floor suites, the ballroom, the roof garden and the library."

"The *library?*"

Sophia smirked. "Yes. If you like books and libraries, then you're going to love it. I think I'll save it until last."

"I look forward to it."

By now, they'd left the various office suites behind and had moved back into customer-facing areas. Sophia smiled politely at any patrons or any members of staff they passed, and Fiona followed suit, all the while drinking in the sights and sounds. By the time they'd reached their first destination, Fiona had counted at least six famous people, and common sense told her that just because she didn't recognise anyone else, didn't mean they weren't important. The place was probably packed to the rafters with businesspeople, politicians, dignitaries, members of royal families and anyone else with serious means. She was way more likely to get the opportunity to chat up Prince Harry here than she was at The Royal Oak.

"Okay, here's the ballroom." Sophia had stopped at a set of grand wooden doors with ornate handles. She pushed one door and gestured Fiona in ahead of her, then followed.

Fiona was silent for several moments. She really should have learned already, but it seemed she hadn't—yes, she'd been expecting impressive, but this went beyond that. She'd long since lost track of whereabouts they were in the building, so she didn't bother to try to work it out. The ballroom was huge—of course—and very light and airy. The height of the room went up several stories, and a glass dome in the centre of the ceiling let in much of the light. Two sides of the room were glass walls, which afforded views of a garden. The other two walls were cream and a very deep red, and the floor was marble. It looked like something out of a stately home.

"Wow," she eventually said.

Sophia laughed. "Yes, that's the reaction most people have when they come in here, guests and staff alike. This is where we hold the really exclusive events—celebrity weddings, charity balls, banquets and the like. We have lots of other function rooms tailored for different types of event, but this is the jewel in our crown."

"I can certainly see why. It's beautiful. I'm honoured to even be standing here!"

"Just part of the tour. Ready to see the spa?"

"Can I just have another moment, please?"

Nodding, Sophia waited patiently while Fiona tip-tapped over to the nearest window and peered out to the garden beyond. It wasn't a huge area, but then she hadn't expected it to be. They were in the middle of London, after all. Space was at a premium.

What they did have, they'd made the most of. Tall trees lined the garden, ensuring complete privacy, and giving the impression of being a secluded haven in the middle of nowhere. The rest of the garden was kept pretty simple. The borders were filled with riots of colourful flowers and bushes, and the middle had a large, neat lawn, with a gorgeous fountain off to one side. A perfect space for pitching marquees, and the fountain was a great backdrop for photos.

Smiling, she tore her gaze away from the pretty garden and walked back over to Sophia. "Okay, take me away before I sit down on the floor and refuse to leave. I'm in love!"

Chuckling, the woman replied, "You think you're in love now? You haven't seen anything yet."

Chapter Five

Several days passed and Fiona could do little but think about her interview at The Portmannow Hotel. She'd been impressed with the hotel, the role, and Jane and Sophia, but had they been impressed with *her?* They'd promised to be in touch by early the following week, so all she could do, once again, was wait.

In the meantime, good news had come to another in the flat.

"Guess what, Fiona?" Gary said as she walked in from a lunchtime shift at the pub.

"Judging by the huge grin on your face and the fact your eyes look like they're going to pop out of your head, I'm guessing it's something good?"

"Yep. Thanks to you, I've got an interview!"

She was drained from the lacklustre time spent at work, but her excitement for her friend was genuine. "Oh, cool! Where? When?"

"Sit yourself down and I'll make some tea and tell you all about it."

"That sounds like the sort of thing an old granny would say."

Gary shrugged as he skipped over to switch on the kettle. "I don't care. I only just found out. I'm really excited and you were the first one to walk through the door. Plus, it's down to your magic touch on my CV that I've even got the interview at all, so I wanted you to be the first to know."

Smiling, Fiona flopped down onto the sofa. "I'm glad I could help out. And even gladder—I think I just made up a word there—you've now got an interview. Things are looking up in this household, aren't they?"

"Seem to be. I take it you haven't heard from The Portmannow Hotel yet?" He looked over from where he was making the tea to gauge her response.

With a wry smile, she replied, "What do you think? If I had, you'd have known within minutes of me putting the phone down on them—or reading the email. Oh!" She couldn't believe the thought hadn't occurred to her before. They'd said they'd be in touch, but hadn't specified how, so for some reason, she'd assumed it would be a phone call. But email was just as likely.

Delving into her handbag, she drew out her phone and opened the email app. She waited impatiently as it downloaded her messages, scanning the sender and subject line of each as it appeared on the screen. *Junk, junk, job alert, online shopping, junk, job alert...* When the emails had all appeared, she sighed and began deleting them all.

"Bloody nothing," she muttered, stabbing at the phone's touchscreen way harder than necessary. "Fuck's sake." She glared at the device, then put it down on the arm of the sofa.

Gary appeared next to her and held out her cup of tea, which she took with a grateful smile. "I take it they haven't emailed?"

"Thanks. No, they haven't. Anyway, never mind that for now. Tell me your news." If anything would take her mind off her dream role, it was good news from her friend.

"They will. Just be patient." He settled down beside her. "So, as you know, once you made my CV the best the world has ever seen, I blasted it out to a bunch of recruitment companies, uploaded it to the various job websites, made some direct applications… Of course, I got a load of the usual form rejections, but I also had a couple of interesting replies." He grinned, then blew lightly on the surface of the tea before taking a sip. "One turned out to be a bit of a time waster, but the other was an interview offer for this fantastic role in Covent Garden."

"That's awesome. Doing what?" Gary's degree in film, while a little more specific than hers, still had lots of scope for different career paths.

"Working in production for a small film company. The money's not exactly going to make me rich, but it's more than I'm earning now. And, most importantly, it's a rung on that all-important career ladder. Even if there's nowhere for me to progress with the company, I'll stay for a good while and get as much experience as possible, then hopefully get a promotion somewhere else. Anyway," he took another gulp of tea, "I'm getting a bit ahead of myself here. It's an interview, not a guaranteed job offer, but it's something!"

"Absolutely. Well done! Before I even applied to The Portmannow Hotel, I figured an interview was a good thing, even if I don't get the job. It's interview experience, and probably like most things, practice makes perfect. So next time I have an interview somewhere, I'll be better at giving answers, impressing people and so on." She'd been enjoying her own brew as Gary chattered away, and she took another warming swallow now.

"You're talking as though you haven't got it. You shouldn't be so defeatist."

Shaking her head, Fiona replied, "I'm not. Not at all. I'm

staying as neutral as I possibly can. I want it, but I don't want to get too excited, just in case—"

The trill of her phone interrupted her mid-sentence. Glancing at the screen, she saw it was a London number. *Could it be…?*

She was vaguely aware of Gary relieving her of her mug as she reached for the device. Taking a deep breath and sitting up straight, she swiped the screen to answer. "Hello?"

"Hello. Is that Fiona Gillespie?"

"Speaking." She thought she recognised the voice of the person on the other end, and her heart began to pound.

"Oh, hi. This is Sophia Lowrey, from The Portmannow Hotel."

"Hi—good to hear from you!" She'd meant the words to sound genuine, enthusiastic, but couldn't help wondering whether they'd come out as too excitable. Didn't matter, it was too late.

"Are you okay to talk?"

"Yes, absolutely."

"Fantastic. I'm just calling to let you know that, subject to a trial period, we'd very much like to offer you the role."

Her mouth dry, Fiona managed to squeak, "You mean you don't want me to come for a second interview?" *What are you saying, you bloody idiot? Don't give them the chance to change their minds!*

Sophia seemed nonplussed by Fiona's reaction. "No. There's no need. Jane and I agreed you were the standout candidate, and there's nothing we felt we could learn in a second interview that we can't learn during a trial period. Am I to take it that you are still interested?"

"Oh, yes! Most definitely. Thank you so much!"

There was a definite hint of amusement in Sophia's tone as she replied, "That's good news. I'm glad to hear it. I'll send you an email with all the pertinent details, which you can go through at your leisure and let it all sink in. Your notice period at your current employment is two weeks, correct?"

"Yes, that's right." She could actually walk out any time she liked since she didn't have an official contract, but she didn't want to put The Portmannow Hotel off her by giving them the impression that she was in less than above-board employment.

"Okay, that's fine. I'll propose an official starting date for you in the email. In the meantime, we will have a background check done on you. Nothing to worry about. This is standard procedure for all new employees, as I'm sure you can appreciate. Subject to that all being okay, which I'm sure it will be, then I'm delighted to welcome you on board. Congratulations."

"Wow, thank you, Sophia! I just don't know what else to say. I'm really happy. Oh," she gasped, "is it okay to call you Sophia?"

"Of course. We'll be working together, after all."

"Fantastic, I can't wait."

"I'll get that email drafted now, Fiona, and have it in your inbox by the end of the afternoon. If you could get back to me when you can—though no later than the end of the week, if possible—that would be great. We can get things moving then."

"Yes, no problem at all. Thank you again, and please pass on my thanks to Ms. Cresswell. I look forward to working with you."

"Don't thank me, Fiona. You earned it. Goodbye."

"Goodbye."

After pressing the 'end call' button, she put the phone back down on the arm of the chair and turned to Gary, her mouth hanging open.

His expression was a mixture of impatience, curiosity and excitement. "Well?" he prompted. "I take it that was good news?"

She nodded, too stunned to say a word.

Rolling his eyes, Gary handed her mug back. "Get that down you, then tell me what happened. Come on. Stop keeping me in bloody suspense here!"

Doing as she was told, Fiona sipped at the cooling drink, grateful for the opportunity to get her whirling, bouncing, excitable thoughts into some kind of order so she could actually form coherent words and make them come out of her mouth.

Finally, she put her empty mug down on the table, then turned to Gary with a smile, and repeated the conversation with Sophia.

"Bloody hell!" he said when she was finished, putting his own empty mug down. "That's absolutely fantastic. Well done, gorgeous! You deserve it. I think this is a cause for celebration, don't you? And this time, tea just isn't going to cut it. I'll nip to the shop and get some lager."

"Hey, wait," she said, putting a hand on his arm as he stood. "Let me give you some money. It's my news we're celebrating, after all."

"Yes, and that's why it's my treat. You can return the favour once I've scored an awesome job."

It all seemed a bit back to front to Fiona, but once Gary got an idea into his head, there was generally no way of stopping him. She knew that, despite him 'nipping' to the shop, he'd be gone a while, given his propensity for talking rubbish to anyone he bumped into. So she decided to take advantage of the alone time to go and have a shower, get into some clean clothes, then put on a load of laundry.

She'd just settled back onto the sofa and was checking her emails to see if anything had come through when Gary reappeared. There'd been no email yet. She was a little disappointed, but reminded herself Sophia was a busy woman. She wouldn't necessarily have had the time to sit and draft the email straight after finishing their telephone call. She'd said by the end of the afternoon.

"All right, gorgeous?" Gary said, his grin wide as he held a plastic carrier bag aloft. The material of the bag was so thin that she could clearly see the brand of lager he'd gone for.

"Wow, you've pushed the boat out, haven't you?" It wasn't exactly expensive, but it was one step up from the crap they usually ended up drinking.

"Nothing but the best for you, babe. This is seriously good news, so it needs seriously celebrating."

"Fair enough." She got up and went over to the docking unit beside the TV. Once there, she slipped her phone into the cradle and set some music to play, but turned the volume down so she and Gary could chat without having to shout.

By now, he'd retaken his seat and held a can in each hand.

He passed her one as she sat down, and they opened them at the same time, then clinked them together.

"Cheers!" they said in unison, then took several long gulps of the liquid, which was generally the only way to cope with the taste—if you quickly downed enough for a little bit of a buzz to kick in, the taste wasn't quite so horrendous. Though at least the more expensive stuff didn't make her want to gag.

As her taste buds slowly got used to the assault, Fiona couldn't help but think that, in a few short weeks, she'd be able to leave the dingy flat and scrimping existence behind. She'd miss her friends, but that was about it.

Chapter Six

Lying on the bed in her new accommodation, Fiona realised she'd read the same page of her book about ten times and hadn't absorbed a single word. It was hardly surprising, though. She was just too excited.

It was Sunday evening, and she was due to start work the following morning. She'd spent the past two days moving her stuff across London—easier said than done when she didn't have a car and couldn't afford to hire a van. Fortunately, Gary had managed to persuade one of his workmates to lend him his car and between the two of them and their other flatmates, Jenny and Ben, they'd managed it. It had involved some very creative packing of the little Peugeot, not to mention some rather hairy journeys through the centre of the city.

She'd never said a word in front of Gary or the others—they were doing her a massive favour, after all—but she'd been a bit embarrassed each time they'd pulled up outside The Portmannow Hotel in the crappy vehicle. She wasn't a snob, but she couldn't help feeling the ancient, rusting motor and its occupants didn't belong in Mayfair, much less carrying stuff inside the most exclusive hotel in the area.

Naturally, they'd been using a staff entrance, rather than the front doors, but it still felt wrong—forbidden almost. And as her friends gasped and gaped at the finery of The Portmannow Hotel and wondered aloud what kind of people stayed there, Fiona also considered whether *she,* in fact, belonged.

Now, though, she'd come to the conclusion that it didn't

matter. Her contract was signed—subject to the trial period. She was set up on the payroll, and she'd moved into her room in the staff accommodation. Granted, it was nothing like the guest accommodation—not even the tiniest bit—but it was still a huge step up from the shared flat in east London.

For starters, it was hers and hers alone. It was a studio flat, with little more than a double bed, wardrobe, kitchen area, small living area and a bathroom, but what more did one person need?

Despite the relatively small scale of it, it was clear to Fiona that the hotel didn't scrimp on the cost of decorating and furnishing their staff accommodation. There were no sparkling chandeliers, marble floors or expensive art, but everything was well done. The décor was neutral and spotless, the carpets thick and clean, the wardrobe and cupboards solid, the appliances top of the range and clearly well looked after. There was even a small desk and chair in one corner, and access to free, high-speed Wi-Fi. She wanted for nothing and was feeling incredibly lucky… and she hadn't even officially started work yet.

After slipping the bookmark inside the pages, she closed the book and placed it on her bedside table, then allowed a huge smile to take over her face. *God, this is really happening.* She still wasn't quite sure how she'd gone from working in a dingy pub in a dodgy area of London, living in an equally dingy flat in the same area, to working *and* living in a super-expensive, super-beautiful part of London. Somehow, she'd fallen on her feet, and was determined to make the most of it.

Tomorrow, she'd begin her career, and do her very best to

ensure Jane and Sophia believed they'd made the right choice in her. She'd learn, be enthusiastic, work hard and grasp every opportunity that was thrown her way. They'd already said that, far from her inexperience going *against* her, they'd seen it as a way to take on someone who had the basic skills they required—that was where her degree came in—but no previous habits. They could train her on the job, so she'd be learning about PR, but more specifically, PR for the hotel business—the high-end hotel business. She was very much a clean slate, and Fiona was more than happy with that, especially since at some point there was the potential to take some exams to gain more formal PR qualifications on her CV.

For now, though, she was trying—and failing dismally—to relax. The move, though it had been a bit of a nuisance, had gone well and she had nothing else to do or to organise. All her clothes were clean and ironed, including the outfit she'd chosen for the next day. She'd found homes for all her belongings, and there was no further preparation she could make to give her a head start for tomorrow. She'd even called her mother and let her know she was all moved into her new home.

The thought of her mother made Fiona smile again. She'd been so excited when Fiona had called to let her know she'd got the job at The Portmannow Hotel.

"I knew you could do it, chick!" she'd said. "You've always been one for getting something once you put your mind to it. I'm so proud of you. This is just the start of something wonderful for you, sweetheart, and I hope you enjoy every moment of it. You deserve it." After a beat, she apparently couldn't resist adding, "And I'll be glad to see you out of that horrible flat."

Rolling her eyes, Fiona had responded, "Yeah, me too, Mum. It's not the nicest place, but I've made some good friends here and I'll be sad to leave them."

"No boyfriend yet, darling?"

Her mother had been surprised when the answer had been in the negative, and Fiona had had to hold herself back from blurting out what had happened when she'd celebrated her good news with Gary.

Their celebratory lager had turned into another, and another, and the booze had done its usual job of loosening tongues and lowering inhibitions. They'd been talking all kinds of rubbish about everything and nothing, and during the course of the chat, Fiona had sunk lower into the sofa, in a state of lazy, hazy happiness.

"I'll really miss you, you know." Gary's statement had come completely out of the blue.

"Eh?" She'd turned her head to look at him. His expression was deadly serious. "I'll still be in London. I'm not moving to Mars. We'll still see each other. Meet up for drinks. I can pop round here. I'm not sure what the situation is with personal visitors at the hotel, but I'll make it a priority to find out."

"I hope so, 'cause I don't want us drifting apart. I think we've got a good thing here, you and me."

Frowning, she'd replied, "You make it sound like we're in a relationship."

"I wish we were."

Had she not already been sitting down—or, more accurately,

slouching—that comment would have put her on her backside. As long as she'd known Gary, he'd always been a bit of a flirt, and not just with her, so she hadn't thought any more about it. She certainly hadn't got the impression he wanted any more from her than just friendship, and once he'd thrown it out there, she'd had no idea how to react.

"Um, where's this coming from, Gary?" Struggling to push herself into a more upright position, she'd peered at him confusedly.

He'd shrugged, and taken another sip from his can. "Dunno, really. Seemed like a day for sharing news, so I thought I'd mention it."

Blinking, Fiona had shaken her head. "*You thought you'd mention it?* That's a bit random. I had absolutely no idea you, uh… liked me, and you've just sprung it on me as though it's no big deal."

With what seemed to be a superhuman effort, he'd turned and met her eyes. "Is it a big deal? For you, I mean?"

"I don't know! I haven't even had time to process this. It's all just so—"

"Fiona," he'd cut in, still gazing at her intently. "It's not difficult. You either like me in that way, or you don't. We've known each other for long enough for you to have come to that conclusion, I'm sure."

"I…" Running a hand through her still-damp hair, she'd scrabbled around for a suitable response. The fact she'd never even considered it before told her everything she needed to know. She'd never thought of Gary that way, and attraction didn't just switch on and off like a light. If she liked him that way, she'd have been aware of it for a while. But how to tell him without coming across as a complete bitch?

Turned out she hadn't needed to. "Your silence speaks volumes."

She'd opened her mouth to say something, though she wasn't quite sure what, but he'd held up a hand to stop her.

"Don't. Don't apologise or try to say something nice. I get it, and it's all right, honestly. I pretty much knew that was going to be your response, anyway. I hadn't got my hopes up or anything, I just figured that since I was feeling a little bit brave—damn you, lager—I'd put it out there, just in case. You never know unless you try, and all that. Now, if you'll excuse me, I'm going to go to my room and feel sorry for myself for a bit."

"Gary, I—"

"Seriously, it's okay. You don't have to say anything." He'd unfolded his lanky frame from the sofa, then leaned down and pressed a kiss to the top of her head. "Congratulations on the job, gorgeous. You deserve it. It'll be my turn next, just you wait and see."

He'd loped off in the direction of his room, leaving Fiona feeling confusion, surprise and regret all in one go. She'd left him alone, though, and when he'd emerged later on, he'd clearly been playing the forget-we-ever-had-that-conversation game, and she'd been happy to go along with it. After all, there had been nothing she could say to help. He liked her, but she didn't feel the same, and that wasn't going to change.

She was glad to leave that incident behind her, both

emotionally and physically. Although Gary hadn't mentioned it since, it had, unfortunately, still had an impact on their friendship. They weren't *quite* as comfortable with each other as they had been previously, and he'd toned down what she'd always thought of as harmless flirting. If the others had noticed, they'd kept quiet about it, and her incredible news had overshadowed everything else, in any case.

A flurry of activity had followed—responding to Sophia's email when it arrived, then working from there to get everything organised. Handing in her notice, both at the pub and with her landlord, helping the others put the word out that a room was coming up for rent, talking to those who were interested in taking her room to weed out the most undesirable folk.

After all of that, though, there had been some fun. She and Jenny had hit the shops in order to get her kitted out with some suitable clothes for her new job. A single interview suit wasn't going to cut it. Thankfully Fiona's parents had sent some money to help her out in that regard, and she'd managed to make the budget stretch to enough items that she could mix and match without looking as though she was wearing the same stuff again and again. That would last until her first payday, and on her much-improved wage she could gradually start adding items to her wardrobe.

Her send-off from the flat had been emotional and bonkers at the same time. It had been sad because she was leaving, but also a celebration of her getting her foot on the first rung of the career ladder. The weird mix of emotions had resulted in an incredibly drunken evening with the four of them—plus Ben's girlfriend

Megan and Jenny's on-again, off-again boyfriend José—vowing to make sure they kept in touch, met up as often as possible and so on.

It'd be difficult, Fiona knew, because she'd no doubt be crazy busy with her new job and learning the ropes, but she felt it was important to keep her friends close. Maybe a little bit of time and space would help mend the rift between her and Gary too. She hoped so.

Her current excitement and anticipation wouldn't allow her to concentrate on a film any more than a book, so she decided to explore the hotel a little. Rolling off the bed and grabbing the shoes she'd left by the door, she figured she'd find her way from her room to the PR & Marketing Suite. It'd be closed, of course, but at least she'd know where she was going in the morning. She didn't want to be late on her very first day.

Chapter Seven

Four weeks later, and Fiona still occasionally got lost in the hotel, but otherwise things were going well. The job itself was incredible. She was constantly learning and improving, and she'd found she had a genuine interest in—and liking for—PR. It helped, of course, that the very thing she was aiming to get publicity for was an amazing, unique hotel in a worldwide chain of amazing, unique hotels. It meant that press releases she wrote, pitches she made, and phone calls she engaged in weren't simply a mish-mash of carefully placed words and phrases designed to make the place sound great. It really *was* great and pretty much sold itself.

But it wasn't the only luxury hotel out there. Mayfair was full of them. London was full of them. The UK was full of them. So it was up to her to get creative, to find new ways of getting the press interested in writing about the place or featuring it in some way, in order to catch the eyes of potential guests. Sophia helped a lot, as part of her training, but Fiona was eager to stand on her own two feet, to come up with something completely her own and really show Sophia and the rest of the team what she was made of.

This plan found her wandering the rooms, corridors and public areas of the hotel, a tablet in her hand and a thoughtful expression on her face. She wanted to create a campaign that would entice more regular folk to come and stay at The Portmannow Hotel. Yes, they still had to make sure their standards were such that their usual clientele would continue to stay with them whenever they were in the area and recommend them to friends, colleagues and business associates. But these were people for whom money was no object.

The biggest, plushest suites were full all the time—even during the week. What Fiona wanted to do was pull in people who'd stay in one of the regular rooms—though even those were a far cry from a Premier Inn or Travelodge—and still find it to be a completely amazing, luxurious experience.

The angle she needed was that these people would be treating themselves, splashing out. Special birthdays, anniversaries, engagements, honeymoons. Causes for celebration. Maybe even a staycation for people who either didn't want to—or for some reason, couldn't—leave the country. They could still have a fantastic time away, get pampered, be looked after, relax… just as they would if they'd zipped off somewhere abroad.

London, of course, had the added bonus of having an abundance of things to do. If guests wanted to stay inside the hotel and take advantage of the world-class facilities, so be it. But if they wanted to venture into the city, they would have endless choices of entertainment—there was certainly something for everyone.

Her brain whirring with the possibilities, she tapped away on the screen, making notes, and flipping to the camera function every now and again to take a snap of something that stood out to her or inspired her in some way. It was an insane jumble of photos and text she'd be downloading to her computer when she returned to her desk, but it was a jumble that would hopefully spark her creativity and allow her to come up with something awe-inspiring.

It was easy enough to put herself into the mindset of someone who wasn't rich, but who would be staying at the hotel. So it was a simple task to look around her and imagine how people would want to spend their time. Sipping exotic cocktails at the bar, maybe. Indulging in afternoon tea. Having beauty treatments, massages, saunas. Swimming. Leafing through weighty, rare tomes in the library. Wandering in the private gardens. Admiring the stunning views from the rooftop garden, even.

Her own wandering had brought her closest to the bar restaurant just off the lobby, so she decided to go and tuck herself away in a corner there, do some discreet people watching, make notes and maybe pick up some more inspiration. She was glad she had the kind of boss who would let her go off and do this sort of thing, rather than being chained to a desk all the time and expected to churn out sparkling copy and snappy press releases. But then, she supposed that was the nature of being in a creative role. Not everything was as simple as putting fingers to a keyboard and hoping something awesome appeared on the screen.

Plus, if Sophia thought she was the type of person who'd use this time to slack off, she wouldn't have been offered the role in the first place. Yes, she was being given some freedom, but she was also expected to get the job done—and done to perfection. Naturally, perfection was Fiona's aim, but if she couldn't quite achieve that, she'd be more than happy with doing her very best.

She'd barely parked her bottom on a chair when one of the waiters whizzed over. She'd seen him around, but didn't know him. The hotel was so big that she was sure it'd take a while before she'd met all the other members of staff, never mind memorised their names. Thankfully, name badges were part of the uniform for customer-facing personnel, so she took a peek.

"Hi, Jeremy," she said, smiling at him.

He looked a little taken aback at being spoken to before he'd had a chance to greet her. "Oh, hello, madam."

Still smiling, she waved a hand dismissively. "I work here, Jeremy. You don't need to call me madam." She indicated the tablet. "I'm the new PR assistant. I've been having a good explore of the place—getting lost is becoming less frequent, luckily—and thought I'd tuck myself away here and do some people watching to get some inspiration for a campaign."

"Oh, I see," he replied, grinning. "You don't, uh, have a name badge."

Heat came to her cheeks as she realised her mistake. "I'm so sorry. I'm Fiona." She held her hand out, and they shook. "It's nice to meet you. I've seen you around, but there are just so many people working here. I can't keep track of everyone."

"Yeah, I get it. I was the same when I first started. Fortunately, staff turnover here is really low, so you'll get there in the end. It's nice to meet you too, by the way. Can I get you anything?"

She nodded. "That would be great. If I look like a regular customer, people might not notice me people watching. Can I have some fruit juice, please? I don't mind what flavour."

"Ice?"

"No thanks."

With a nod, Jeremy zoomed off to get her drink. Fiona gave a contented sigh as she thought about the perks of her job. Although what she ate and drank wasn't free, exactly—an amount was taken from her salary for her board and lodgings—it was heavily subsidised. She was paying less 'rent' now than she'd been in the flat, and needless to say, her living standards had increased. After all, she hadn't had unlimited use of two swimming pools, spa facilities, saunas, steam rooms, gym equipment… The list went on. She wasn't sure she'd ever feel the need to have someone else shine her shoes—however, it was fun to know the option was there.

The best part was that all the facilities were open twenty-four hours, so if she didn't finish working until nine o'clock at night—though her contracted hours were nine to four-thirty, sometimes she had to work extra time to get projects finished or take care of urgent requests—she could still go and have twenty minutes in the sauna and a nice, relaxing swim or perhaps chill out in the Jacuzzi for a while.

It was something it had taken her a while to work up to, though. Despite knowing it was allowed, Fiona felt a bit like an impostor using facilities that were for paying guests—paying guests who were often famous or very important. Sometimes both. Not that those people knew she *wasn't* important, but she still couldn't shake the feeling of being out of place.

She was slowly growing used to mingling, for want of a better word, with the guests while using the various facilities, and it was also how she'd been slowly meeting and getting to know other members of staff. Not the sort of person to go and knock on her neighbour's door and say hello, Fiona had waited until she'd more organically bumped into someone before introducing herself. And this had happened a few times in the sauna, pool area and gym.

Made sense, really. Why would anyone go somewhere else, pay a monthly subscription to a gym, when there was an absolutely top notch one available to use at any time, absolutely free?

Jeremy returned shortly with her drink, placing it beside her with a discreet wink before moving off to look after the other patrons. It really was an ideal existence. She was enjoying a life that was somewhere in between being an ordinary girl from Birmingham and being rich and famous. It had many of the perks and none of the downfalls. Nobody recognised her. Nobody harassed her. Nobody requested selfies or autographs.

Not that anything along those lines took place on the premises, anyway—certainly not that she'd seen, or heard about. Anyone who even gave off the remotest hint of being paparazzi wouldn't even make it over the threshold, and genuine guests had better manners than to stare at others or to interrupt them while they were relaxing or having dinner—even if it happened to be their favourite footballer, actor, singer, royal or whatever.

Just about to chastise herself for allowing her thoughts to meander so, she suddenly realised she was on to something. Closing her eyes and grabbing hard onto the trail of the train of thought she'd been pursuing, she tugged it back into the forefront of her mind.

Yes! She opened her eyes. That was it. That was her angle. The wording would need work, serious refinement, but the basic idea was there. *Treat yourself to a once-in-a-lifetime stay in the ultimate luxury hotel. Enjoy rooms, spaces and facilities fit for royalty.*

Typing the snippet into the tablet's note-taking app before she forgot it, she grinned. It was good—really good. Once polished up, expanded on and worked into press releases, sound bites, competition copy and advertorial copy, she was sure it would result in lots of coverage, not to mention bring in plenty of guests. The concept might even be used in TV, magazine and radio advertising. Now that would be seriously cool—a way for her to be famous, without being famous. Her idea, her baby, up in lights!

After tapping in a few more notes, she saved her progress, then stopped to take a drink of the fruit juice. It was then she noticed she wasn't quite as secluded in her corner as she had been before. Two businessmen had settled down two tables away. Nothing unusual in that, except that as she allowed her gaze to linger on them, she quickly realised they were, in fact, a little out of the ordinary. The majority of the businessmen and women she saw here were middle-aged or older, which made sense. They'd had longer to climb the career ladder, achieve higher positions, earn more money and therefore attend meetings or stay over in places such as The Portmannow Hotel.

These two, however, looked like they had less than a decade on her—late twenties, possibly early thirties. And the thing that made them the most unusual was the fact they were *hot*. A subtle glance around the room confirmed she wasn't the only woman who'd noticed them, either.

Chapter Eight

Continuing to surreptitiously peer at the men over the rim of her glass, it hit her that this was the first time in months she'd looked at a man with interest, much less two men—and at the same time! She was ready to snatch her gaze away if one of them happened to glance at her, but it wasn't surprising the pair had attracted her attention.

The tailored business suits would draw the eye even on someone unremarkable. But on these two, the fine clothing was practically an orgasm for the gaze. They sat opposite each other, and their angle to her meant she had a view of both their profiles—lucky her.

The one to her right had very dark, almost black hair, with a bit of a curl to it, a long straight nose, a trimmed goatee and, if she wasn't mistaken, deep blue eyes. It was hard to tell for sure from this distance and perspective.

The one on her left had lighter, shorter hair, stubble that by some magical feat still looked smart, and the most sinful lips she'd ever set eyes on. And speaking of eyes, she thought perhaps his were green. What she wouldn't give to go and check both of them out close up, preferably naked.

Shocked at her own sudden lustful thoughts, she inhaled more than drank another sip of the juice. Unfortunately, it hit her throat all wrong and she almost slammed the glass down as she started to cough. She tried so hard to suppress the cough, eager not to draw attention to herself, that she made it worse. Snatching up the thick linen serviette from the table, she held it to her mouth as she spluttered in a most embarrassing manner, and tears began to roll down her cheeks. By now, she was sure the whole damn restaurant was staring at her, and she wished the tablecloths reached the floor, like the ones in the restaurant upstairs, so she could hide under the table until she regained her composure.

Swallowing repeatedly to try to soothe her irritated throat, she gasped as a gentle hand laid on her shoulder, which set her off all over again.

"Oh God," came a voice. "I'm so sorry. I didn't mean to make you jump. I just wanted to make sure you were all right. See if I could help."

Unable to speak, Fiona waved a hand to try to signal that she'd be okay, but unless the guy was a mind reader, he'd have no luck figuring that out. Blinking through the tears that marred her vision, her urge to hide underneath the table grew stronger. Christ, it was only the hottie with the blue eyes. And, if she wasn't mistaken, his sexy friend with the green eyes was also hovering close by, concern etched into his handsome features.

Managing to drag in a breath, she huffed out, "Thank you."

Just then, Jeremy arrived with a carafe of water, complete with ice, and poured her a glassful. "Here you go, Fiona. Drink this. Are you all right? Anything else I can get you?"

She picked up the glass and took a tiny sip of the freezing cold liquid, hoping it wouldn't make her cough again. She seemed to have got a handle on it, though her now-sore throat wasn't at all happy with her. After taking several more tiny sips, she let out a sigh of relief—it seemed her mortifying coughing bout was over. Then she moved on to bigger gulps, buying herself some time to think of something witty to say, anything to convince the three men looking at her that she wasn't some kind of imbecile who couldn't even manage a glass of juice without choking.

Unfortunately, her creative brain, which had been on fire up until she'd started lusting over the hotties, had taken its leave. So she decided to opt for the truth. "I'm so sorry. I didn't mean to disturb you. My juice just went down the wrong way, that's all. I'm fine, really. I'll just finish my drink and be on my way. Thank you for the water, Jeremy." She aimed a weak smile in his direction.

Blue Eyes turned to Jeremy. "Yeah, thanks, buddy. If you need to get on, we'll keep an eye on her for a bit, make sure she's okay. Don't worry."

A little warily, Jeremy looked at the two men, then at Fiona. "Are you going to be all right, Fiona? Do you need me to call someone and let them know you'll be late or anything?"

She shook her head. "Honestly, Jeremy, I'll be fine. It was just a coughing fit, that's all. No lasting damage, except maybe to my makeup. And no, nobody will be missing me yet. It's fine. Thank you so much, though."

"Just give me a wave if you need me," he said, backing away.

"Will do."

With that, he morphed from concerned acquaintance into efficient waiter in an instant and went back to looking after his tables and the patrons frequenting them.

Knowing she'd now have to address the two men who'd

caused her blush-worthy incident in the first place, she took yet another huge gulp of the icy water, then dabbed at her face with the serviette. Putting it down, she turned to Blue Eyes, who still stood by her side, but had removed his hand from her shoulder, with a wide smile.

"I'm so sorry," she said again. "Please excuse the state of me, I'm sure I must look terrible. Thank you so much, both of you, for coming to check on me, but I'm really fine. No Heimlich manoeuvre required. I'll just finish my drink... drinks... and be on my way. Please feel free to go back to your meeting."

Green Eyes stepped a little closer. "You look just fine, sweetheart, except for being a little flushed, but that's no bad thing." He shot an almost imperceptible glance at Blue Eyes, and Fiona had to wonder if she'd imagined it. And if not, what on earth did he mean by that, anyway?

"Yes," his friend chipped in, moving around so that he, too, could look at her face. "You look great. We'll be just over there if you need us, all right? Don't you hesitate to call out or wave, okay?"

Fiona wished they'd stop making such a fuss. But they were just being polite, she supposed. So, fixing the smile back on her face, she said, "Thank you. And I will. I promise."

She waited until they'd retaken their seats before she started to make preparations for leaving hers. She didn't want to dash off straight away as that might concern them further and send Jeremy into a tizzy, so she acted as coolly and calmly as possible, finishing the water, then the juice, as she continued making notes on her tablet. Finally, feeling able to leave without raising any eyebrows, she got up and collected her things.

Her movement attracted the attention of Blue Eyes and Green Eyes, and she gave them both a smile and a nod before moving off. She didn't see Jeremy, who must have been in the kitchen collecting something, so she made a mental note to thank him when she next saw him. That was the downside to posh material serviettes and electronic devices—it meant there was no paper or pen handy to scrawl him a little note with.

She wasn't quite ready to head back to the PR & Marketing Suite yet, at least not until she'd fixed her no doubt ruined makeup—which would raise a few eyebrows and spawn some questions—so she decided she'd dash up to her room for a few minutes and sort herself out.

After pressing the button for the elevator, she swiped through some of the photos she'd taken on the tablet as she waited for it to arrive. A couple of minutes later, the car arrived with a ping and a swish of doors. She stepped in, pressed the number for her floor and moved back. Just as the doors began closing, she realised the table the two men had been sitting at was visible from her position.

They were still there, and she was glad no one could see or hear her reaction as she looked at them, only to find two pairs of very arresting eyes looking right back at her—with interest.

And, as her view of them grew narrower and narrower until only a sliver was left, Blue Eyes flashed her a positively wicked grin just before he disappeared altogether.

Clinging onto the brass handrail behind her to steady herself, Fiona willed herself to get a grip. She'd been having a really good day, right up until those two had somehow awakened her hormones and made her bloody fruit juice go down wrong. And the way they'd clearly been watching her... and that *smile!* Shaking her head, she wanted desperately to believe they were some kind of dodgy perverts who frequented hotel restaurants to prey on lone young women, but common sense and cold, hard facts told her that wasn't the case.

For one, what had they done? Offered help, and concern. That was all. What had they gained? Nothing, except maybe peace of mind in knowing she was okay. Her tablet and phone were still in her possession, so they weren't thieves. Dodgy folk didn't spend time in The Portmannow Hotel. It just didn't happen.

So if they weren't dodgy perverts and were just two relatively young businessmen, why had they been watching her like that? Their expressions, the looks in their eyes, indicated something altogether different from innocent concern for her wellbeing. The smile Blue Eyes had thrown her had been nothing short of sinful. Lustful, even. One Lucifer himself would have been proud of.

God, was it possible that they... found her attractive? She wasn't the sort of girl who had no self-confidence and thought nobody would ever like her in that way—though, admittedly, Gary's admission had pulled the proverbial rug out from under her—but guys like those two were way out of her league. Yes, she'd gone up in the world from a horrid flat and a crap job, but she wasn't rich, famous, royal, or cultured. She didn't have friends in high places or rare, sought after skills.

She was just an ordinary girl from Birmingham, a PR assistant in a world-famous luxury hotel. They were clearly very successful businessmen with their whole lives ahead of them to become even more successful. They could date princesses, models, actresses... In fact, looking like they did, they could date anyone they damn well pleased.

So why the hell had they been looking at her like that? There had to be something she was missing. There just had to be. One of them looking at her would have been weird enough. But both of them? That was just plain freakish and confusing.

The lift opened at her floor and she scurried out, heading for her room. She'd get her face and hair sorted out, then return to the office and get stuck into her work. Wondering about motives for other people's behaviour was a waste of time—especially, she realised, as a virtual light bulb popped up over her head, since the answer was so bloody obvious.

Of course! Blue Eyes and Green Eyes had been *drunk*. It was the only feasible explanation. They'd indulged in a liquid lunch. *Over*indulged.

Heaving a sigh of relief, she let herself into her room and dove for her makeup box. Time to get freshened up, face the world again and forget about the unfortunate incident in the restaurant once and for all.

Chapter Nine

Entering the upstairs bar of the hotel, Fiona looked around for the work colleagues—whom she was gradually starting to think of as friends—who'd invited her to join them for a few Friday night drinks, which generally started in the bar as people gathered, then moved out into the city.

Soho was popular, with its variety of pubs and clubs, not to mention its laid-back vibe and gay-friendly establishments, which were exactly where several of Fiona's new work buddies wanted to be, in order to find like-minded people, and potential dates. Fiona generally just went along with whatever everyone else fancied doing and had always enjoyed herself, so she figured tonight would be no different.

That was, until she turned from the bar, holding her gin and tonic, and saw Blue Eyes and Green Eyes seated on the other side of the room, by the windows. They didn't seem to have noticed her, so she forced herself to walk casually over to the table her workmates had commandeered and take a seat where she'd be hidden from their view.

She was greeted with enthusiasm, then everyone fell back into the conversation they'd been having before she arrived. Fiona sipped her drink as she listened and caught up on the chatter, which seemed to indicate that, once again, Soho was the destination of choice. Happy to go along with the majority, Fiona let her attention drift, and she found herself leaning slightly to the right to get a view over to where the two hotties sat.

Or *had* sat, anyway. They'd gone, and by the looks of their empty glasses, which were just about to be cleared away by Carlos, one of the barmen on duty, they weren't coming back. *Oh well, at least I don't have to worry about them seeing me.*

Shrugging, Fiona returned her attention to what was happening at her table, only to discover she'd obviously missed something, because everyone was downing their drinks. She hurriedly followed suit, managing to catch up and place her empty glass on the table within milliseconds of the others.

"Okay, everyone," said Wyatt, the flamboyant, bossy guy from the admin department who generally took charge on nights out and was the main reason they frequented so many gay bars, "let's go have some fun!"

En masse, they headed for the elevators. There was no one else waiting—decorum and training dictated they'd let paying guests go in ahead of them—so they piled into two cars and zoomed down to the ground floor before scurrying out into the Mayfair streets and heading east.

Just under an hour later they were ensconced in Wyatt's favourite club, which, despite his protestations, everyone knew was his favourite because he had a thing for the manager. It didn't matter, though. It was a fun place to be and the drinks weren't too expensive. Fiona, starting to wind down, followed a bunch of her workmates onto the dance floor, and began enjoying herself—swaying, jigging and bopping away to the cheesy music. Soon, the fun, the atmosphere and the alcohol made her busy week and its period of weirdness fade away into insignificance.

***

Usually, they rolled back into the hotel—through the staff entrance, of course, so as not to risk having their drunkenness on display to the patrons—any time between two and four a.m. But due to one of the girls from Accounts, Sorcha, having an argument with her boyfriend by text message, then getting falling-down drunk as a result, Fiona was back just after midnight. She was buzzed from what she'd drunk so far, but was still well in control, so she'd opted to make sure Sorcha got back to the hotel in one piece and safely into bed.

She'd been aided by Olivia from Housekeeping, who wasn't much of a night owl anyway. So much so that she, too, had gone straight to her room after dropping Sorcha off, leaving Fiona to waver between going to bed or heading back to the bar for a couple more drinks and to chat with the bar staff for a while. Choosing the latter, five minutes later Fiona perched on a stool in the bar, keeping Carlos and Rafael company in between them serving customers and clearing tables.

She'd spent quite a bit of time in the bar over the weeks she'd been working at The Portmannow Hotel and had found it a good way to get to know her colleagues. It was easier than going out in a huge group and trying to make conversation with everyone. In the bar area, she could just talk with the two or three staff members currently on shift, grabbing snippets of conversation between them serving customers. As a result, she was pretty friendly with all the bar staff.

A sudden influx of patrons meant that Carlos and Rafael's attentions were on mixing and pouring drinks, leaving Fiona to amuse herself. She subtly watched the guests, wondering if she could guess what they'd order, and what had brought them to the hotel. Her curious nature and active imagination were soon conjuring up all kinds of situations, most of which she was sure were way off the mark. But making stuff up was keeping her entertained.

That was until a hand on her shoulder made her jolt and spin around on her stool, her heart pounding so hard she worried it'd turn her ribs to dust. Clutching at her chest, she said without thinking, "Fucking hell, you scared the shit out of me!"

A second later, which was a second too late, she realised it wasn't any of the group she'd gone out with returned to the hotel, but Blue Eyes. He stepped back, holding his hands up. "Whoa, I'm sorry, Fiona, I didn't mean to startle you. I did speak, but you were obviously in your own little world." He gave a wry grin. "I just came over to see if you wanted to join us."

Glancing to where he indicated Green Eyes sitting at a table, she nodded politely in response as Green Eyes raised his glass to her in acknowledgment. "I'm so sorry," she said, her pulse still skipping. "Please pardon my language. You startled me, and I thought you were one of my friends. I apologise."

Shrugging, Blue Eyes said, "Don't worry about it. My language is bluer than the Atlantic Ocean. Think nothing of it. So… would you like to join us?"

Fiona was torn between the answer she wanted to give, and the one propriety dictated she give. Figuring the latter was a great deal more sensible, she replied, "Thank you for the kind offer, but I don't want to gatecrash your evening. I was just chatting to my colleagues here, until they got busy."

"I know. I saw. But you won't be gatecrashing, because you've been invited. Come on. We're quite interesting, really. I'm Logan, by the way. Logan Chisholm."

Shaking the hand that was offered to her, Fiona tried not to let her brain linger on the fact his hand was large and strong, and would probably feel amazing on her—

"Fiona Gillespie," she forced out with a smile. "Nice to meet you, officially."

"You too. I take it you're okay after your incident earlier in the week?"

Glad the dim lighting would disguise much of her blush, she replied, "Yes, thank you. Absolutely fine. Thank you again for being so kind."

"No problem at all. It was my pleasure. Now, at the risk of sounding like a broken record, will you be joining us or are you going to send me back to my buddy with my tail between my legs?"

Giving her puppy dog eyes and a pout, Logan clearly knew how to win people round, which probably went some way to explaining his apparent success.

Laughing, she slid carefully from the stool, picked up her drink and her bag and said, "All right, all right. You win. But you'd better be as interesting as you say."

Logan didn't respond, but his arrogant smirk and the glint in his eyes kindled a heat low in Fiona's abdomen. Damn, that was all she needed—her hormones to start getting involved again. Look what had happened last time. Falling into step behind Logan, she took a couple of deep breaths and resisted the temptation to scurry to the elevator while his back was turned and bolt for the safety of her room.

Unbidden, her gaze dropped to his backside. Today, he was dressed more casually, but was still smart in his jeans and deep-blue shirt. And, just like his suit, his jeans appeared tailored too, so perfectly did they mould to his high, firm-looking arse cheeks. Cheeks she'd quite like to grab great big handfuls of, preferably as they were naked and thrusting—

This time, her smutty thought process was cut off by their arrival at the table. Green Eyes stood as they approached and pulled out a chair for Fiona, pushed it in as she sat down, then retook his own seat. "Hi," he said, holding out a hand, which she took. "I'm James Kenrick. I'm glad you decided to join us. It's nice to meet you properly."

"You mean when I'm not having a coughing fit." Heat overtook her cheeks again as she released his hand and wished like hell her mouth wouldn't run off so often without consulting her brain, especially not in front of two of the most gorgeous guys she'd ever seen. Guys who, for some unknown reason, wanted to speak to her, spend time with her.

"Well," James said, shrugging, "yeah. I mean, if that's what floats your boat, so be it. But I'd rather have you talking to me than coughing at me."

Smiling tightly, she lifted her glass to her lips before

mentally reminding herself to slow down, take it easy. Chugging down the drink to hide her embarrassment could set off a repeat of the other day, giving all three of them a serious case of déjà vu. Not sexy. Sipping carefully, she enjoyed the mild burn of the gin as it slid down her throat, savoured the pleasant buzz, then put the glass on the table. "Fair enough. So what would you like to talk about? Logan assures me you're both very interesting, so I look forward to hearing about you."

"I didn't say *very* interesting," Logan interrupted, that smirk on his face again. "I said we were *quite* interesting."

Rolling her eyes, she shot back, "Huh. Silly me. I should have held out for conversation only with *very* interesting men, shouldn't I?" She wasn't entirely sure where her sudden sassiness was coming from, but a splutter of laughter from James spurred her on. "You pair had better not be dullards, or I'm leaving as soon as I've finished my drink."

"Bloody hell," Logan held his hands up again, "you drive a hard bargain, Fiona. Well, as long as you don't cheat and down your drink in two seconds flat, James and I will do our best to up our game from quite to very interesting. Deal?"

"Deal."

Fucking hell, what am I doing?

Chapter Ten

"Great." Logan slapped his hands down on the table, which was sturdy enough that none of the glasses were in danger of toppling over, then picked up his pint. "Well, to make sure we're more interesting, we'll have to loosen our tongues a little. Let me go and get some more drinks in, all right? Can I get you one, Fiona?"

Eyeing her own glass, which was still half full, she said, "No, I'm all right, thanks. Maybe on the next round. If you're still interesting, that is."

Logan grinned, downed the rest of his drink, then glanced at his friend. "James? I'm going on to Jack and Coke. You?"

"Yeah, the same. Thanks."

They watched Logan for a couple of seconds as he strode towards the bar, then turned back to each other. "So," James said, his sinful lips curving up into a smile that should have been illegal, "what interests you, Fiona? Got to make sure I'm barking up the right tree, here."

She shook her head, ignoring the increasing heat low in her abdomen. "You'd better not start making stuff up. I don't want any fibs. Why don't you start by telling me about the two of you—where you're from, how old you are and what brings you to The Portmannow?"

Shrugging, he said, "Okay, that's simple enough. I'm James Kenrick. I'm twenty-nine and from Cambridge. He's Logan Chisholm, also twenty-nine, also from Cambridge. We work in property development—have our own company. We're actually pretty regular visitors to The Portmannow. Although we're based in

Cambridge, we have to travel a fair bit, for site visits, business meetings and so on. London, of course, is the centre of the frigging universe, so we're here a lot—meeting clients, wining and dining them, pitching for their business. Sometimes we stay here en route to heading out for international flights. Did that answer your questions?"

It most certainly had answered her questions, but it had also raised plenty more—and not ones she could voice without being rude. *How in the hell do two twenty-nine year olds end up with their own business, one so successful that they are regular visitors to a luxury hotel?* Maybe she should hang around with them for a little longer. Perhaps their business acumen and success would rub off on her.

"Yep." She took a sip of her drink before continuing. "And I'm still interested so far. Not fascinated, but not bored, either. Tell me more about the business, then. How did that come about?"

James was rattling off the story when Logan reappeared, placed the drinks down and settled into his seat. Smiling at Fiona, he stayed quiet as his friend talked, speaking only when James appeared to have finished.

"So," Logan said, turning his gaze onto her once more and making her feel as though she'd had her bottom glued to the chair, "that's us in a nutshell. Now are we allowed to ask about you?"

Gulping to try to relieve her suddenly dry mouth, she nodded. "Y-yes. What would you like to know?"

"The same as what James just told you. I'm guessing you got the basics before the business info."

"All right." It didn't take long. She, after all, didn't have an incredibly successful business to speak of, and her career was in its infancy.

"Ah," Logan said when she was done. "That explains why we haven't seen you around here before. We suspected you were a newbie. How are you finding it here, so far?"

"Great. I'm incredibly lucky to have landed the role, and even luckier to discover I like it and am good at it—or at least I think I am. My boss, Sophia, seems pleased with me."

"Fantastic. It certainly helps when you've got a genuine passion for your job. So, if you don't mind me asking, why are you all dressed up, yet were sitting in here chatting with your colleagues behind the bar? Not that this place isn't amazing, but London's full of nightlife. Shouldn't you be exploring a little further afield?"

Fiona rolled her eyes. "I *was* enjoying that nightlife not so long ago. A bunch of us—staff, I mean—were in Soho. But one of the girls had an argument with her boyfriend, then proceeded to get incredibly drunk. Me and one of the others decided to bring her back here before she passed out, threw up or got arrested. We put her to bed, and I decided to have a couple of drinks in here before calling it a night myself. Then you appeared and scared the crap out of me. What about you guys?" She didn't confess to having seen them earlier. They'd have no doubt wanted to know why she didn't speak or at least acknowledge them.

"The same, actually." It was James who spoke this time. "Well, not *exactly* the same. We were in Soho too, and some drunken arsehole kicked off in one of the pubs. It turned ugly and a bunch of people started fighting. We weren't involved, but we witnessed the whole thing. As soon as we could safely leave, we did. Didn't feel like going anywhere else after that, so we thought we'd have a couple more quiet ones in here before heading to our suite."

Fiona wrinkled her nose. "Ugh, yeah, I can understand why you wanted to get out of there. Not good. You certainly wouldn't see that kind of behaviour in here. No wonder you guys like staying here so much, especially if you have a suite." As she said the words, their implication sank in. If they had a suite, then they weren't just successful, just well off. They were *filthy rich.* Again, she asked herself why the hell they were talking to her. And—if she hadn't got it totally wrong—flirting with her a little, too.

"Oh yeah," Logan said. "We always have a suite. We take up quite a lot of room." It was then she noticed he'd almost finished his Jack Daniel's and Coke. "And it certainly helps that the suites are soundproofed." He let out a bark of laughter and grinned at James, who returned the smile, but his looked forced—more like a grimace.

Clearing his throat, James returned his attention to a confused Fiona. "So, where are we currently on the interesting scale? Do I need to start dancing on the table?"

Tutting, she replied, "*That* sort of behaviour wouldn't be allowed in here, either. I dunno… You're somewhere between 'quite' and 'very', I guess." Then her curiosity got the better of her. *Dead cats be damned.* The hotel was enough off the beaten track that traffic noise wasn't an issue. "How about this? If you tell me why having a soundproofed suite is such a good thing, I'll let you buy me another drink."

The men glanced at each other, and James glared at Logan momentarily, before altering his expression to a charming smile. "Oh." He waved a dismissive hand. "That's nothing interesting, I'm afraid. *He* snores."

Logan's resultant indignation and spluttering told Fiona everything she needed to know. She shook her head. "No way! If that were true, why would Logan have mentioned it with a big grin on his face? People don't publicise the fact they snore—much less to the extent that soundproofing is necessary. Come on. What is it? Wild parties? Loud music?" She lowered her voice. "Crazy monkey sex with supermodels? Swinging from the chandeliers?"

After several seconds of silence, in which the two men alternately shared uncomfortable eye contact and finished their drinks, Fiona thought perhaps she'd gone too far, been overfamiliar. But then, they'd been the ones who had wanted the conversation in the first place and had agreed to volunteer information. They only had themselves to blame if she'd unearthed the truth about their kinky sex games, or whatever.

Something didn't quite make sense. She'd only ever seen the two of them together, not with anyone else. And yet they were neither confirming nor denying that they had orgies in their luxury suite. Unless their orgies took place with people much more interesting than supermodels… Maybe they were involved in a full-on sex scandal? Married women, royals, dignitaries… In a place like this, with clientele like this, the possibilities were endless. Particularly since she defied any straight woman to turn these two down—or even one of them. She certainly wouldn't.

"Well," James said, standing and shooting a meaningful look at his friend, who also slid back his chair and got to his feet. "It's been really lovely talking to you, Fiona, but I think we're going to call it a night. Would you like us to walk you back to your room?"

"No," she said coolly. "That won't be necessary, particularly as we're not done here. You," she waved her index finger between the two of them, "started this. You took us down this path, and now you won't answer me. I have a wild imagination, you know. So if I'm not right about orgies or supermodels, then what the hell are you two up to? Something illegal? Drugs? Porn? People trafficking?" Panic made her brain spin with the potential transgressions. "Is that why you're loaded? The property development just a front for your more nefarious activities, is it? Christ, and here was me thinking there was only a certain type of clientele that frequented this place!"

She got up too, only she shoved her chair back so hard it fell over. Not bothering to pick it up, she snatched her bag, downed the last dregs of her drink and turned sharply on her heel, but not before throwing over her shoulder, "I'd say it's been nice chatting with you, gentlemen, but I don't think *any* part of that sentence is true. Goodbye."

The swirl of emotions battling inside her didn't leave room for worrying about anyone else witnessing the display. She was far too concerned with the thought that these sexy yet shady characters were clearly using the premises for their dodgy business deals. What the hell was she supposed to do? Keep quiet and pretend she didn't know anything? Go to the hotel manager? The police?

As she strode to the elevator, she quickly discounted the last two options. She had no concrete idea of what was going on, only speculation. What if she pointed the finger and there was no evidence in James and Logan's suite? She'd end up looking ridiculous and could get into trouble for calling into question the integrity and reputation of two of the hotel's regular clients.

But she wasn't happy with leaving things alone, either, not when she could have stumbled across a prostitution ring, or the supply of illegal drugs. Her conscience wouldn't allow it.

Stabbing the elevator call button, she willed it to hurry up and arrive. She wanted to be as far away from James and Logan as possible. For all their good looks, nice clothes and impeccable manners, they weren't people she wanted to be associated with.

There was a flurry of movement behind her as the doors opened, and by the time she realised they were crowding into the car with her, it was too late to do anything about it.

Ignoring them, she lifted her hand to press the button for her floor, before thinking better of it. She didn't want them to know which floor she was on, much less in which room. No, she'd wait for them to exit the elevator, then head back down to her own accommodation. She dropped her hand.

Logan reached out and selected the top floor, then sighed and ran a hand through his hair as the mechanisms kicked in and they began to rise through the innards of the building. "Fiona. Whatever you're thinking, you've got it wrong. I have no fucking idea what's going through your head, but I guarantee we don't do anything illegal."

"So you just screw supermodels, princesses and politicians," she said dryly, some of the panic trickling away. Logan seemed more exasperated than worried—like she *had* got it wrong, rather than thinking she was about to expose some criminal activity and blow their operation wide open.

"No, not even that. Look, this is going to sound even more dodgy than what your imagination has probably already come up with, but can we just show you? In our suite? It's much easier to show you than to try to explain. Please, just stay long enough to understand, then you're free to leave whenever you like. We won't stop you. You have my word. In fact, why don't you text one of your friends or colleagues and tell them exactly where you're going, so they know where to find you if necessary?" He peered at her earnestly. "It won't *be* necessary, but if it makes you feel safer—"

"No need. Just show me what you're going to show me. Let's get this over with, so I can at least go back to my accommodation with a clear conscience and sleep without having nightmares about God knows what."

Huffing out a breath, Logan nodded. "Yes, okay. We can do that. Thank you."

Snorting, she shot back, "Don't thank me yet. Who knows what I'll do with the information I'm about to receive?"

Neither man replied, and the rest of their skyward journey was made in silence, punctuated only when the elevator pinged its arrival on the hotel's top floor.

Chapter Eleven

Logan stepped out of the elevator first, and James indicated Fiona should go in front of him. Tentatively, she followed Logan, despite feeling as though she was trapped between them—the filling in a very sexy sandwich, but a dodgy sandwich, nonetheless.

She'd been to the top floor of the hotel before, but not often, and only for short periods of time. On her first tour of the building she'd seen the rooftop garden, one of the huge suites, and the world-famous restaurant—complete with world-famous chef—that were up there. She wasn't keen on having her view of the ultimate in luxury suites sullied, but she didn't feel as though she had much choice. Logan and James insisted they weren't up to anything illegal, but she wasn't going to take their word for it. Only first-hand evidence—or lack of it—was going to put her mind at rest. So she just had to suck it up, get on with it, then walk away. The place was big enough that she could easily avoid them in future.

Surreptitiously wiping her clammy palms on her skirt, she waited as Logan unlocked the door to their suite, opened it and stepped inside. He beckoned to her.

"Leave the door open," she commanded as she moved further into the room, peering anxiously around, just waiting for something—or someone—to jump out and prove one of her theories.

"Um, that's gonna be a problem," James said, pausing with his hand on the door handle.

Turning and fixing him with a withering look, she replied, "I thought you said I could leave whenever I wanted."

"You can," Logan interjected, moving to stand beside her, so close she imagined she could feel his body heat. And the scent of his cologne was real enough. It had been present in the elevator, albeit mixed with James's, but now it was individual, unique. Intoxicating.

Shit. Keep your head, Fiona! These guys are fucking dangerous. What the hell are you doing here?

"So why can't you leave the door open?"

"Because what we're going to show you is… kind of sensitive. Not for the public gaze," Logan replied.

"I fucking knew it! Come on. Just stop playing games, will you, and get on with it?" *Not for the public gaze? Christ!*

"We can't. Not until you agree we can close the door. I promise you, no harm will come to you. You know how these doors work. They lock from the inside, but there's nothing to stop you from turning the knob and walking right out. We won't lay a hand on you."

Sighing, she took a couple of steps away from Logan, hoping that putting some space between them would help slow her racing heart. She wasn't even entirely sure why it was pounding or why her hands continued to sweat. What exactly was she scared of? Them? What they were going to show her? Or the fact that, in spite of their apparent nefariousness, she still found them magnetic, captivating, and utterly gorgeous.

God, is it the thought of a bad boy? Two bad boys? They'd never done much for her in the past, but the ones she'd encountered were the more traditional kind—tattooed, motorcycle-riding or fast-car-driving types with vague employment records and a string of crazed ex-girlfriends.

James and Logan were a different breed altogether—suave, successful, stylish and smouldering—but still bad boys. And everyone knew bad boys were good for nothing but an amazing screw and a broken heart. Just as well she'd be leaving them firmly in her rear-view mirror, then. Though it was a pity to skip the amazing screw.

"Fine," she bit out, defeated. "Close the door. But soundproofing or no soundproofing, you do anything I don't like and I'll scream until my lungs explode. I also have a mobile phone and a can of pepper spray in my bag. I *will* fight you."

Logan and James exchanged a look, and she thought she saw the faintest glimmer of a smirk on Logan's face. But before she could call him out on it, it was gone. He cleared his throat loudly—exaggeratedly, she thought—and said, "Hearing you loud and clear. Ready, James?"

Nodding, James quietly closed the main door, then crossed the room and headed into one of the bedrooms.

"Okay," Logan said, his tone even, but betraying something she couldn't quite place. Strain, perhaps? "I'm going in there, too. Come on in after a couple of minutes. Stay by the door if you wish. But just promise me one thing?"

Sniffing, Fiona replied, "I don't think you're really in a position to be asking me that."

"I have to, otherwise this isn't going to work."

She rolled her eyes. "All right. What is it?"

"Promise you'll stay long enough to absorb what it is you're actually seeing. Don't make a rash judgment and leave straight away. To understand, you need to *see*."

"I promise." The cloak and dagger crap was starting to get to her, now. The delays, the anticipation—her imagination continued to run away with her. But, for some reason, she wasn't scared. Nervous, yes, but not scared for her life or her wellbeing, not even for the wellbeing of others. Her gut told her that whatever the fuck was going on here, it wasn't, to paraphrase James, for public consumption. So what the hell was it?

"Remember, give us a couple of minutes at least, then come on in."

Fiona inclined her head and watched as Logan strode after his friend. She hadn't heard anything since James had gone into the bedroom, and she didn't hear anything now. But then there was what felt like a mile between where she stood and the door they'd disappeared through and left standing open.

Dragging her attention from the men, she then turned it to the room in general. When else was she going to get the chance to poke around in one of the hotel's most beautiful suites? Particularly when it was inhabited. That, after all, was what made the rooms so interesting. Not the facilities, not the décor, not the furniture—but the thought of what people would do within the four walls. A room was just a room… But add life, love and lust, and you had a heady cocktail indeed. Heady and hopelessly addictive.

She crossed over to the windows and peered out. As the building was an older one, it was far from being a skyscraper. In fact, it was the same sort of height as the places adjacent, and so the view was of the heart of Mayfair only. She couldn't see Hyde Park, which was just a couple of minutes' walk away, on the other side of Park Lane. She couldn't see Grosvenor Square or Berkeley Square. She definitely had no chance of glimpsing Bond Street, Savile Row, Piccadilly or Oxford Street, but it didn't matter. It was enough to know they were there.

She kind of liked the fact that London wasn't laid out before her, as though she was on Mount Olympus, perusing all that was below. It meant she felt very much a part of it, instead of being above it, detached from it. And she'd rather have a gorgeous old structure with stunning period features than an ultra-modern glass and steel monolith like The Shard any day. That was what made the place so unique—the perfect blend of traditional and modern, resulting in a charm that was unparalleled. Clearly she wasn't the only one who felt that way either, as The Portmannow Hotel was always busy, always sought after, and customer feedback was consistently spectacular—even from guests for whom luxury was the norm.

Moving back towards the centre of the room, she admired the glittering chandelier, which sparkled so much it looked brand new. Not a smear, not a speck of dust to mar its magnificence. The lovely flocked wallpaper on two walls stood out against the other two walls, which were painted in an off-white—a wonderful background to the expensive paintings hung upon them. Fiona, not being much of an art buff, had no idea who the artists were, but it didn't matter. The guests would probably know, and that was what was important.

Off to one side, the sitting area alone could have easily encompassed her apartment. Huge, sumptuous sofas looked as though they'd be more comfortable than the average bed, and between them stood a coffee table plucked directly from the pages of *Perfect Homes* magazine. More realistically, it had probably been plucked from the furniture department of Harrods or Selfridges—or even custom designed and made. She resolved to find out. Such details were useful when it came to showing off the hotel in press releases and other copy. It was the sort of thing that would pull patrons in.

A bar was situated next to the sitting area. Not quite the size of the bar she'd just left, but impressive nonetheless. This was no mini-fridge. It was fully stocked, by the looks of it, and the only evidence of use were two empty glasses on the shiny black surface.

A large table took up another corner, complete with four chairs and a pull-down projector screen mounted on the wall beside it. For business meetings, she assumed.

Opposite the room the men occupied was another door—to another bedroom, probably. That was why suites were popular with businesspeople. Colleagues and associates could stay close, but still have their own space and privacy.

Which begged the question, why had James and Logan gone into the same bedroom, and what the hell were they doing in there?

She'd been nosing around for longer than the couple of minutes Logan had requested she wait, so she decided to forgo any further exploration and find out what all this palaver was about.

With a glance at the door leading out of the suite to reassure herself it was within reach, she moved towards the bedroom, careful not to snag her heels on the plush carpet and send herself sprawling to the floor.

Signs of life, of movement, were audible as she drew closer, but that was all she could figure out. It was them, she knew, but it wasn't conversation. Maybe just the occasional word, or sound—and a noise she couldn't identify. Frowning, she took in the changing view as she approached—the different carpet in the room, the edge of a wardrobe, another plush sofa, a second glittering chandelier, the base of an enormous bed.

Her attention remained on the bed as it became apparent there was movement from that area. Two bare feet appeared, two calves, two thighs, a delicious naked arse. Pausing briefly to push through the shock, she observed that limited view for a couple of seconds longer, before moving over the threshold and taking in the scene in its entirety.

As her brain processed the information her eyes were feeding to it, several emotions hit her at once—understanding, relief, confusion, surprise... and arousal.

Frozen to the spot, Fiona watched, open-mouthed, as James and Logan's so-called nefarious activity played out right in front of her. Only it wasn't nefarious at all. It was beautiful, stunning, and knicker-wettingly hot. So hot it probably should have been illegal... but definitely wasn't.

James was naked, face down on the large bed, his arms and legs spread, each limb bound to the nearest corner post using what looked like black, silky rope. Logan loomed over him, also naked, with an ominous-looking black whip thing in his hand. It had a thick handle, with lots of stringy pieces coming out of it. With a regularity of rhythm clearly born of practice, he brought the strings down on James's backside with a *thwack*. Then again, and again. Not just on his bottom, either. Blows landed on his shoulders, his sides, his back, his thighs. His skin was pink and fast turning red.

As the pieces of the jigsaw in Fiona's head fit together with a resounding *clunk,* she found that, once again, although some questions had been answered, what was unfolding right before her eyes raised many more. Ones she knew wouldn't be answered for a while yet.

After all, it couldn't possibly be good manners to interrupt someone getting whipped in order to assuage one's curiosity, could it? And, if she was honest with herself, she didn't want to interrupt—far from it. She wanted to watch, and find out what happened next. Was this just some kinky pain thing, or would they have sex, too?

Chapter Twelve

Continuing to drink in the supremely erotic sight before her, Fiona was lulled into a kind of trance by the repetitive motion of the blows Logan was laying on James. She had next to no knowledge about whipping or bondage, but she was learning on the fly. The most obvious thing was that both men were deeply into what they were doing.

Since she'd appeared in the doorway—though neither of them had acknowledged her presence, she sensed they knew she was there—Logan had gradually increased the force of his blows. Probably he hadn't wanted James to make too much noise until she saw for herself what was happening. Hearing sounds wouldn't have been enough. As Logan had said, she needed to *see*. But now, there was nothing to stop James screaming until his lungs exploded—hence the need for soundproofing.

And the *noises*. They were just as arousing as the sights. Logan was letting loose the odd grunt and groan, and every now and again she heard a heavy exhalation of breath, as though he was breathing deeply. Exertion, or trying to keep a handle on his emotions and physical reactions? Possibly all of the above.

James, on the other hand, was creating a cacophony. As he wriggled and jerked on the Egyptian cotton bedding, he moaned, gasped, yelped and growled. But above all, he begged.

"Please," she heard him say, his voice muffled by the duvet. "Please, Sir. Harder. *Harder.*"

Fiona herself gasped as Logan acquiesced. He raised his muscular arm high, gripping the implement, then brought it down with such speed and force that it *whooped* through the air before landing on James's backside, which was now criss-crossed with angry-looking red lines.

With a shout, James bucked into the mattress, then, apparently enjoying the sensation, did it again.

"Hey," Logan said, pinching James's left buttock. "None of that, please. You'll come when I say—and no sooner."

"S-sorry, Sir. I just—"

"I know exactly what you *just*. You'll have to wait. But not for long, because I need to fuck that tight hole of yours."

One of Fiona's questions, at least, had been answered. They were lovers, too. She'd suspected as much on seeing them like this, but given how wrong she'd already got the situation, she'd forbidden herself from jumping to any further conclusions.

But now she couldn't help wondering why everything that had gone before, everything that had caused her to be standing here now, had happened. Checking she was okay in the restaurant after her little coughing fit, fine. That was just what any decent person would have done. But to approach her in the bar, ask her to come and drink and chat with them, then proceed to flirt with her…? What was that all about? She had nothing to offer them, either professionally or intellectually, and certainly not physically. She didn't have the right equipment, after all.

Shaking her head, she chastised herself for getting it so wrong. Maybe it had been the alcohol. She hadn't had all that much, but enough to relax her, to give her a nice buzz, so perhaps that was why she'd thought they were interested in her in that way. How utterly ridiculous. She wouldn't make that mistake again.

Deciding it was time to leave—she'd seen what they'd wanted to show her, and she was now surplus to requirements—she allowed herself a couple more seconds to commit the delicious image to memory. She'd never really thought about what it would be like to see two men making love, but she had overwhelming first-hand experience now and had reached the conclusion it was the most sensual, erotic thing she'd ever seen. And they hadn't even got properly started, yet.

Since declaring his intentions, Logan had discarded the whip thing, then crawled up to the head of the bed—giving her an amazing view of his flexing backside, and the thick, heavy cock visible between his thighs—and retrieved a small bottle from the top drawer of the bedside cabinet. He scooted back down, then knelt between James's spread legs, flipped the lid of the bottle—which she could now see was lube—and held out the first and index fingers of his right hand.

Fiona backed away. It was time to go. She'd seen enough. They'd made their point. They were doing nothing wrong, and she now had enough fantasy fodder to last a lifetime. Staying any longer would be an intrusion of privacy. That, and she was already in danger of spontaneously combusting. Any more of this, and she'd be forced to pull up her dress, stick her hand inside her knickers and stroke her clit, which was already aching for attention. Her pussy lips also felt terribly swollen, and a veritable lake was forming in her underwear.

Thankful she had a private apartment she could hurry back to in order to spend some time alone with her battery-operated boyfriend and give herself some much needed relief, she took another step back and turned to walk towards the door.

She'd barely gone two steps when a hand grasping her wrist made her squeal. She spun back around and was faced with a full-frontal view of Logan. And, as was to be expected, he was still fully aroused. Forcing her gaze to his face and fighting hard to keep it there, she said, "What? I'm leaving. I think I've seen enough." She tugged out of his grip. "You said I could leave any time and that you wouldn't try to stop me."

He held his hands up—apparently a trait of his—and replied, "Yes, you're right. And I would never attempt to keep you here against your will. But I wondered, *we* wondered, if perhaps you'd like to… stay?"

Fiona wrinkled her nose. "What the hell for? You've made your point. I get it now. I don't need to stick around and watch any more."

"We don't want you to stay so you can *watch*." A tiny frown line appeared between his dark eyebrows. "We want you to join in."

"What?" she squeaked, then cleared her throat. "Me? But I'm…" Unable to make herself state the obvious, she glanced down at her body.

Logan's frown deepened. "You're what? Utterly gorgeous? Wearing a dress? Look, if you're not, um… interested in us, that's absolutely fine. But we kinda got the impression you were. And we're definitely interested in *you*. I mean, what red-blooded male wouldn't be?"

Fiona pinched the bridge of her nose, squeezing her eyes tightly shut. Then, after taking a deep breath and releasing it, she opened her eyes and said, "Are you trying to tell me you're both into girls, as well as each other?"

"Is that so unbelievable?"

Opening her mouth, Fiona realised she didn't know what to say. *Was* it so unbelievable? The way they'd acted around her, the fact she hadn't got the gay vibe from them at all, at least until she'd walked in on them butt naked on the bed…

"No," she eventually said. "I guess not. And I do think you're both very attractive. Don't get me wrong, but I don't know if I'm into all… that… you know."

"The flogging?" Logan chuckled. "That's fine, sweetheart. Not a problem. It's not for everyone. Sure, if you want to try it out, I'll be more than happy to oblige, but if you just want to indulge in some good old-fashioned fucking with the two of us, we'll both be happy to oblige."

"Both?" Her brain hadn't got that far ahead. It was having a busy time of it. One minute she'd been drinking with a couple of sexy guys she'd have happily slept with. The next she'd wanted to get as far away from them as possible as she'd thought they were criminals. And now, she had discovered they were lovers, played kinky games together, they liked girls, *and* they both wanted to have sex with her… at the same time.

Rubbing at her temples, she looked Logan in the eye, not entirely surprised to see amusement glinting there. "I'm sorry," she said, her voice laden with sarcasm, "I'm having a little trouble keeping up. I've a few options available here, from what I can gather. I can still leave. Or I can join in with your… flogging. Finally, I can have some good old-fashioned sex with the two of you." She paused. "Presumably, if I wanted to, I could just have sex with one of you?"

Raising his eyebrows, Logan gave a shrug. "Yes, of course." His expression turned wicked, his blue eyes suddenly full of mischief and promise. "But you won't go for that option."

"Oh? And why's that?"

With a snort, he replied, "Because you're attracted to both of us. So why on earth would you settle for just one? One man, a single portion of pleasure—albeit extreme pleasure—or two men, double the pleasure, double the hands, the mouths, the tongues, the hands, the cocks… I think you get the idea. Come on, Fiona." He held out his hand. "What's it to be? Only I can't leave poor James lying there like that for much longer. And I'm in need of some relief myself."

Unable to stop herself, Fiona raked her gaze down Logan's body—a delicious example, and one she could happily stare at all day long—and stopped at his crotch. Throughout their conversation, his cock had remained erect. Standing proud from its nest of well-groomed dark hair, it curved up towards his belly button, long and swollen, looking mouth-wateringly good. A huge part of Fiona wanted to drop to her knees on the thick carpet and suck it.

Instead, she took the proffered hand and allowed Logan to lead her back towards the bed, where James remained spread-eagled and face down on the mattress.

Escorting her to a nearby chair, Logan indicated she should

take a seat. "Be with you in two ticks, gorgeous."

As if to emphasise his point, he leaned down and pressed a kiss to her lips. An all-too-brief kiss that was warm and sensual, that did nothing to whet her appetite and everything to make her want another, much longer kiss—and much more besides.

"Change of plan, baby," Logan said, aiming his words at James as he moved to the nearest corner of the bed to untie the restraints. "Looks like we've got a guest for the evening."

Turning his head so he could look at her, James smiled. "Excellent news. I'm glad to hear it. S'been a while since we had a girl in bed with us. I'm already looking forward to sucking on those nipples, caressing those delicious tits of yours and eating your pussy—"

He stopped abruptly when Logan landed a sharp smack on his arse cheek. "Oi, enough of that. As much as I agree with what you're saying, you don't want to scare our guest off before we've even begun, do you?"

He looked over at Fiona with a smile. "We're kinda fond of dirty talk, I'm afraid. Like some of our other favoured activities, we know it's not for everyone."

Fiona shrugged. "It's all right. You go ahead. I have no idea how this works, so I guess I'll have to go with the flow, be led by you guys." She paused, nibbling on her bottom lip. "I don't suppose I could get myself a drink, could I? The booze from earlier has most definitely worn off, and I could do with a bit of Dutch courage."

"Certainly not," Logan shot back, releasing James from the last restraint, then immediately pulling the man close and rubbing at his ankles and wrists in turn, presumably to make sure he was okay. "If you could give me a moment to attend to James, *I'll* get you a drink. I'd like one, and I'm sure James would, too. But, just to be absolutely clear, it'll be one drink, and one drink only. I understand you might be a little nervous—though I assure you, you have no need to be. We'll take the best possible care of you—but I want you fully in control of all your faculties. Including, most importantly, your capacity to say no. If you want out at any point or you change your mind, you speak up. All right?"

For fuck's sake! He'd spent all this time persuading her what a good time she'd have with the two of them, and now he was trying to talk her out of it? She wished he'd make his bloody mind up.

Chapter Thirteen

"Fiona." Logan's tone was firm, commanding. "Do you understand what I'm saying?"

She stifled a sigh. "Yes, I understand. I just don't get why you're trying to talk me out of it."

Giving James a brief kiss on the lips before releasing him, Logan stood. Shaking his head, and flashing her a wry smile, he said, "Are you frigging insane? I am certainly *not* trying to talk you out of it. I'm just making absolutely sure this is what you want, that's all. Despite your earlier comment, I *am* a gentleman—well, most of the time, anyway. Once you're naked and in bed with the two of us, I make no promises."

As he turned on his heel—still gloriously naked—and strode out into the main room, she watched him go. The arousal that had been ebbing and flowing for goodness knew how long now flared up again, big style. Logan and James were just so... affecting. Handsome, yes. Well dressed, yes. Intelligent, yes. But more than that, they had a confidence that was very attractive and, in Logan's case, not a small amount of arrogance. But she supposed that was what made him such a good businessman.

Movement from the huge bed snagged her attention, and she turned to look at James, who'd rolled over onto his back and was settled against the mountain of pillows at the head of the bed. He gave her a lazy smile, and she returned it innocently before realising what he was doing. His movements were so slow, so languorous that she hadn't noticed he'd fisted his still-erect cock and was stroking it.

She shouldn't have been surprised, though. She had, after all, managed to disrupt their almost-sex by attempting to leave, causing Logan to stop her. Both men had been aroused for some time now and hadn't—unless she'd missed it while still in the main room of the suite—climaxed. A small part of her felt sorry for them, but a much bigger part thought they deserved it for treating her to such torment. She, too, had been on a slow burn—since Logan had approached her in the bar, in fact—so they were all in the same predicament. It was a nice touch that they'd all be getting off together very soon. Hopefully.

Her pussy and clit throbbed almost painfully as she continued to watch James touch himself. Dutch courage or not, the temptation to strip off her clothes, jump onto the bed and sink that luscious cock inside her grew stronger by the second. She was sure it'd fill her nicely, stretch her, stroke her in all the right places and, ultimately, make her come. And that was before she even took into consideration any kissing, any foreplay and the fact there were two of them.

A tall, dark and gorgeous reminder came into the room just as she arrived at that thought, skilfully carrying three drinks. He crossed over to Fiona first. "Yours is the nearest one to you. A gin and tonic, no ice, like earlier. I hope that's okay."

"Yes, thank you." After removing the glass carefully from his grip so as not to cause him to drop the others, she took a sip, once again savouring the gentle burn and buzz that followed. Reluctantly—though she kept the information to herself—she agreed that Logan was right. A little bit of Dutch courage was okay, but if she was going to do this—which she absolutely was; she wasn't *insane*, after all—then she didn't want to be totally plastered. Why have an amazing experience like a threesome with two gorgeous guys, but be so drunk she couldn't remember a damn thing? No—just a smidge of booze, enough to stop her being a Nervous Nellie, was fine. She also knew, somehow, that if she was to get totally plastered, neither man would do anything with her, anyway. Now she understood them a bit better, she realised they were, in fact, complete gentlemen.

Except, as Logan had so sexily and seductively reminded her, when it came to being naked and in bed, all three of them. A wave of arousal crashed through her, further increasing the swollen, aching need between her thighs and making her knickers even wetter. God, she hoped the reality lived up to the fantasy.

She had a sneaking suspicion it would.

By now, Logan had walked back over to the bed, perched on the edge and handed James his drink. They sat together in a companionable silence, quenching their thirst. A few moments later, having placed his now-empty glass on the bedside table, Logan got to his feet and said, "Okay, I'm going to use the bathroom. Then, unless anyone has any objections, I'd quite like to have some more fun." He fixed his gaze on Fiona. "No more interruptions."

Fiona felt as though her brain was the ball in a pinball machine. Or perhaps it was just the situation that was pinging around in random unpredictable directions.

Blinking a couple of times, Fiona then shook her head and downed her drink in a couple of gulps. No more pinging around—what was the point? They were three consenting adults and that was all that mattered. She placed her glass on a nearby end table, then slipped her bag from her shoulder and her shoes from her feet. Finally, she waited for Logan to return from the bathroom.

A few minutes later, having used the toilet, cleaned up, freshened her makeup and gargled with some of the minty mouthwash the hotel supplied to all guests, she returned to the bedroom. James and Logan were sprawled against the pillows, with a gap between them. A Fiona-sized gap. She also noted the bumper-sized box of condoms that had appeared on the bedside cabinet.

Glancing between them, she took in their identical grins, their equally luscious physiques and their semi-erect cocks. Looking back up to each of their faces in turn and enjoying the arousal she saw in their eyes, she then screwed up her courage and began to undress. The grins grew wider. Like Tweedle-Dum and Tweedle-Dee. Only, you know, hot.

By the time she had removed her dress, bra and thong, the arousal had turned to pure hunger, and the cocks had waved goodbye to their semi-erect status and were full-on raring to go. *Christ*, she thought, as she approached the bed and climbed onto the huge mattress, *where the hell am I supposed to start?*

Sensing her hesitation, Logan patted the bed. "Come on, gorgeous. Don't worry. We'll take care of you."

"Yeah," James concurred, his green eyes burning with intensity, "in more ways than one."

As gracefully as possible—which wasn't very, because how did one crawl gracefully up a bed?—she moved into the space between the two men, immediately struck by the heat their bodies were giving off. She took longer than necessary to settle into position, hoping the tremble of her hands wasn't apparent.

In a move that could have been choreographed, James and Logan turned on their sides to face her, still smiling. The body heat was now almost overwhelming, and her nostrils picked up the scents of their various shampoos, shower gels and colognes, as well as the visceral scent of raw masculinity, laced with a not-inconsiderable amount of arousal. She was surrounded by it, drowning in it, and they hadn't even touched her yet.

That was soon rectified. Logan reached out and tucked her hair behind her ear, caressed her cheek. "How do you want this to play out, Fiona? Do you want to tell us what you do and don't want to do? Or do you want to just lie back and let us do our thing? Go with the flow?"

Her pulse fluttered in her neck. "Just… um… do your thing. Please."

His breath was warm on her cheek as he replied, "Okay, we will. I'm looking forward to it."

Then his lips touched hers, softly at first, and she had to twist a little to return the kiss. She felt bad, half-turning her back on James, but she couldn't give equal attention to both of them all the time. Some of the time, they would simply have to take turns. But others…

She groaned. God, were they thinking of double penetration? The thought both petrified her and turned her on beyond belief. But she was soon forced to turn her attention back to Logan, whose tongue now sought entrance to her mouth as he cupped her jaw.

James's hands weren't idle, either. He ran one down her flank, stroking her hip, the side of her thigh and her bum, then sweeping back up and over to squeeze her breast. She moaned into Logan's mouth as James continued massaging her soft flesh, her stiff bud brushing his palm. James then released her breast, only to concentrate on her nipple, rolling it between his fingers, pulling and pinching it. He was gentle at first, testing how much she could take, how much she enjoyed.

Juices pooled between her thighs, soaking her skin and threatening to run down onto the expensive bed linen. She could scarcely believe what was happening—two gorgeous guys focusing purely on her pleasure, and there was so much more to come. She just knew it.

Sure enough, Logan's kiss grew more passionate, almost violent, as he plundered her mouth, nibbling her lips, sucking her tongue, exploring her thoroughly.

At the same time, James had shifted closer. His body was now flush against hers, his rigid, hot cock pressed enticingly to her bottom and upper thigh. It meant he could reach further over her body, slipping his hand between Fiona and Logan to treat her other breast to the same erotic treatment. Caressing, kneading, cupping. Pinching, pulling, rolling.

Suddenly, she gained enough control of her lust-fogged mind to realise she was being somewhat of a passive participant. Sure, she was kissing Logan back, but her hands had remained by her sides, when they could be doing something *much* more interesting—or one of them could, anyway. Her position half on her side meant the arm trapped beneath her was all but useless. But the other…

Since she was already kissing Logan, she figured James deserved some attention. She reached behind her, seeking the stiff dick that she could so easily manoeuvre into her slick pussy. She wouldn't, of course, not without protection, but she could certainly tease him the way he was teasing her.

Finding James's cock, she dragged her nails along its length, smirking against Logan's mouth as James gasped. She repeated the motion, then circled her fingers around his shaft and got her hand into a position where she could stroke him. It was a little awkward, but she figured out a way, and began shuttling her fist up and down his thickening length, gratified at the sounds her actions elicited from those sinful lips.

In return, he swept aside her hair and pressed said lips to the side of her neck, the hollow beneath her ear, the crook between neck and shoulder. He alternated delicate kisses, light sucking and running his teeth over the sensitive skin. All the while his stubble scraped against her. It set all the tiny hairs on her body standing on end, especially when he pulled her earlobe between his lips and nibbled it, his breath hot and giving off a mild scent of whiskey.

God, she was already going into overload. She was kissing Logan, who was now tugging lightly at her hair to change the angle of their caress and also to expose more of her throat to James. James played with her breasts and titillated her neck. And she, in turn, was playing with a very erect cock that was leaking precum onto her backside.

Neither of them had so much as looked at her pussy yet, and

she felt as though she was on the very edge of climax. Not that it would matter if she came, though. It wasn't like she'd come once and it'd all be over. She was definitely up for multiples.

She smiled to herself. What an incredibly lucky girl she was.

Chapter Fourteen

The tension increased rapidly between the three of them as they continued to fool around, giving and receiving pleasure in a delicious cycle that felt like it could go on forever. Fiona certainly wouldn't have minded if it did. They could order food and drinks from room service, and have clean clothes, condoms and anything else their hearts desired sent up until the end of time.

Suddenly, a strong hand grasped her wrist, and James muttered into her ear, "Hey, stop. Amazing as that feels, you need to stop, unless you want me to come all over your back."

Fiona wouldn't have minded that, either, but there were much more creative ways to make a man come. Hopefully she'd have the chance to explore more than one of those ways, given she had two eager cocks to experiment with. She released James's shaft and reached for Logan's, only to have another hand grip her wrist.

"Uh-uh," Logan said, breaking their kiss. "I've got a much better idea."

After gently pushing her shoulder to encourage her to lie back on the bed, Logan placed his fingertip on her bottom lip, then ran it from there, all the way to her cropped pubic hair. "You're so beautiful, Fiona. You know that?"

It didn't seem like a question that warranted a reply, so she didn't give one. Instead, she waited to see what would happen next, all the while enjoying the delicious view of two perfect male bodies. She wondered whether she would have the opportunity to see them make love to each other, as well as her. She certainly hoped so. What she'd observed earlier had got her so hot that it was clear the two of them full-on fucking would be mind-blowing.

Logan's next question, however, most definitely warranted a reply. "I'm thinking of fucking your mouth while James eats your pussy. You okay with that?"

Nodding enthusiastically, she forced out a strangled, "Yes!"

God, it sounded so rude when he just came out with it like that, the smooth, cultured accent enunciating the dirty words. But maybe that was what made it so sexy.

Chuckling, Logan replied, "All right. I'm very glad to hear it. But there's something I have to do first."

Leaning over her, he slipped his hand behind James's neck and pulled him in for a rough kiss. James responded with enthusiasm, and their mouths mashed together in an embrace that looked almost painful, and yet the grunts and groans they came out with said that, painful or not, it felt good.

It looked pretty damn amazing too and, far from being jealous or feeling left out, she was content to watch them express the way they felt about each other and enjoy the incredibly erotic scene. And hell, if they happened to get carried away and forget about her, then she'd stick her hand between her legs and stroke herself into blissful oblivion over the sight of their sweaty, entangled bodies. Either way, she won.

After a few more minutes the boys parted, eyes blazing, spots of high colour on their cheeks, and lungs grabbing at precious air. Then, with barely a pause, James moved up the bed and kissed her, his lips feeling every bit as luscious as they looked. He kissed differently to Logan, somehow, but was neither worse, nor better.

Just as sexy and arousing as his lover, he explored and possessed every millimetre of her mouth, leaving her melting beneath his caress and gasping as he pulled away with a wicked grin.

"Just had to do that, gorgeous. Thought it'd be rude to kiss your pussy without having kissed your lips yet."

Shifting back down the mattress, he left Fiona grinning dazedly at the spot he'd vacated, which was soon filled with an impressive view of Logan. The ridges of his abdomen appeared, and she snapped out of her stupor as he straddled her chest. She raked her gaze over his arms, chest and abdomen, then allowed herself a nice, long look at his cock. Standing thick and proud, a slick of precum sat at its tip, and she wanted to lick it while stroking his shaft. But, pinned into place as she was, her arms by her sides, she could do neither.

She also couldn't see James, and therefore had no idea what he was doing. Rebelling against having her choices taken away from her, she shifted her arms enough so she could reach up, grab Logan's delectable arse cheeks and force him closer to her mouth.

Clearly surprised, he shot out his hands to break his fall, and they landed on the soft pillows above Fiona's head. Without giving him the chance to move again, she closed her lips around the tip of his dick, savouring the sensation of thick, hot cock in her mouth, and tonguing the juices seeping from its tip. The taste exploded, tart and salty, over her taste buds, and she hummed happily as she used her hands to pull him further into her mouth.

Though apparently a fan of being in charge, Logan seemed to have been rendered powerless by her act of defiance, unable to make himself shift away from her lapping tongue. He'd said he planned to fuck her mouth, but was instead holding himself still as she sucked it.

She was just establishing a rhythm when she felt James's hands on the insides of her knees, creeping higher and pushing her legs apart at the same time. Momentarily distracted, she paused and gasped around Logan's cock.

It was enough. He took the opportunity to reset the balance of power, and he began doing what he'd promised—slowly rocking his hips so his shaft slipped in and out of her mouth.

Fiona, knowing she was beaten, relaxed into the movement, letting saliva coat Logan's hot, thrusting cock, while settling her lips over her teeth so she didn't hurt him when he increased his speed, which she was certain he would.

After a few moments, she was very glad Logan had taken the reins, because now James had reached the apex of her thighs, her brain was more focused on what was happening down there. His hands had shifted higher and higher, until she was spread rudely before him. Given his stillness, she suspected he'd simply looked at the wanton display for several long moments, before diving in and beginning to tease and titillate her.

His hot mouth was just as skilful between her legs as it had been on her neck, shoulder and lips, and not being able to see what he was doing served only to heighten the sensations. With an enthusiasm that told her he enjoyed being with women just as much as men, he ran his tongue the length of her slick seam, delving deep. Murmuring contentedly, which caused little tremors to run across her swollen labia and clit, he parted her pussy lips and gave a long, slow lick, before pulling away and blowing on the wet skin.

Chills skated across Fiona's entire body, and her pussy clenched. Christ, he knew how to tease! And she couldn't even encourage, plead or beg, because her mouth was otherwise occupied.

It was obvious the two of them had done this before. It was a tried and tested method, one that left the lucky woman they were sharing in a position where she had to lie back and take it. But Fiona was most definitely not thinking of England. In fact, she could barely think at all. She was being bombarded by sensation, and she was sure the moment James's tongue touched her clit, she'd be spiralling into an orgasm she'd been building towards for hours.

Apparently, she wasn't going to find out if she was right. Not just yet, anyway. James moved his mouth away, and his thick fingers entered her pussy, probing and stretching, though she was so wet he could have penetrated her with his cock with no trouble at all. She'd have accommodated him easily and, more than anything, was what she desperately wanted at that moment in time. There was a cock in her mouth, jerking away and continuing to lace her taste buds with salty precum, and she wanted one in her pussy, too.

Digging her nails into Logan's pert buttocks, humming around his shaft and tilting her hips in one movement, she hoped to spur the two men to some kind of action. She was suspended on the very edge of climax, her arousal rapidly turning to frustration. She just wanted to come, just once, then they could carry on doing whatever they wanted. But the pressure building inside her wanted out, and fast.

Bucking her hips again and clawing at Logan's buttocks, Fiona now grunted around the invasion between her lips. *Come on!* she screamed silently. *For Christ's sake, make me fucking come!*

Sucking in a breath through his teeth, Logan slowed his movements and let out a chuckle. "Seems we've got a little wildcat on our hands here, doesn't it, mate?"

"It does," came the reply. "She's jerking against my face like she's in a fucking rodeo or something. Think she wants to come?" He continued to finger-fuck her as he spoke, feeding more and more pleasure into her system, but not quite enough to tip her over.

"I think she'd *love* to come," Logan all but purred, pushing his cock deeper into her throat than he'd ventured before, making her fear for her gag reflex. But he was apparently a pro in that department, too, and didn't go too far. "And you know what? I think she's probably earned it, don't you? Just one orgasm, to get her started."

Get me started? Holy fuck, how long are these two planning to carry on for?

"All right," James said amenably. He angled his fingertips to stroke and press at her G-spot, then took her clit between his lips and began sucking. Lightly at first, which fanned the embers of her climax and turned them into gently flickering flames. Then, satisfied she was used to the sensation, he licked the aching bud, getting it plenty wet. Over and over he licked, before closing his lips around her again and sucking harder, increasing the pressure at the same time as he upped the speed with which he stimulated her G-spot.

The gently flickering flames grew higher, brighter, hotter,

and Fiona sucked in shaky, hasty breaths through her nostrils as her chest heaved. She was hanging over the edge now, the merest thread stopping her from plummeting into the abyss.

"She's close," James said, his voice husky, laden with his own arousal. "Really close."

"Good," Logan replied, his own voice a little shaky. "I am, too. I'm going to come between these sweet lips any second—" He stopped, let out a strangled sound. *"Now!"*

Fiona's world tilted on its axis. At the same time her mouth was being filled by hot cum, her own climax ripped through her with a sudden, unexpected force that left her wildly grabbing for air. Black spots danced before her eyes as her abdomen undulated, her core clutching and spasming around James's fingers and the flames now an inferno that raged along every nerve ending, leaving her completely burnt out.

"Shiiit," James said, apparently the only one of them capable of speech. "If that's the way she starts, I can't wait to see how she carries on."

***

A little while later, feeling brave, Fiona voiced something that had been playing on her mind. "You know…" She smiled, heat coming to her cheeks in a mixture of embarrassment and arousal. "I haven't actually seen you two, um… *together*."

Both men glanced at her, and Logan raised an eyebrow. "You mean, *together* together?"

Sure he was deliberately winding her up, or trying to make her say the actual words, she refused to give him the satisfaction. "Yes. That's precisely what I mean, and you know it."

Mischief glinting in his eyes, he said, "Well, not that we need an excuse, but I'm game if James is."

Simultaneously flicking their gazes to James, they watched as he rolled lazily onto his stomach, his lips curving up into a lascivious smile. His still-pink backside was on tempting display, welcoming Logan's attentions. No verbal answer was necessary.

Logan reached for the lube, encouraged Fiona to swap places with him on the bed, then moved in for the kill. He used plenty of the liquid to slicken James's rear hole, before positioning himself between James's legs and pressing the meaty head of his cock against the puckered entrance. With a hiss, he pushed inside.

Fiona remained silent, her mouth and eyes wide as she observed the scene unfolding before her. Her right hand, seemingly on autopilot, crept between her legs. Finding herself wet and hot once more, she stroked her pussy and clit, tormenting and teasing herself slowly towards orgasm as James and Logan made sensual, passionate love.

Chapter Fifteen

Several days later, Fiona was still walking on air. From the moment she'd agreed to the seriously sexy threesome with James and Logan to collapsing into her own bed in the early hours of the morning, it had been truly unforgettable. They'd spent what felt like forever—in a good way—teasing and pleasing each other in a variety of positions and pairings. She'd had sex with both of them, sucked them, had them lick her, stroke her, rub her, pinch her. There'd been sixty-nines, moves she wasn't sure even had proper names, and lazier moments where they'd lain in a tangle of limbs and touched each other, languidly continuing to explore sweat-dampened skin.

And now, the men having departed several days earlier, Fiona was left with lasting memories so supremely erotic that replaying them in her mind felt like watching custom-made porn. She didn't really need to replay them, however. Her body still ached and buzzed from the sexual acrobatics, and the release of hormones must have stimulated her brain somehow, too, because she'd written some of her best-ever copy and come up with the smartest ideas in recent days.

Sophia had noticed. She strode over to Fiona's desk, leaned her curvy bottom on its edge and gave her a narrow-eyed stare.

"W-what's wrong?" Fiona asked. "Have I done something?"

Drumming her French-polished nails against the wooden surface beneath her, Sophia replied, "That's what I've come to find out. You've been good, almost from day one. But these last few days, you've been something else. On fire. Your mood has been as buoyant as your work has been amazing. Have you got yourself a boyfriend… or girlfriend?" she added hastily, covering all her bases.

Colour raced into Fiona's cheeks, and she found herself hoping Sophia might attribute that to the compliment, rather than the query. "N-no, I haven't. I like men, by the way. But I haven't got a boyfriend. I just… I dunno—maybe I'm getting into my stride? I've had a good tutor, after all. The best!" She laughed, mentally keeping her fingers crossed that her deflection tactics had worked. The last thing she wanted was anyone asking questions about her private life. Not that she had one—not since that night—but she didn't want it getting out. No way was she going to risk losing her job over a one-night stand with a couple of guests, albeit the best one-night stand in the history of everything, ever.

Narrowing her eyes further, Sophia tilted her head to one side. "Hmm… I'm not sure it's just getting into your stride. But whatever… It's none of my business. As long as it's not illegal, you carry on doing it and coming out with these strokes of genius. We're seriously loving your work, Fiona, and your dedication and enthusiasm. I know you've not been here that long, but keep it up and you could soon be in line for promotion."

Beaming, Fiona replied, "Really? That's fantastic! Yes, for sure I'll keep it up. You know how much I love this job, how much I appreciate the opportunity I've been given. I want to progress, and I'll work my backside off to help that happen."

Returning Fiona's smile, Sophia stood. "I know you will, sweetie. You're a great addition to the team, and we love having you with us. Now stop your gossiping and get back to work." With a wink, she went back to her office, leaving Fiona open-mouthed and red-faced in her wake.

Bloody hell. She hoped she could keep coming up with the ideas and copy that had so impressed her boss. Perhaps she should invest in a shitload of high-powered batteries for her vibrator, then masturbate herself into oblivion each night to keep those happy hormones flooding her system? She sure as hell couldn't conjure up a nightly threesome. Well, actually, this was London—with the assistance of technology, she probably could. But definitely not with two smart and sexy businessmen who indulged in all kinds of kinky shit, as well as screwing each other *and* women. It'd take more than the wonders of the internet and hook-up apps to conjure up a combination like *that*.

Shit. Battery-operated oblivion it was then. Or was it? Perhaps it was time to get her kicks somewhere else.

Although it had only been the tiniest part of their evening together and hadn't involved her directly, Fiona often replayed in her mind the part where Logan had used the flogger on James's gorgeous naked arse. She also now knew—due to extensive pillow talk when they'd been catching a breath—it had been tame compared to what normally happened between the two of them. They were heavily into BDSM, and Logan often spanked, whipped and caned his lover, making it uncomfortable for him to sit down for days, in spite of Logan's loving aftercare. And they *adored* it. It was a big part of their relationship, though they'd been eager to add it wasn't necessary all the time, that they were happy to indulge in good old-fashioned vanilla fucking, either with or without a third party.

Something about it had sparked Fiona's imagination. It was cheesy, but her night with them had truly been a revelation, one that had opened her eyes wide. She'd been thrown in at the deep end, presented with seemingly endless opportunities, and had enjoyed every last second. And now she'd had time to absorb it all, go over it in her head, figure out her feelings on the matter, she knew she'd do it all again in an instant if given the chance.

But she also wanted more. She'd been bitten by the experimentation bug, and although she wasn't up for taking any stupid risks, she had to know about the darker side of James and Logan's relationship—the side that involved handcuffs, gags, blindfolds, whips, floggers and all manner of things she had no idea about.

In an ideal world, she'd ask them if they were interested in showing her, but that wasn't an option. They'd upped and left without so much as a goodbye, and she had no way of contacting them, not without exploiting the hotel's information system, and she wasn't willing to do that. It'd be way too easy to get caught and would be a gross invasion of privacy—a sackable offense. She'd already played with fire by spending the night with them and had got away with it. She wasn't about to get burned by trying to repeat the experience, especially since she had no idea whether they would want to. Perhaps they were happy to leave things at one decadent, debauched night, and move on.

Much as the idea disappointed Fiona, she figured it was probably the case. Otherwise, why would they have checked out and not tried to get in touch with her or found a way to pass on their details? No doubt if she did risk contacting them, she'd make a complete fool of herself. They might not even remember who she was.

Resolving to leave things well alone with James and Logan, she made a mental note to start researching BDSM. She knew from passing comments by friends and colleagues that there were many fetish events all over London and its wider suburbs, so she'd just have to find one or two that appealed, and check them out. See where things went from there.

Nodding to herself, she took a couple of deep breaths and got her brain back into work mode, determined to come out with something genius to dazzle her boss. Private life and multiple orgasms be damned—she'd been told from the moment she started her creative writing degree that skill could not be taught. It seemed she had a knack for it. It was just a matter of bringing it out, nurturing it and improving upon it. She wasn't short of determination or ambition, either. She could do it, *would* do it.

Putting fingers to keyboard, she began to type.

***

Later, as Fiona lounged in the bath with a book, she found her mind wandering. It was nothing to do with the quality of the writing, the storyline or the characters, and everything to do with the curiosity that seemed to be constantly burning away in the back of her mind. It had now crept to the forefront and demanded to be noticed.

How did it feel for Logan when he flogged James? How did it feel to swing his muscular arm with varying degrees of force, knowing that when the blow landed, it was going to hurt the man he loved? To leave marks that would grow angrier and more painful the longer he went on?

And what about the reverse? What did James experience, other than the obvious pain, when Logan flogged him? Or whipped him? Or plain old spanked him?

It had to feel good—for both of them—otherwise they wouldn't do it. And she'd seen with her own eyes the evidence that it aroused both of them immensely.

They'd talked a lot about the surrender of control, of letting go, but she hadn't fully grasped what they'd meant, and supposed she wouldn't until she'd experienced it for herself. It was clearly about much more than giving and receiving pain.

After putting the bookmark in, she placed the novel on the floor beside the bath. Then, shifting so her pale thighs were out of the water, she lifted her right hand and brought it down, hard, on her right thigh. The sound was shocking, amplified by the water and the tiled room. It took a second or two for the physical sensation to hit. A sharp bloom of pain across her skin. She gasped. Granted, she hadn't hit herself very hard, but it had still stung.

Repeating the action on her left side, though with more force, she experienced the same physical reactions, with more intensity. Pink marks had appeared on her skin, her blood rushing to the surface, and suddenly, as the mild discomfort morphed into something darker, more delicious, she began to understand exactly why this sort of thing floated James and Logan's respective boats.

Chapter Sixteen

Having finally managed to cross Park Lane—which, to a pedestrian, was akin to crossing a busy motorway—Fiona was swallowed into the relative peace and immense greenery of Hyde Park. She'd found that, providing there were no big events on, it was a great place to go running. So large it never seemed crowded—big events notwithstanding—but always having people around, it felt safe.

Keeping to a gentle jog until she got away from the busier area of Hyde Park Corner, where tourists gathered as they entered and exited the Tube station, Fiona was careful not to collide with any of the people peering at maps, guidebooks and phones.

Soon, though, as the area opened up and path after path filtered big groups into smaller ones, couples and solo folk, she picked up her speed. Her feet pounded the well-maintained walkways, and she was able to relax, empty her mind as she travelled metre after metre.

Today was Friday, and a rare day off during the week, so she didn't have to rush. Four weeks had passed since That Night, as she'd dubbed it, and the last two of them had been crazy. A bunch of meetings among the upper management had resulted in lots of new things being passed down the chain of command—improvements to be made, changes to plan and put into force, and approval of ideas pitched now needing to be actioned.

Only the latter had affected Fiona and her team, and one of Fiona's own ideas, much to her delight, had been not only accepted, but highly commended. So she'd been given the major responsibility—though still being overseen by Sophia—of getting things going. It had been a mammoth task, one that had required her to work a great deal of overtime, but she'd loved every minute. Seeing her ideas come to life, having them appreciated and admired by others… It had definitely been worth all the hard work.

As a result, though, she'd barely left the hotel in two weeks, as she'd either been working or so exhausted from work she couldn't muster the energy to head out. Which was why Sophia had, the previous day, called her into her office and notified her she was having the following day off—no arguments.

Her body clock had still woken her at the usual time, much to her chagrin. But she felt rested, and after tossing and turning a while, then coming to the conclusion she wouldn't get back to sleep, she'd got up, dressed in her exercise gear, then headed out. The brilliant sunshine had been very welcome, and Fiona enjoyed it now as it bathed her skin, albeit in spits and spots as she passed in and out of the shadows of the huge trees filling the park.

She decided to head as far as the road bisecting The Serpentine and The Long Water, follow it up to the north side of the park, then loop back around to Speakers' Corner and Marble Arch, cross back over Park Lane and go through the thick of Mayfair to return to the hotel. She'd likely get snarled up in foot traffic around the Marble Arch area, but once she left Park Lane and disappeared down one of the side streets, it'd soon fall quiet again. Not many tourists seemed to penetrate that far, which was a shame for them, as they were missing out on amazing squares, restaurants and architecture—not to mention celeb-spotting, if that floated their boat.

Immediate plans made, Fiona allowed her brain to consider her evening's entertainment. She was heading to a fetish event. Weeks of indecision and a heavy workload meant her research into the kinky lifestyle James and Logan had given her the tiniest glimpse of had been difficult, to say the least. It hadn't been as simple as a Google search and job done. Once she'd opened up the search engine, she'd fallen into a digital rabbit hole with a seemingly endless choice of websites, venues and events. So much so that she'd had to go on a bookmarking frenzy, then go through each website over the course of several evenings until she'd found what seemed best for her.

Being given the day off had helped make her decision. In her naïveté, Fiona had thought she could just rock up at one of the clubs whenever she felt like it and walk right in. However, her research had revealed that most of the events only happened on certain dates, and pretty much all of them had strict dress codes. Turning up in her trusty little black dress wasn't going to cut it, apparently, but although this particular evening's event had been top of her to-attend list, she hadn't thought she'd have time to go shopping.

Now, though, with oodles of free time laid out ahead of her, everything was falling into place. She could go shopping, find something that would pass the dress code without making her too self-conscious or look ridiculous, then attend what had been lauded *London's friendliest fetish event*. Fiona hoped the emphasis on 'friendliest' wasn't exaggerated. She was going alone, which was nerve-wracking enough, without having the shit scared out of her by other attendees. She wished she had someone to go with, but she hadn't been brave enough to ask any of her colleagues, or Gary, Ben or Jenny, and she'd still not seen hide nor hair of James and Logan, so it was alone or not at all. And her patience wasn't going to hold out much longer. She had to find out what the hell this was all about, whether it was for her or not. Then at least she could move on.

A spike of irritation flared as she thought of James and Logan, but rather than allowing her mind to continue down that path, she picked up speed, forcing her brain to engage wholly with her body, to push it to its fullest potential. Grass, trees, bushes, flowers and people whipped past in a blur, but she managed to maintain her speed for a good while, until screaming lungs and muscles forced her to take a break and flop onto a wooden bench in the shade of a huge old oak tree. Gulping at her sports drink, she quickly regained her equilibrium. Then she stood up and continued her run at a more manageable pace, the thought of a nice long shower dangling like an invisible carrot in front of her.

***

Two hours later and Fiona was showered, changed, briefly rested and back out on the streets of London. The run had helped clear her mind, cast off her worries and sharpen her focus on the night ahead, which was why she was now heading south of the river to a specialist shop she hoped would help get her kitted out without breaking the bank. Granted, her wage was much better these days, but she didn't want to spend a fortune on something that might end up being worn once then relegated to the very back of her wardrobe, never to be seen again.

Her eyes widening as she caught sight of the window displays, Fiona took a deep breath before pushing open the shop door and crossing the threshold. Somehow, she knew the most outrageous stuff wouldn't be in the window, and that the things she saw in the shop would be nothing compared to what she'd clap eyes on at the event. So she had to hurry up and get used to this kind of thing, otherwise she'd spend the whole evening resembling a goldfish. Not sexy.

An attractive blonde-haired woman dressed in a black and red corset and black leggings was tidying a rack of outfits. She smiled as Fiona entered. "Hi, honey. You need help finding something, or are you just looking around?"

Contemplating whether she looked as nervous as she felt, she replied, "I'm just looking for now. I don't quite know what I want, really."

"No problem at all. If you need any help, or have any questions, just let me know. I'm Divine."

Yeah, Fiona thought, *you are, actually. If I was into women…*

Smiling politely, she thanked Divine and glanced around, wondering where to start. At least there weren't any other customers to observe her discomfort. Steering away from racks full of black PVC and chains, she headed for the rails with colourful items on them, hoping to find something a little more beginner-friendly. Soon, she discovered a black and white PVC schoolgirl outfit. Okay, so it wasn't terribly original, but she reckoned she could wear it without being too embarrassed, and it was the sort of thing one might wear to a hen party. It was sexy and slutty, sure, but it didn't scream *I'm going to a fetish club!*, which was the main thing.

After grabbing one in her size, she screwed up her courage and walked over to the counter, which Divine now stood behind, clicking away at the computer.

"Hi," the woman said, looking up immediately as Fiona approached. "You all right?"

"Yes, thanks. I'm just wondering if it would be possible to try this on, please?" Then, glancing doubtfully at the outfit, added, "And if I get stuck, will you help me get out of it?"

Giggling, Divine nodded. "You ain't gonna get stuck, honey, but yeah, sure. Just shout 'mayday' and I'll come running. Okay, head through that red curtain." She pointed. "Changing rooms are just through there."

"Thanks."

A few minutes later and Fiona was not only dressed in the slutty schoolgirl outfit, but was actually admiring herself. Fortunate to have the figure to pull the tiny skirt and white vest top off, she clipped the collar-and-tie ensemble around her neck and peered into the mirror. She looked a million miles away from the PR professional image she gave off most of the time. In fact, she barely recognised herself. If she added pigtails, some hipster glasses, knee-high white socks and sexy shoes, she reckoned her own mother would walk right past her. Perfect.

It was only as she was changing back into her regular clothes that she thought to check the price. She had no idea what this sort of stuff cost. She heaved a sigh of relief when she seized the tag. Even at full price it wasn't too bad, but as luck would have it, it was on sale. Figuring it was meant to be, Fiona gathered up the items and her bag and made her way back towards the counter.

Another couple of customers had arrived in the meantime. A middle-aged guy was looking at the PVC and chains she'd thus far avoided, and a woman who looked to be in her late thirties was having some purchases rung through the till. Fiona tried not to look, but couldn't resist a glimpse. Black PVC bra and hotpants, black PVC ankle boots and red fishnet stockings. Suddenly, Fiona had the feeling she might very well see the woman again in the not-too-distant future.

As the woman took her purchases and turned to leave, they exchanged polite smiles, and Fiona stepped forward to put the things down on the counter.

"You didn't need rescuing, then?" Divine asked, looking a little disappointed.

"No. You were right. It's fine. But I was wondering about… accessories?"

"Okay. You have anything in mind?"

"I'm pretty new to this, but I was thinking some fake glasses, knee-high socks and maybe some shoes? Also, I noticed this was on sale…" She indicated the outfit.

"Gotcha. You're after some bargains."

Heat flared in Fiona's cheeks. "I can afford… I mean—"

"Hey, don't worry about it, honey. I love a bargain myself. There's no shame in that. And if it means you've got some budget left over to come back and see me soon, then I'll be a happy girl."

Tipping Fiona a wildly flirtatious wink, she stepped out from behind the counter. "Come on. Let's see what we can do."

Chapter Seventeen

Even though the sun was slipping from the sky and London's streets were dropping into shadow, cooling rapidly, it was still way too warm for a coat, much less a long one. Still, Fiona had no choice. She couldn't be spotted leaving the hotel dressed like she was, and she didn't want to travel through the city with people staring at her, either. She hurried from the building, lest someone see her and engage her in conversation, then get to wondering where she was going so heavily made-up, and with her blonde hair in pigtails.

So, wrapped in the coat, Fiona made her way through the Mayfair streets, the red-brick and grey stone buildings beautifully dappled with light and shade, in the direction of Green Park Tube station. She grumbled to herself that it'd take her longer to walk to the station than it would to get the Tube the three stops to Vauxhall, in spite of the flat shoes she wore. Figuring there was no easy way to hide knee-length white socks and sexy skyscraper shoes, she'd opted to carry those in a tote bag and put them on when she arrived at the venue. For now, her unremarkable ballet pumps would do. Hopefully that innocent method of footwear would stop people wondering why her coat was longer than whatever she had on underneath it. The socks would have definitely given the game away.

It was even warmer in the bowels of the Underground system, and Fiona huddled at one end of the platform, wafting the lapels of her coat to try to cool down and giving the Jack Daniel's poster on the curved wall opposite her quite the view.

She became aware of someone in her peripheral vision, so she snatched the lapels close again, hiding herself and staring resolutely at the poster. Soon, the train arrived and she stepped on and sat down, shifting her bag into her lap and holding it and her coat tightly to her. She couldn't help peering around, though. Always a fan of people-watching, she wondered how many of the folk around might be heading to the same place as her. The events were clearly popular, so *someone* had to be going. They couldn't all go by car—driving in London wasn't the most desirable method of transport, not even on a Friday night. And who wanted to drive, anyway, on a night out like this?

Disappointed, she shifted her gaze back to her lap. She hadn't spotted any latex, PVC or leather anywhere. And there was no one else huddled into outerwear that could be hiding such things, either. Everyone she'd seen was dressed in regular gear or office wear. Damn. Maybe she was too early? Maybe no one turned up until much later and she'd end up standing there by herself, like a total moron?

Only the fact that the venue was a mere twenty yards from the Tube station stopped her from getting off the train at Vauxhall, crossing to the opposite platform and going back the way she'd come. If she was right, she could be on a northbound train within ten minutes, maybe five. But she had to find out, first, just to be sure. She'd come this far. She couldn't turn back now.

Exiting the station, she headed for the arches beneath the nearby bridge. The website she'd been on had been pretty descriptive. A couple of minutes later and she knew she was in the right place, and that there'd be no need to scurry back to the station just yet. A queue of people waited to get into one of the doors, over which was the sign for the club. *Excellent.*

However, on walking past the queue to join it at the rear, Fiona grew more and more confused. There were a few people dressed in club or fetish gear, but for the most part, they wore regular street clothes. What happened to the strict dress code she'd read about?

After a beat, the penny dropped and she wanted to kick herself. Of course—most people were carrying large-ish bags, which presumably held their outfits. And maybe, just maybe, some of the folk were so scantily clad *underneath* what they wore that they'd step inside, strip off their outer layers and get right on with partying.

Bloody hell! Why hadn't she thought of that? It would have saved an embarrassing, sweaty and stressful journey. Still, at least she knew now, and if she were to return to this event or attend a different one, she'd stash her outfit in her bag and change on arrival.

The queue moved at a good pace. Fiona guessed the people running the show probably got to know the patrons, so only new people or potential troublemakers would be thoroughly searched and checked out.

She fished in her bag for her purse, which held the required ID and cash. Finding it, she clutched it tightly, ready to retrieve whatever was asked for first. It turned out to be the identification. A friendly-looking woman in a skintight black PVC dress checked it, nodded with satisfaction, then waved her in. "Have a good evening, honey. Just pay at the desk, leave whatever you like with the cloakroom staff and head on in."

"Th-thanks." Heaving a sigh of relief to get off the street,

Fiona hustled in and did as the woman had said, as well as swapping her cute shoes for the knee-high socks and heels. Then, feeling much better now she'd discarded the coat and large bag, replacing the latter with a smaller bag containing only her purse, phone and other essentials, she entered the venue proper.

There, she let out another sigh of relief. The place was already half-full—and, judging by the still-growing queue she'd just left, that would soon change—and the outfits on display meant she didn't stand out. In fact, she fitted right in. She was perhaps a little younger than most of the people she could see, but that didn't matter. As far as she was concerned, this was a research trip, to find out first-hand what happened in these places and whether her curiosity would remain as just that, or whether she, like James and Logan, wanted to make kink a regular part of her life. At this stage, she was completely open-minded.

Thanks to the things she'd seen in the shop where she'd bought her own outfit, the get-up other people wore wasn't quite so shocking. On the occasions it was, she managed to hide her reaction. PVC as far as the eye could see, shining even in the dim lights, tight clothing, leather, plenty of corsets—and, despite her best efforts, she couldn't help but stare at the male pensioner she saw sporting one, *very* tightly cinched—and some gear so skimpy it was impossible to tell what it was made of.

Teetering a little on the shoes, which were cute and sexy all at once, with their black background and pink and white polka dots, she headed for the bar. She'd eaten a good meal before coming out and had limited herself to two drinks. Like That Night, she required a little Dutch courage, but needed to have her wits about her, so getting drunk wasn't an option.

A couple of men in what could only be described as hotpants, thick black collars and nothing else stood aside to let her get to the bar. Her research indicated that these were submissives. Whether they thought she was a… What was it? A Dominatrix, or Domme, she didn't know, but she smiled politely and thanked them, before placing her order with the barman, a cute guy around her age in leather trousers and matching waistcoat.

She paid for her drink—a lurid-blue alcopop, which she'd bought because she figured it wouldn't spill if someone nudged her—thanked the barman and turned back to face the room. Okay, what the hell should she do now? She'd got this far, and was proud of herself for having done so without chickening out, but being a wallflower in this area wasn't going to give her much information. It seemed this was where people just hung out and danced a bit—like in a regular bar or club, but with considerably less—or more outlandish—clothing.

To have any idea of what these events were *really* about, she needed to bite the bullet and get to where the action was. After taking a few pulls on her drink, she wandered away from the bar, deeper into the room, and looked around some more, trying to work out what was happening, and where.

Some helpful signs on the wall indicated where to find the toilets, the dungeons, the playrooms, the smoking area and, most intriguingly, the performance area. Figuring that was the best place to watch without being expected to join in, Fiona made her way there.

Passing down the narrow corridor was a bit of a squeeze, with queues for the bathrooms, and people milling here, there and everywhere. She'd never understood why people couldn't just adopt the rules of the road whilst walking—if everyone just kept left, things would be much easier. She finally emerged from the melee and spotted a sign indicating that the next door on her right led to the performance area.

She was just about to step into the darkened room when a hand lightly gripped her arm and a surprised voice said, "Fiona? What the fucking hell are you doing here?"

Heart pounding, she spun to face the owner of the voice. *Holy fuck!* James stood there. His appearance was a million miles away from his usual smart-casual or business attire. He had on leather trousers and a thick, black leather collar, which had a silver ring attached to the front of it.

She'd been so busy taking in the sight of the man she'd been naked and in bed with just a month ago that she'd forgotten he'd asked her a question. He, however, was determined to get a reply. "Fiona?" He shook her arm gently. "Are you listening to me?"

"Uhh…" Her mouth suddenly dry, she took a sip of her drink, swallowed, and tried again. "Sorry, I'm just a bit, um… surprised to see you here."

"*You're* surprised?" He led her to one side, out of the way of the milling people. "You know about me and Logan and our extracurricular activities. But you… Well, you said you didn't have a clue about any of this stuff when I last saw you. So I think I've got more reason to be surprised."

"James, what are you—?" Logan appeared, then abruptly stopped speaking. His gaze fixed on Fiona's face for a moment, before raking up and down the length of her body.

Oh, fucking hell. Just like before, her traitorous body reacted to a mere look. But this time it was heightened, more immediate, fiercer, probably because now, unlike last time, she knew exactly what this man—what both these men—were capable of. Of doing to her, with her, in front of her.

"Fiona?" Logan sounded even more shocked than James had. In fact, he sounded—and looked—utterly dumbfounded. She suspected he'd have been less surprised to see the Pope standing there.

"Yes," she replied, more steadily than she felt. "Hello, Logan. How are you?"

"How—*how are you?*" The words sounded as though they were being forced through a mangle. Good God, was he going to grab her by one of her pigtails and drag her out of here? The mixture of shock, confusion and fury on his face made him look as though he was capable of anything, and she really had no idea which way he was going to go.

Shooting a glance around and noting a few people were giving them more than a passing look, she said, "Could you relax, please? We seem to be making a scene, and I've only just got here, so I'd appreciate it if you didn't get me kicked out. Some of us don't have bulging bank accounts—I'd like to get my money's worth before I head home."

Pressing his lips together in a firm line, Logan looked over at James and indicated he should answer her. Apparently when it came to *situations,* James was the level-headed one.

"Sweetheart," James said, running a hand through his hair, "though I don't pretend to read Logan's mind, I know him pretty well, and I suspect he's feeling just the same as I am. Are you here alone?"

Fiona nodded, and James's kissable lips pursed momentarily before he replied, "Well, that's even worse."

"It is?" she said, standoffishly. "So, just 'cause I'm dressed like this means you get to treat me like a naughty little girl, does it?"

Spluttering, he shook his head. "No, nothing like that. We're just surprised to see you here—and concerned. And even more concerned you're here alone. Do you have any idea what you're doing?"

"Not a fucking clue," she spat. "And whose fault is that?"

"Right," Logan interjected, the low level of his voice brooking no argument from either of them. "We're leaving—now." He held a finger up to stop Fiona interrupting. "*Now.* I'll reimburse you the fucking entrance fee. Clearly, we need to talk."

Chapter Eighteen

Despite being safe in the knowledge that neither James nor Logan would ever hurt her, Fiona experienced more than a frisson of fear as Logan led her back along the corridor, towards where she'd come into the club. James was close behind, and although he didn't look as stern as his partner, a glance told her he was far from happy. She really was *not* looking forward to the talk Logan had in mind.

Fifteen minutes later and James and Logan were back in street clothing, and she'd replaced her shoes and socks with the flats she'd arrived in and hidden herself beneath the coat once more. She stared intently at the ground as she was all but frog-marched from the building, cheeks blazing, and handed into the rear of a black limousine.

With a man either side of her, Fiona had nowhere to run, to hide. Her blood boiled with a mixture of embarrassment and anger, and she had no idea how to express either of those emotions for the time being. She'd just have to wait and see what they had planned next, what information the talk uncovered.

Apparently the men either had too much to say, or couldn't decide where to start, because they remained resolutely silent.

Fiona gazed out of the windows, peering at the sights as they passed them—the Thames, with the view down to the Houses of Parliament and the London Eye, the relatively nondescript streets of Pimlico and Victoria, the step upmarket as they glided past the rear wall of the Buckingham Palace estate, up to Hyde Park Corner and eventually back into the quieter, more reserved Mayfair.

As they grew closer to the hotel, Logan threw Fiona a look.

"How did you get out of the hotel like that without anyone seeing you? I can't imagine your bosses would be too impressed with one of their staff going about dressed that way."

She gestured to the coat. "Quickly, and holding onto this bloody thing for dear life. If only I'd known you could get changed at the venue, it would have saved a lot of bloody embarrassment. The Tube journey was horrendous."

She thought she saw the merest flicker of amusement cross Logan's face, but couldn't be sure, because no sooner had it arrived than it was gone, and the stony expression was back. "For all our sakes, I think we should go in separately. Perhaps you should use the staff entrance, Fiona? And take out those bloody pigtails. They're damn cute, but they'll attract attention. You may as well have a neon sign pointing at your head."

Grumbling, she did as he said, stashing the hair ties in the tote bag. "Are you going to get the driver to drop me around the back, then? I assume he's discreet."

Logan eyed her. "I think it's possible he invented the word."

Shrugging, she turned moodily away from him, ignoring James too, and returned to peering out of the windows. They were almost there. "So where are we having this talk of yours, then? I presume not in the bar?"

Glaring, Logan replied, "Certainly not. Would it be convenient for you to come to our suite?"

"And what if it's not?" She was just being awkward for the sake of it now and all three of them knew it.

Logan sighed. "Well then, James and I would have to come

to your room. But I imagine it's much smaller, and if one of your colleagues was to see us entering..." He didn't finish the sentence, didn't need to.

"Fine. Which suite are you in? I'll get changed, then come up."

"You'll come *straight* up, Fiona. This cannot wait." He told her the name of the suite—not the same one as last time, but she suspected it would be just as plush.

"Fucking hell." She turned to James. "Is he always this bloody bossy?"

James, apparently not knowing how to reply without getting into trouble, eventually gave a cute nod and a sheepish grin. "If it makes you feel any better, he's generally right."

"Hmph. Well, you would say that."

A look of hurt crossed James's face, and Fiona wished she could take her words back. She hadn't meant them. It had just been her anger and irritation speaking. She reached out and squeezed his hand by way of apology, then said, "All right, all right. I'll come *straight* up. Let me out then."

They'd pulled up by now, and the chauffeur came around and opened the rear door. Logan exited, then helped her out before sliding back into his place. Giving her a meaningful look, he said, "See you in a couple of minutes."

Thanking the driver—just because his employers were being twats didn't mean she should be rude to him—she turned and made for the staff entrance. Only when the car pulled off, driving around to the main entrance, did she dare risk a glance. She stuck her tongue out at the retreating vehicle, giggled at her tiny act of rebellion, then let herself into the hotel.

As she hung around in one of the service corridors for a few minutes to give them a chance to get inside the building and on their way to their suite, Fiona was glad no one was around. She'd have had a tough time explaining why she was loitering in the first place, never mind if they noticed what she was wearing. Thankfully, though, The Portmannow Hotel relied much more on security personnel than CCTV—the latter mostly reserved for the public areas—so there wouldn't be any bizarre imagery of her skulking around, resembling a flasher, before scurrying up to one of the luxury suites.

Feeling she'd let enough time elapse, Fiona pulled herself up straight, adopting a casual air, and strode confidently in the direction of the nearest bank of elevators. The staff members she passed were busy, so they exchanged nothing more than a polite nod or a quick hello, and she got all the way to the top floor without incident.

As she knocked on the door of James and Logan's suite, however, she had a feeling that was about to change.

The door flung open almost immediately. Logan grabbed her hand and all but yanked her inside before closing the door behind her. She was glad she didn't have the sexy heels on any longer, because the speed at which she'd been propelled into the room would have made her highly likely to fall flat on her face.

"Where the hell have you been?" Logan demanded, relieving her of her tote bag but allowing her to keep the coat. Whether that was for her sake, or his and James's, she wasn't sure.

"Fucking hell," she shot back, jabbing her hands on her hips, "you've really got a bee in your bloody bonnet tonight, haven't you? If you must know, I was giving you chance to get here first. I didn't particularly want to be seen hanging about outside your room, especially dressed like this, all right?"

His ire dissipating, Logan sighed and ran a hand through his hair. It had grown since the last time she'd seen him at the hotel. The almost-curls she remembered were now full-on curls, and she wondered what it would be like to grip them in her fists as his talented tongue played between her legs.

Sounding almost defeated, Logan asked, "Can I get you a drink, Fiona?"

"Yes, please. Since I barely drank half of the one I bought at the club, it's the least you can bloody do."

With a strained smile, he gritted out, "What would you like?"

"A Screaming Orgasm."

A snigger from the bedroom doorway alerted her to James's presence. He must have been in the bathroom when she'd arrived. Giving him a small smile and hoping he'd forgiven her mean comment in the limo, she shifted her attention back to Logan. "Well?"

Coolly, he said, "I take it you are referring to the cocktail."

"Yes. Obviously." Had she not been so pissed off, she might have requested the other kind, too—but not now.

"Fine. James?"

"Ooh, if you're making cocktails, I'll have a Mojito."

Rolling his eyes, Logan said, "See what you've started

here?"

"Well, you did ask. And actually, I thought you'd order from room service."

"I could. But this'll be quicker. I don't want to mess around any longer. This talk is happening."

***

Cocktail in hand, Fiona settled into one of the plush armchairs, while James and Logan sat on the sofa. She took a long pull on the straw, enjoying the mix of flavours as they hit her tongue. She swallowed, then said, "Well?"

Unsurprisingly, Logan took the lead. "Are you going to tell us why exactly you were at that club?"

"Aren't you supposed to be smart? I'd have thought that much was obvious."

"Fiona…"

Spurred on more by James's concerned expression than Logan's firm tone, she said, "Look, this is your fault. After what happened last month, you guys put a lot of ideas in my head. *A lot.* Obviously we were a little preoccupied, so I didn't get the chance to find out more about the whole spanking, BDSM thing, but it intrigued me. However, since you two buggered off without giving me any way of contacting you, I couldn't ask you. So I took matters into my own hands. I went online, did some research, bought this," she pulled one of her coat lapels aside to indicate her outfit, "then went to that club. I thought the best way of finding out what it was all about was to go there and see for myself. I couldn't very well take any of my friends with me, which is why I went alone."

By now, James had dropped his head into his hands, and Logan looked thunderstruck, then angry all over again. "You figure it's *our* fault? How so, when you were the one who upped and left the suite in the middle of the night without leaving your phone number? We couldn't very well get a message to you, not without someone finding out and asking questions, so we had no choice but to check out without contacting you. So, rather than pointing the finger of blame at us, how about you think about that?"

Fiona opened her mouth to snap out a retort, then closed it again. For fuck's sake, he was right. She *had* left without giving them a way of getting in touch. But she'd had no idea they'd *want* to get in touch.

In a small voice, she said, "I'm sorry. I just thought it was a one-night thing and that's how it was going to stay. I had no idea you would even *want* to stay in touch, so leaving contact details didn't even occur to me."

Looking up, James said calmly, "All right, it looks as though we're all partially to blame for this situation. So let's move past pointing fingers and arguing. It's getting us nowhere. I, for one, Fiona, am sorry we left you feeling so misinformed and that you felt you had to find out more about the BDSM and fetish scene by yourself. Had we known, we'd never have let you go alone—"

"But I was fine," she cut in. "I'd only been there a little while and was just about to go into the performance room and see what it was all about. Then you two turned up, and the next thing I know

I'm being hauled out of there like a naughty child. Which reminds me..." She turned her gaze on Logan. "You owe me the entrance fee."

Wordlessly, he stood, pulled his wallet from his pocket, retrieved two notes and handed them over. Then he retook his seat. "All right," he said, "what do you want to know? Where should we start?"

After taking another pull on the straw as she mulled over Logan's question, she swallowed, then replied with a shrug, "From the beginning, I suppose."

Chapter Nineteen

"Fine," Logan said, with a curt nod. "James?"

Also nodding, James said, "Yep, no problem."

"Great." Logan stood and slipped off his shoes, then used his foot to shove them under the coffee table out of the way. "You two finish your drinks. I'll be in the bedroom when you're ready. Don't be too long."

Turning smartly on his heel, he strode into the bedroom, leaving Fiona and James exchanging amused looks. Patting the sofa beside him, James said, "Come sit here, sweetie. Let's chat a while as we finish our drinks."

Doing as James asked, Fiona settled down beside him and continued sipping at her cocktail. "I'm sorry for what I said earlier. You know… in the limo."

"Forget about it," he said with a wave of his hand. "I know you just said it in anger, so let's not mention it again. It's been a weird evening all round. Hopefully now we can improve it exponentially."

"I like the sound of that." Fiona grinned, her mood picking up now she knew James didn't hold her comment against her. Eager to find out what the bedroom had in store, she sucked hard on the plastic straw, then let out a laugh at the loud slurping sound it made in the bottom of the glass. "Oops! Think I'm empty!"

After downing the remains of his own drink, James took Fiona's glass and put them both on the table before standing up and holding out his hand. "Come on. Let's set about righting some wrongs. Your education awaits. Though," he added, as Fiona took his hand and he pulled her up off the sofa, "Logan likes fast learners. So do your best to keep up. Trust me. It'll be worth it."

They stepped into the bedroom and Fiona, hyper-aware of James's comment about being a fast learner, drank in the sights, trying hard to make sense of them, commit them to memory. A series of implements sat, perfectly lined up on the silver silk duvet cover. Most looked to be for corporal punishment, but she also saw some satiny material, some thick leather handcuffs, something else with leather straps and a ball attached and a couple of weirdly-shaped sex toys, one bigger than the other. She reminded herself that the whole point of her being here was so they could teach her all about this stuff. She didn't know what everything was *now,* but she'd be thoroughly educated by the time she left. Hopefully.

Logan had now removed his socks and his shirt, and stood there in only his dark blue jeans, which rode low enough on his hips to offer an enticing slice of his underwear, which naturally led her to fantasise about what was beneath. Just because she already knew, had already *experienced* what was beneath, didn't mean she didn't want to see, taste and touch it all over again.

James's body heat was apparent as he remained just behind her in the doorway, and he reached out, pulled her hair away from the side of her neck and murmured into her ear, "I'm looking forward to this. And to having a proper look at what you've got on underneath that coat. I don't suppose you'll let me relieve you of it?"

Shivering at James's closeness, the whisper of his hot breath on her skin and his words, she nodded slowly. "Okay."

He took the garment as she shrugged it off her shoulders, and she was vaguely aware of him moving away from her as she continued to look at the items on the bed and at Logan. He'd watched the exchange between her and James with interest, and now he grinned as her slutty get-up was revealed once more.

"Can I just say how much I love that outfit?" His eyes glinted with lust, and Fiona, despite her relative inexperience, suspected she already knew what Logan had in store for her.

"You can. Thank you. I'm glad you approve." The rebellious streak still burning within her, she grabbed the sides of the PVC skirt and pulled them out wide as she gave a mocking curtsey.

A sharp inhalation of breath from behind her told her James was back and was either surprised or shocked by her behaviour.

Seemingly choosing to ignore her—or maybe he was saving his response until later—Logan replied, "So, since you're dressed appropriately, how about you be the pupil and I'll be the teacher? You should address me as Sir."

Now this was something she *did* already know about. Submissives often called their Dominants Sir, Master or something similar. It was a mark of respect. Given it was just a game at this stage, though, Fiona was happy to play along. It didn't make her Logan's submissive.

"Yes, Sir. I'm willing to learn."

"Good. Come here, girl, and bring your friend."

Half-turning, she reached for James's hand, and the two of them crossed over to the bed. As she got a closer look at all the items laid out on the silken bedclothes, the pulsing that had begun between her legs back in the club grew stronger. Again, she was reminded of why the soundproofed rooms were so useful.

"Okay. I hope you're paying attention, because we've got a lot to pack in, and I'll be moving on to a more practical demonstration later in the lesson. From left to right, we have whip, crop, flogger, paddle, slipper, cane, tawse, handcuffs, blindfold, ball gag, restraints, two sizes of vibrating anal plug and a bullet vibrator. As always, in the bedside drawer, we have lubricant, condoms and antibacterial cleaning wipes."

The last sentence, she knew, was more to reassure her of her safety without breaking out of the persona he'd adopted than to teach her anything. She appreciated it nonetheless. Nodding, she said, "Okay, Sir. So what's next? Will you be using all of these things on me?"

As the words tumbled from her lips, she found herself hoping the answer was no. Not all tonight, anyway.

Chuckling, Logan said, "No, not all of them. Some of them, yes. But all those corporal punishment devices, plus my hand, would be much too much for your delicate buttocks to take in just one evening. What I propose is a taster of a few of the gentler ones. Then for some of the more painful ones, I'll teach you, using James here as our subject, how to use the items."

She licked her lips as she digested the words. Then, nodding again, she said, "Yes, Sir. I understand, and I accept your proposal."

James's consent hadn't been confirmed, but Fiona figured the two of them had played these kinky games a hundred times over, so it was implied by the fact that he was even here.

"Very good, girl. Now, a big part of BDSM is not doing

anything you don't want to. Or, if you find you don't enjoy something or it hurts beyond the realms of pleasure-pain, then the Dominant will stop immediately. This is achieved by the use of a safe word. You say the safe word, and anything that's being done to you at the time will stop straight away, no questions asked, no repercussions. All right?"

"Yes, Sir." She had known that already, but she didn't want to interrupt him or put him off his stride, mainly because said stride was so damn sexy. She'd known almost from the moment they'd met how bossy he was, but when he morphed into this full-on Dominant persona, she found she liked it, very much. She'd enjoyed it when he'd taken charge, orchestrated the smouldering threesome they'd had a month ago, particularly since the results had been so spectacular.

Despite these feelings, though, she didn't feel very submissive when he was this way. She'd willingly gone along with his plans during their ménage because she hadn't had the faintest idea how things worked, but she'd never felt tempted to throw herself upon his mercy and obey his every command.

How was it possible to find Logan's dominance so hot, but without being submissive?

Even more strangely, she was much more excited than worried about the prospect of having some of the implements used on her—perhaps because she'd only be subjected to the gentler ones—and the thought of using what was left on James was thrilling. Confused, she figured it would be better to stop thinking, and start doing. She could try to work out what it all meant afterwards. Or maybe ask questions. But not now. They were making progress here, were on the very cusp of yet another unforgettable evening together, and she didn't want to delay it any longer.

"Are you still with us, Fiona?" Logan's voice punctuated her decision—a full stop.

"Sorry, Sir. What was that?"

"I asked if you could choose a safe word, please. Something distinctive that you wouldn't normally call out in the bedroom. So not 'no' or 'stop'. For example, James's safe word is 'Supernatural', after his favourite television show."

Giving James an impressed sideways glance, Fiona smiled. "Mine, too," she said, before turning back to Logan. "In that case, Sir, I would like my safe word to be 'Castiel'."

Logan rolled his eyes. "God, both of you? Really? Should I dress in plaid and jeans, stock up on holy water and rock salt and be done with it?" Shaking his head, he continued, "Okay, Fiona. 'Castiel' it is then. Remember, though, this is only if you want something to *stop*. If you want to slow down, or for me not to use so much force, just saying so will be sufficient."

"I understand, Sir." The mental image of him dressed up as a Winchester brother was not unappealing, but she decided to keep that particular opinion to herself.

"Excellent. Let's get started, then. Come with me, Fiona."

He led her to a straight-backed chair with no arms. She wondered why he hadn't picked one of the more comfortable armchairs, but didn't have to wonder for long.

Logan sat down and patted his lap. "I want you over my

knee, Fiona. What sort of underwear do you have on?"

"A-a thong, Sir. A white one."

Closing his eyes briefly and biting his bottom lip, he then said, "That can stay as it is for now. Come on, quickly."

Her heart rate increasing, Fiona approached the chair, then draped herself over Logan's lap, before reaching for the chair leg to help steady herself. As soon as she was in place, he trapped one of her legs between his own, securing her position. Relaxing a little now she didn't think she was going to tumble onto the carpet, she wriggled to get comfortable. It was then she noticed the hardness poking into her hip. Her body responded immediately and shamelessly, heat racing through her every nerve ending and a trickle of juices seeping into the gusset of her knickers. Before long, it would be obvious to both men just how turned on she was, as the scent of her arousal permeated the air.

Biting back a moan, she waited for whatever was going to happen next, excited and tentative in equal measure. She'd wanted first-hand experience of BDSM, and now she was about to get it. From an expert, no less and, even better, someone she trusted and was hopelessly attracted to.

"James," Logan said, "could you please bring me the paddle? I think that would be best to start with, don't you?"

"Yes, Sir," James replied, moving immediately to comply. Handing over the implement, he remained nearby, apparently wanting to watch the show close up.

"Mmm…" Logan lifted the tiny skirt, the timbre of his voice deepening as her backside was exposed. "Such a pretty arse. So pert, so pale. I look forward to marking it. Are you ready, girl?"

"Yes, Sir."

"Your safe word?"

"Castiel, Sir."

"Good. Be sure you don't forget it. I hope you won't need it, but you *must* use it if you feel you need to."

For God's sake, just get on with it, will you?

Out loud, she repeated, "Yes, Sir."

Chapter Twenty

As Logan stroked the cool leather of the paddle over her trembling arse, Fiona couldn't help but wonder how this was going to compare to the self-experimentation she'd indulged in all those weeks ago. Spanking her own inner thighs in the bath had been the very beginning of her education, and it had stung quite a bit, but she suspected it wouldn't come even remotely close to preparing her for what was about to happen.

And yet, she was still much more excited than scared.

That all changed when the first blow hit her arse. The yelp was out of her mouth before she could stop it, and she gripped hard onto the chair leg to stop her snapping her hands up to cover her bum. That would no doubt only get her into trouble. Or, rather, *more* trouble.

"What I'm going to do, girl, is give you four blows with each of the implements I'm planning to use on you this evening. I think that is a fair number—a bearable number—for someone so new to this. I feel I should warn you that I may well leave some lasting marks on your luscious arse. Will this be a problem? I don't want to upset your boyfriend."

Fiona frowned. Why was he was mentioning a boyfriend when she didn't have one? But then she recalled they'd never actually had the discussion, so Logan was probably just covering his back. "It's fine, Sir. I don't have a boyfriend. Nobody will see my bum except me."

"All right," Logan replied.

James muttered, "No boyfriend? Fucking blokes around here

are clearly insane."

The compliment, whether it had been intended for her ears or not, warmed her to the very core and had the added benefit of bolstering her resolve. She could deal with whatever Logan was going to dish out. She'd asked for it, after all.

Blow two arrived soon after, on the opposite buttock. More prepared this time, she didn't yelp, but still sucked in a breath through her teeth, squeezing her eyes closed as the sharp sound faded away. Milliseconds later, the sensation arrived. Stinging, burning, melding gradually into an ache and a throb, which only served to emphasise the throbbing between her thighs.

Smack! Smack!

The next two were given in rapid succession, and the overload of sensations raced through her nerve endings and her veins, leaving her in a weird kind of limbo—did this hurt, or was it the hottest thing she'd experienced in her life? Did she want him to stop, or carry on?

All she knew for sure was that her pussy continued to swell and ache, juices leaking from her core. She could smell herself now—the scent of aroused female unmistakable.

She'd been so focused on what was going on in her brain and body that she'd lost track of what was going on around her. She was reminded immediately when something landed with a wallop on her left arse cheek. Then her right, then left, then right. No pauses this time, no chance for her to get used to the pain or psych herself up for the next spank—just one, two, three, four, in rapid succession.

A slipper landed on the floor, out of reach, but within her

eyeline. She suspected it had been thrown there deliberately so she could see it. Pain bloomed in her buttocks, the skin growing hotter and hotter. Not one millimetre from the base of her back to the crease where cheeks met thighs was free of the burning sting, which seemed impossible after only eight blows. How could he have covered so much ground? But then, she supposed he'd had plenty of practice.

Determined not to be caught unaware this time, Fiona paid attention to what was happening around her. Logan, of course, remained beneath her, pinning her into place, while James returned to the bed and collected the next implement. She didn't know if he was choosing them, whether Logan was signalling somehow, or if there was some premeditated order. Either way, James wordlessly picked up the flogger and walked back over to the chair.

Shit! Fiona bit her lip. If the flogger was one of the gentler implements in the line-up, then she certainly hoped Logan stopped after he'd used it on her. The wickedness of the others wasn't something she felt she was ready for. And did he plan to add in any of the restraints? The gag, or the toys? Or were they focusing only on corporal punishment this evening?

She didn't get the chance to ask, because suddenly Logan was tickling the tails of the flogger over her tortured skin. It didn't hurt, per se, but she suspected anything that touched her flaming arse, however lightly, would garner an unfavourable reaction. Fingernails would be the absolute *worst*.

After a few seconds, the tickling tails disappeared, and Fiona gritted her teeth, preparing for the blows. They came quickly, though not as quickly as those from the slipper, probably because he had to lift the flogger higher to land the hits.

What felt like a thousand tiny pinpricks exploded across her quivering flesh, expanding and joining together until her bum was one giant expanse of raging agony. Multiplied by four, that agony had her clenching her arse and screeching, calling Logan all the names under the sun. And to think he'd probably gone easy on her.

Fucking hell, only twelve spanks and she was a roiling mass of hormones and fury. How in the hell did people do this all the time? And with more force, harsher tools, more blows? It was a wonder James could ever sit down, or even walk properly if Logan tortured his arse like that on a regular basis. But then he was much more used to it than she. Perhaps she'd ask for some tips.

God, what the hell am I thinking? Why do I need tips? I'm never doing this again. No way! She'd taken the spanks she'd all but asked for, determined to do her research thoroughly, and she now had her conclusion. Being beaten was not for her.

Why then were her pussy lips so swollen? Why was her clit screaming out for attention, for stimulation, for climax? If one of the men—or both—threw her to the bed, or even the floor, now and thrust their cock inside her, it would be the best thing ever. Thick, hard flesh penetrating her own, filling her up, stretching her, tantalising all those nerve endings, taking the frustration that had built up inside her and transforming it into the orgasm to end all orgasms.

Christ, she could think of nothing she wanted more. But it seemed, for now at least, she wasn't going to get it.

"Well done, girl," Logan said, stroking her hair, which had fallen around her face like a golden curtain, preventing her from seeing anything except what was immediately in front of her. "You did very well. And," he stuck his hand between her legs, dipped under her thong to the heat and wetness beneath, "it seems as though you enjoyed it, too. Naughty girl." He took a sharp swipe at her with his bare hand. The sound was loud, louder somehow than anything that had gone before. She screeched at the new burn in her bum, more so when he evened the score by smacking her arse three more times.

"Sorry, girl, but I couldn't resist. Your reaction was just so delightful. And beautiful. My cock is fit to burst."

That much was certainly true. Heat blazed at the point where his rigid cock still poked against her hip, even through three layers of their clothing. And, in spite of her annoyance at those final four spanks, Fiona would happily have sunk the thick length of it inside her and ridden him until her legs gave way.

When she didn't respond, he stroked her hair again. "Ready to get your own back, Fiona?"

He'd shifted from 'girl' to 'Fiona', which was clearly significant, though she didn't quite understand how yet.

James appeared at her side to help her off Logan's lap. She accepted his assistance gratefully and stumbled to her feet. Straightening her clothing, such as it was, she grimaced at the sensation of her damp underwear cooling against her skin.

"What's the matter?" Logan asked, his tone laced with amusement. "Arse hurting?"

"No," she shot back indignantly, determined for him not to know the whole truth. "My knickers are stuck to me, that's all."

Raising his eyebrows, he replied, "Well there's a simple solution for that now, isn't there? Hurry. I think James is more than ready for his spanking, don't you?"

Glancing at James's crotch, the meaning of Logan's words was right before her eyes. James's cock tented his jeans. Returning her gaze to his face, she saw his expression was as uncomfortable as his cock appeared to be.

Figuring the sooner she finished her education, the sooner she could have sex with one or both of them, she caressed James's cheek, then kissed him lightly on the lips.

Then she hurried out of her thong, kicked it to one side and crossed over to the bed. She wasn't concerned about the items' order of harshness. James had taken every one of these things more than once, and they'd been wielded by someone much stronger and more experienced.

She grabbed the crop and turned to James. "Clothes off, gorgeous, and bend over the bed."

James complied, and Fiona risked a glance at Logan before she continued. She was momentarily surprised to note he'd freed his cock from the confines of his clothing and was stroking it slowly, so slowly that the action would probably do little more than keep him hard. Which, she supposed, was the point—for now, at least. He wouldn't want to come at this stage. He undoubtedly had much more exciting plans for his cock than masturbation when there were plenty of willing, waiting holes at his disposal.

She licked her lips, then threw Logan a salacious smile. Returning her attention to her task, suddenly she was reminded that earlier the prospect of doing this very thing had filled her with excitement. Maybe everything that had happened since had muddled her brain somewhat, but now, it couldn't have been clearer.

She was going to whip, crop, cane and tawse—was that even a proper word?—James's delightful backside, and she was going to love every last moment of it. How she knew this without having done it yet, she had no idea, but it didn't matter.

After wafting the crop around in the air a little to get used to the feeling and weight of it, she gripped it tightly, then moved into position.

"Fiona," came Logan's voice.

She turned. "Yes?" No need for 'Sir' now, if she was no longer 'girl'.

"Just be careful, all right? James is experienced in this, but you're not. So take it easy to begin with, get used to the feel of the crop in your hand, how James is reacting. And, James?" he added.

"Yes, Sir?"

"Be sure and use your safe word if needed, all right? Fiona, remember James's safe word is 'Supernatural', okay? He uses it, you stop. Understand?"

She nodded, then remembered James couldn't see her. "Yes, Logan, I understand. I'll be careful, and I'll stop immediately if James uses his safe word."

Turning back to James, she pulled in a deep breath. Then, taking aim at his right buttock, she drew her arm back then immediately snapped it forward, a whoop filling her ears as the crop cut through the air and landed on its target.

To her surprise, James let out little more than a hiss. Repeating the action on his other bum cheek, but with more force, she hoped for a stronger reaction. Instead, she got more of the same. She hadn't been told she could only lay four blows with each implement, though, so her best option was to use his high, muscular buttocks as target practice until she hit James's specific buttons. If she was going to get anything out of this, she wanted to give *him* pleasure. Surely that was the whole point?

Getting into a steady rhythm, Fiona built up the force and frequency of the hits, growing to enjoy the power she had more with each passing moment. It was heady, having someone completely at her mercy, someone she could do pretty much anything with or to, someone who'd take whatever she wanted to give. And as Logan was his Dominant, Fiona figured there was nothing her imagination—despite its fertility—could come up with that James wouldn't accept. There was no way she'd be able to make him use his safe word.

Not that she wanted to. All she wanted was for them both—and Logan—to have fun. Judging by the increase in James's breathing, and the occasional moans she'd finally managed to elicit from him, he was.

After a few more strokes, she dropped the crop, moved up next to James and reached for his cock. It stood rigid and red hot, straining up toward his belly button, with precum beading at its tip. With her other hand, she stroked his arse, which radiated scorching heat. At the contact, James winced a little and his cock leapt in her hand.

Oh yes, he'd enjoyed that. And her still-throbbing pussy attested to the fact that she had, too. She was in no mood for dissecting the whys and wherefores, however.

She released James, then strode over to the bedside cabinet and retrieved a condom. As she returned to him, she removed the rubber from its wrapper, so it was ready to roll down his length, which she promptly did. Once it was seated securely at the base of his swollen dick, she bent over the bed beside him, flipped up her skirt and said, "James, please fuck me. Now."

As James moved to do her bidding, the blunt head of his cock slipping easily through her slick folds and into her entrance, Logan piped up, a tinge of surprise in his tone. "Well, James, I think we have ourselves a switch."

Chapter Twenty-One

The words reached her ears, permeated her brain, but she was far too focused on James's thick cock easing inside her to react to them. Instead, she filed away the comment, determined to ask what the hell he was talking about when she and James were finished.

And that wouldn't be for a little while yet. He had more restraint than she—again, likely down to practice—and rather than hurrying to fuck her, he was taking his time. Tingles raced up her spine as he inched his way inside her, setting off a chain reaction of delicious sensations as he did so.

The remaining tools and toys were still lined up beside her, unused, but she didn't care. Logan had made his point, and she'd made hers—she could take pain *and* give it out. Besides, the thoughts and feelings she'd had while spanking James would be no different, whatever tool she used. And, since their three-way relationship—or whatever it was they were doing—was apparently no longer a one-off, she'd get her chance to play with some of the other things in future.

Closing her eyes, she let her other senses take over. The scent of sweat and sex filled her nostrils, only serving to make her hotter. The sounds, for now, were minimal. James was still rocking slowly in and out of her grasping hole, so there was no skin slapping against skin, no grunting, growling, screeching or swearing. But that would come soon enough. Instead, elevated breathing and quiet moans were all she picked up.

Wait—what? Quiet moans? James was right there, his body in hers, on hers, against hers. He was making sounds, sure, but not that quietly…

Fuck! She twisted to look over at the chair where she'd left Logan. He was still touching himself, but much faster than he had been before. His hand, gripped tightly around his ruddy shaft, shuttled up and down at a steady speed as he watched the scene playing out before him.

Their gazes met, and he flashed her a decadent grin that, had she not already been in the middle of a glorious shag, would have made her wet and weak-kneed. Smiling back, she continued to watch him pleasure himself as James treated her to a slow, smouldering screw.

Logan broke eye contact and raked his gaze over her and James, apparently enjoying the sight of them together. He increased the pace at which he fisted his dick, and bit his bottom lip. Closing his eyes, he let his head loll back on his shoulders as he wanked. The sight was so enticing, so utterly sexy that overwhelming need filled Fiona. She *needed* to come, but James, who apparently wasn't quite so submissive when it came to Fiona, was intent on teasing her, on drawing out the experience.

But the teasing wasn't enough. She turned back to the bed, her gaze alighting once more on the toys. Grinning, she grasped the bullet vibrator, pushed the button at its base, switching it on, and inserted it between her legs, seeking the swollen, slippery bud that so eagerly awaited her touch.

The motion of their bodies and the slickness of her pussy meant it took a couple of attempts to press the buzzing toy to the right place and keep it there. But once she did… *Wow*. She had no idea whether the thing had more settings, more power, but it was already stimulating her clit to perfection, sending her rocketing towards her much-needed climax.

"James," she gasped, holding tightly onto the bedclothes with her left hand as her right kept the tiny vibe pressed against her tingling bud. "Please…"

Without responding, James moved one hand from her hip and used it to grab her hair. Winding it around his fist, he tugged her head back, exposing her throat. Still fucking her at that maddeningly sedate pace, he leaned in and said next to her ear, "Better hold on tight, gorgeous, if you want more."

"Yes," she forced out, prickles of pain dancing across her scalp. "Yes, please."

With that, he straightened and, using her hair and hip for leverage, upped his pace. His lean, powerful hips pistoned faster and faster, his delicious cock filling her over and over, making her scream and screech and yell as bliss rushed through her. The increase in speed and ferocity made it nigh on impossible for her to keep using the bullet on her clit. Its shiny surface, now slick with her juices, became difficult to hold, and her vulva was so wet and swollen that accuracy just wasn't happening.

With a growl of frustration, she tossed the still-buzzing toy onto the bedspread and replaced it with her hand. Immediately, James released her hip, grabbed her wrist, shifted her hand away and used his own instead, his long fingers moving confidently between her labia and finding her clit.

Fisting the sheets with both hands, Fiona held on tightly as

James used his cock and fingers in tandem to drive her ever closer to climax. Christ, but she needed it. Every part of her strained towards it, silently begged for it. Even being fairly certain it wouldn't be her only orgasm of the evening didn't make her want it any less or increase her patience. She'd been tormented and stimulated for so long that she could barely think of anything else.

Fortunately, it seemed James was willing to give her what she wanted. Either that, or he was ready, too. Rubbing her clit, he pounded into her hard and fast, panting and grunting. Fiona used the leverage of her hands on the bed to shove herself back against him, urging him deeper, and harder and faster still, her head forced back by the hand still gripping her hair.

In a sudden change of pace, James began jerking shallowly in and out of her, fast and furious. Then, pinching her clit hard, he sent her plummeting over the edge, following immediately afterwards.

Torrents of sensation slammed through every fibre of Fiona's being, and only the increasing soreness of her throat told her she'd been calling out. What she'd said, or screeched, she had no idea, and she didn't really care. All she cared about was the blissful sensation of orgasm, the amazing buzz that raced through her nerve endings.

James bucked and jerked away behind her, still riding out his own climax. Soon, he collapsed over her back with a loud exhalation of her name, his damp skin hot against the exposed areas of hers, and the scent of fresh sweat permeating her nostrils.

"Wow…" was all she could manage

James chuckled. "Yeah. My sentiments exactly. You all right?"

She nodded. "Yes, thanks."

He released her hair, then caressed her scalp. "Good. Just give me a moment and I'll move."

"No rush." She was in no hurry to get rid of him—he felt damn good pressed against her, after all, though it'd feel even better if there wasn't a layer of tacky PVC in the way.

Suddenly, a movement caught her eye. Logan was walking over to the bedside cabinet. What was he…?

The penny dropped when he reached for the antibacterial wipes, pulled one from the packet and wiped his softening shaft and his hands before tucking himself away. After dropping the wipe into the nearby bin, he grabbed another one. Snagging the bullet vibrator, he then turned it off and cleaned its shiny surface.

Having returned the toy to the bed, he discarded the second wipe, then advanced on the two of them. Leaning down, he captured Fiona's lips in a brief but delicious kiss, leaving her breathless, before repeating the process with James.

"That was fucking hot," he said, grinning widely. "*So incredibly* hot. When you've regained the use of your legs, why don't you both join me in the bathroom?"

It wasn't a question, not really, but they nodded, turning their heads to watch him walk away. After pausing in the doorway to discard his clothes, Logan crossed the threshold. Moments later the sound of running water was audible.

With a contented sigh, James slowly disentangled from Fiona. He removed the condom and binned it. Then, slipping his arm around her waist and tugging her upright, he said, "Come on, you.

Let's get cleaned up and chill out for a bit. I think we all need it after that."

Chill out? Since when was one climax apiece enough? Last time they'd got together, she'd lost count of how many times she'd come.

Her confusion must have registered on her face, because James let out a short laugh. "Hey, don't worry. I'm sure we'll still have some more fun and games before the night is out, gorgeous. And if you're free, we've got all day tomorrow, too."

All day tomorrow...

Now that was an offer only a lunatic would refuse.

After allowing him to help her out of the remains of her outfit, then lead her into the bathroom, she wasn't entirely surprised to see Logan already relaxing in the large Jacuzzi. Offering a lazy grin, he said, "Get cleaned up, you guys, and hurry. It's lonely in here by myself."

They responded by hurrying into the massive shower cubicle with its four waterfall heads and pulling the door closed behind them. James switched on the water, which was hot right away, thanks to Logan having just been in there. He then handed her a bottle of complimentary shower gel, took another for himself, and set about washing.

Fiona followed suit—equally eager to settle into the hot tub and ease her aching muscles and stinging backside. Granted, it would have been sexier to wash each other, but it'd have taken a damn sight longer. They'd likely have become distracted and forgotten all about the Jacuzzi.

She laughed to herself as she realised the idiocy of that thought. The Jacuzzi alone was tempting enough, but since it contained a naked and gorgeous Logan Chisholm, forgetting about it was completely impossible. Ridiculous. Ludicrous, even.

Having rinsed the last of the suds from her hair and body, she nodded to James to turn off the spray, then scampered after him over to the tub.

Logan watched silently, amusement glinting in his eyes as they gingerly lowered themselves into the hot, bubbling water. Once they were seated, he reached over the edge of the tub and lifted up a bottle of champagne. "Bubbles, anyone? Or should I say *more* bubbles?"

"Yes, please," Fiona said, hoping she'd hidden her surprise at the label on the bottle. This was no middling brand—it was the crème de la crème, and although it was pretty commonplace in the hotel, she'd never thought for one moment she'd have the opportunity to try it out for herself.

She took the glass Logan handed her with thanks and had the tiniest of sips. She'd been so careful up until now to keep a clear head—she didn't want to lose it now, not for the sake of some expensive champagne. It was nice, yes, but the experiences she was sharing with these two men were better, and she hoped they weren't over yet.

As she relaxed and sunk a little deeper into the bubbles, contentment and satisfaction seeped through her. A sexual education, a toe-curlingly amazing shag, followed by some time in a Jacuzzi with a glass of champagne—how awesome was that? If she conveniently ignored everything that had gone before the education part, she'd deem it a perfect evening.

And if this was the way things were going to be, how the hell was she going to cope when the two of them buggered off again?

As she took a thoughtful sip of the champagne, she remembered something. "Uh, guys?" They looked at her. "What the fuck is a switch?"

Chapter Twenty-Two

Fiona had just settled down at her desk with her first cup of tea of the day when one of the reception staff appeared in front of her, a huge bunch of flowers in her arms.

"Morning, Lisa," Fiona said, smiling. She was getting to know Lisa pretty well. They were around the same age, both lived on-site and partook fairly regularly of the Friday night gatherings. "Nice flowers. Who are you looking for?"

Lisa narrowed her eyes and placed the blooms down on Fiona's desk. "Morning, Fiona. They're for you, actually."

"*Me?*" she squeaked. "But who are they—?" She stopped as the answer presented itself, not wanting to have to explain to Lisa. After all, how exactly *could* she explain her current situation? "They're beautiful. Thank you for bringing them."

Lisa looked as though she was about to start asking questions, but, in an amazing stroke of luck, Fiona's desk phone rang. "Sorry," she said, hoping her expression looked more regretful than relieved. "Catch you later?"

Nodding, Lisa gave a little wave and left. Fiona picked up the handset. "Hello?"

"Fiona…" came Sophia's voice, her tone suspicious. "Who are those divine flowers from?" One of the perks of working in what was essentially a huge glass box meant Sophia didn't miss a damn thing.

"I don't know," Fiona lied. "I haven't had a chance to read the card yet." Well, at least that part was true.

"Hmm… All right. I hope you're not holding out on me,

sweetie. Gotta go, I have a call waiting. Bye."

"Bye!" Fiona replaced the handset, then stared at it incredulously. Christ, it was tough to keep anything secret in a place like this. Honestly, she was amazed her trysts with James and Logan hadn't been discovered yet. After they'd found her in the Vauxhall club, she'd spent that night, as well as most of the following day, with them. They hadn't ventured from the room, spending their time indulging in mind-blowing sex and just chatting, and it was only after considering phoning for room service for the third meal in a row that Logan had called time.

"Okay, enough's enough. Much as this has been amazing, I need to get out of here for a bit. Plus," he'd added, a salacious grin on his face, "if I don't give it a bit of a rest, my cock may well drop off."

Fiona had known what he meant. She herself had been exhausted and ached, inside and out. A change of scenery would do them all good—and would force them to keep their hands off one another for a little while, at least. "Okay," she'd said brightly, though she hadn't really wanted to leave them, "I second that motion. I need to get going, anyway. I need a shower, clean clothes and a *proper* rest." She'd mock-glared at the two of them. "I'm heading out with my old flatmates later on, so maybe we can catch up again before you leave?"

At that, the men had outlined their plans for the following days, and a flurry of typing phone numbers and email addresses into various devices had ensued. There was no way they were going to risk losing touch again.

By the time that particular stay at the hotel had ended, Fiona had spent more time in their suite than her own room.

Smiling at the memory, she glanced over her shoulder to see if Sophia was looking. She wasn't—whoever was on the phone obviously had her undivided attention—so Fiona quickly searched among the flowers for the card. All her other colleagues were either out on errands or engrossed in their various tasks, so once she found the tiny envelope, she opened it and read the message inside.

Gorgeous Fiona,

Just a little gift to make you smile. And your smile is way more beautiful than these flowers.

JL xx

She frowned when she got to the signature line. *JL?* What was L? Neither of their surnames began with L.

After a moment, she got it. Not JL, but J *and* L. But, appreciative of her need for subtlety and discretion, they'd signed it to look as though the flowers were from just one person. And, reading back through the message, she realised it had been worded in such a way that the words 'I' or 'we' weren't needed.

Smart *and* considerate. She was a lucky girl. It had only been a day since they'd checked out, promising to let her know in advance when they next had business in town, and already they were sending lovely reminders to make sure she didn't forget them.

As if. Smiling, she put the card back in its envelope and tucked it safely into her purse. Then, figuring she could come up with some fabricated sender of the flowers for the next person who asked, she continued supping at her tea as she began reading her emails.

It wasn't until much later that she got the opportunity to express her gratitude for the flowers. She'd had a busy morning with admin, followed by a post-lunch internal meeting to discuss an upcoming event the hotel was hosting—some huge international conference to do with climate change and global warming. Publicity support was minimal, given it was a meeting of world leaders, diplomats and various important folk, so they only needed to boost the profile of the event itself, rather than trying to encourage attendance.

Given its importance, Sophia had said she'd handle the publicity, freeing Fiona up to start brainstorming their next big campaign. So, immediately after the meeting, she stuffed her tablet and a notebook and pen into her handbag and scurried off to her favourite place in the hotel—the library. Well, her favourite place *after* whatever suite James and Logan happened to be staying in when they were around, anyway.

Her love affair with the cavernous room had begun as soon as she'd first laid eyes on it—way back when Sophia had shown her around on the day of her interview. It was a stunning room, clad in a classic style. The only nods to modern life were the free Wi-Fi access and the row of computers at one end of the space. Replica antique tables and chairs were dotted around, as were coffee tables situated next to sofas and armchairs. It was wonderful—comfortable, relaxing and functional, all at once. And the best part was that, even though it was more akin to a private library than a public one, the guests seemed to keep to the unwritten rule about being quiet.

This made it the perfect place for her to go and work on occasion. Although she loved the hustle and bustle of the office, the chatter, the bouncing ideas off one another, occasionally silence and solitude were the order of the day. And right now, it was exactly what she needed.

She was pleased to see her preferred spot was available and snagged it quickly. It was at the far end of the room, hidden from the door by several rows of shelving, and had plenty of natural light, thanks to the huge skylight. It meant she had to turn the brightness on the tablet up to its maximum to be able to see the screen, but that was a small price to pay to work in such magnificent surroundings. It was a place of learning, of education, of expanding one's mind—and that, in addition to the unequalled scent of books, both old and new, seemed to get Fiona's synapses firing like nowhere and nothing else. Except maybe sex.

Settling into the comfortable old leather armchair, she resisted the temptation to kick off her shoes and tuck her feet up beneath her. She was still on duty, after all. Just because she'd earned the perk of being able to disappear off and work wherever she liked on occasion didn't mean she should take advantage or let her professional manner slip. There were guests in and out of here all the time. It wasn't exactly the most popular destination on the premises—which was another reason she liked it so much—but it *was* visited.

After popping her handbag on the table, she retrieved her

mobile phone and typed out a message to Logan. He seemed to check his phone more often than James, and they were pretty much joined at the hip, anyway, so she knew James would see the message soon after Logan did.

Hope you're both okay. Sorry I've not texted before now. Things manic here today! Just managed to escape to the library for a bit for some brainstorming. Anyway, just wanted to let you know I received the flowers and they're beautiful. Thank you so much, F xxx P.S. Talk later.

She hit the send button, then switched the device onto silent mode, returned it to her bag and grabbed her tablet. It had automatically logged itself onto the library's Wi-Fi network—God bless technology—and was ready to go.

She opened the web browser, then cringed to herself as she started typing in the phrase. It was *way* too early to be thinking about Christmas, but she had no choice. It was the nature of her job—yes, some publicity could be gained on the spot in response to things that had happened, but for those things that rolled around each and every year, campaigns had to be brainstormed, planned and executed, the wheels set into motion many months in advance of the actual event. And, in the hospitality trade, Christmas was a biggie. The biggest, really.

Gritting her teeth, she pressed search, then waited. After the results came up, she flipped to the image results and focused on what came up, waiting for a kernel of inspiration to take root. Most of the time, she had absolutely no idea where her ideas came from, but, thankfully, they always seemed to come. Even if they weren't quite what she'd been looking for, they were a good enough jumping off point, and the creative side of her brain raced away with itself, providing phrases, imagery, plots and plans so quickly that she could hardly keep up. But she couldn't complain. It was better to have too many ideas than not enough.

Sophia still seemed pleased with her work too, which, far from making Fiona complacent, spurred her on to work harder and smarter, to keep impressing her boss and hopefully inspire more talk of courses and promotion. She'd well and truly settled in at The Portmannow Hotel, and she adored it. In her eyes, the only way was up.

Smiling to herself, Fiona wished the people who had thought a creative writing degree was a waste of time could see her now. Granted, some of her success had been down to pure luck and the early rapport she'd established with Sophia, but if she hadn't been up to the task, she wouldn't have passed her probationary period.

Those people didn't matter anyway, not now. The people who *did* matter had supported her all along and were pleased for her.

Which reminded her… She was due to go home at the weekend, and work had been so crazy that she still hadn't booked her train tickets. She navigated away from images of baubles and snow-covered fields, went onto her preferred rail travel website and began inputting her details. As she did so, she smiled at the thought of seeing her family. It had been a while, and although they understood she was busy, she was way overdue a visit. Some girly time with her mum and some time out walking the dog with her dad was definitely on the cards. She could hardly wait.

Chapter Twenty-Three

Leaving the clothing store and heading back into the heaving crowds in Birmingham's Bullring shopping centre, Fiona glanced at her watch, then turned to her mother. "Want to go and grab some lunch? I could do with a break, a drink and something to eat."

Caroline Gillespie nodded to her daughter. "Sounds like a plan, chick. Nando's?"

Twenty minutes later, having battled through the throngs of people with their many shopping bags, the two women were seated in the restaurant, had placed their order and were supping at the drinks that had just been brought to their table.

"Ahh," Fiona said with satisfaction, putting the glass of sparkling flavoured water down on the table. "That's better. All that shopping has made me totally parched."

Her mother smiled. "I'd have thought you'd be competing at Olympic level by now—having all those amazing shops on Oxford Street and whatnot nearby."

Chuckling, Fiona shook her head. "You're having a laugh, aren't you? I don't have much time for shopping in London—which is just as well, really. There's too much temptation… I'd spend a fortune!"

"Sounds like the job's still keeping you busy. I hope you're getting some time to yourself, though, to relax. I know you've got your eye on a promotion, but you don't want to burn yourself out."

"I know, Mum." Fiona returned her mother's smile. "And don't worry, I am getting time away from work. Weekend work is once in a blue moon—if something major is happening—and I put in reasonable hours the majority of the time. But yeah, I'm flexible because I want them to know how keen I am on progressing."

"So what do you do to relax? Do you still see your old flatmates?"

"Oh yeah, definitely. Not as much as we'd all like, unfortunately, due to clashing schedules, but as often as we can. Mostly I chill out in my room, reading, watching TV and films. Friday nights I generally go out into town with a bunch of work colleagues. I go running in Hyde Park, sometimes alone, sometimes with a colleague or two. I go to the cinema, the theatre. I'm working my way through London's tourist attractions, the museums, art galleries and so on, though I'm seriously beginning to think I could live in London for the rest of my life and still not manage to see all it has to offer. Once you've checked all the obvious places off the to-visit list, you get down to the quirky museums, random ruins and stuff further away from the centre."

Nodding thoughtfully, Caroline replied, "It sounds wonderful, darling. I'm glad you're making the most of the opportunity. So," she continued, way too casually for her words to actually *be* casual, "no boyfriend yet, then?"

"Mum!" Fiona shook her head. "Were you not listening to a word I just said about how busy I am and what I get up to in my spare time?"

"I was listening, darling, and I couldn't help but think that the vast majority of those outside-of-work activities could easily, and indeed preferably, be enjoyed with someone else. So you go to the cinema and theatre alone, do you? Visit museums and art galleries by yourself?" Caroline's eyebrows were raised, and her tone bordered on sarcastic.

"Sometimes, yes," Fiona replied defensively, folding her arms. "But like I said, I go out with friends or colleagues, okay? No boyfriend." Well, she wasn't lying. She hadn't gone anywhere with James and Logan yet, and even if she had, she wasn't sure she could put a label on their relationship. She certainly wasn't going to mention them to her mother. How could she?

I may not have a boyfriend, Mother, but I do have two gorgeous, successful men who are in a long-term relationship with each other and stay in the hotel on a fairly regular basis. And the last two times they've been in town, I've shared their bed. Oh, and they're also into BDSM, have taught me the basics, decided I'm a switch—which means that sometimes I like to be dominant and other times submissive—and are going to take me to a fetish event next time they're in London. How's that for a relationship status?

Shrugging, Caroline said, "All right, all right. No need to get snappy about it. I'm just checking, darling. I only want you to be happy. Though," she said quietly, as though her words weren't really intended for her daughter's ears, "I still think you're holding out on me." She picked up her drink and took a sip, glancing around as if to see if their meal was on its way.

"I *am* happy, Mum," Fiona replied, deciding to ignore her mum's last sentence. After all, it had been muttered, so it was perfectly reasonable to draw the conclusion that Fiona hadn't heard it, and therefore didn't need to respond to it. "I love my job. Living in the hotel is great. I mean, come on—I've got world-famous restaurants and spas at my fingertips, my colleagues are great, both in terms of work and going out on the town, and exploring London is awesome. I don't need to be in a relationship to be happy. But when I have someone I'm serious about, Mum, you'll be the first to know."

"Ah-hah!" Caroline said, way too loudly, drawing glances from the tables nearby. "So there *is* someone. You're just not sure if you're serious about him yet!"

Shit. Dropping her head into her hands, Fiona groaned, then straightened and looked her mother in the eyes. "That's not what I meant, Mum. I just don't see the point in letting you know every time I go out on a date, or for a drink or a coffee with someone. I could mention someone to you, and yet never see them again because there was no chemistry or whatever. Wouldn't you rather I waited to tell you about someone who's actually important, who I might bring home to meet you at some point? Or would you prefer I told you about every single man who so much as smiles at me?"

"Of course not." Now it was Caroline's turn to be defensive. "I'm just interested, that's all. You don't want to tell me things? I can't make you. Now, I think we ought to change the subject before we end up having an argument."

Thank fuck for that.

"Okay, Mum. Sorry." She reached across the table and squeezed her hand, giving a placating smile.

"Hmph. I'm sorry too, I suppose."

They were saved from any further grovelling—or arguing—by the arrival of their food. After thanking the waiter, the two women began eating in silence, glad of the opportunity to let their irritation wane before attempting further conversation.

"So!" Fiona said brightly, as they picked up their shopping bags once more and prepared to head back into the bedlam of the shopping centre. "Where next? I could still do with a couple more outfits for work. What about you?"

"I don't mind, sweetheart. Wherever you like. I'm just enjoying spending time with you."

Way to make me feel guilty, Mum. Worst daughter ever, or what?

Stuffing her guilt deep down inside, she smiled. "Me too, Mum. I know I don't get home often enough. But you and Dad should totally come down to London at some point. Maybe before Christmas, so you can do your shopping, see the city in all its pretty lights and decorations, possibly go ice skating at Somerset House or the Natural History Museum?"

"Oh, yes, that sounds like a fabulous idea. Though," she frowned, "I don't think we'll be able to stay in your hotel. It's a little out of our price range."

Giggling, Fiona nodded. "I know, Mum. Don't worry, I wasn't expecting you to. My staff discount isn't *that* good! Maybe once I'm running the place," she tipped her mother a wink to show she was joking, "I'll treat you and Dad to a weekend there. But for now, a cheap hotel will have to do. It won't matter, anyway. London's a big place, but the Tube makes it small. As long as you're staying somewhere pretty central, you can be anywhere within twenty minutes or so. I sometimes find it takes as long to get to a

Tube station as it does to get to your final destination. You should ask Charlie if he wants to come, too. Make a real family thing of it."

"Ask him yourself later, darling." Caroline checked her watch. "He should be at home right about now."

"Oh, seriously?" Fiona let out a little squeal. As long as it had been since she'd seen her parents, it had been longer still since she'd seen her brother, who was away up north in York at university. "He's home this weekend? You kept that one quiet!"

"I know." Her mother grinned. "We did it deliberately. We wanted it to be a surprise. It'll be nice to have all four of us in the same place at the same time, won't it?"

"Absolutely! Come on, let's go and get the rest of these shops tamed, so I can see my troublesome little brother."

"It's a good excuse to buy a non-work outfit, too—we're going out for dinner tonight."

"Even better." Hoisting her handbag higher onto her shoulder and gripping her purchases more tightly, she galvanised herself. "Right, let's get on with it, then."

***

"I love it," Charlie said the following morning as they walked the family dog, a Cocker spaniel called Maverick, in the park near their childhood home. It was the first chance they'd had to chat alone since he'd arrived the previous afternoon, and Fiona had mentioned the London-before-Christmas plan. "Actually, it could take a weight off our minds."

"It could?" Fiona frowned, then exclaimed as she almost fell over Maverick, who'd stopped dead to sniff something in their path. Giving his tail an affectionate wiggle to chivvy him along, she said, "What do you mean?"

"Well, you know how Mum and Dad are a complete nightmare to buy presents for?"

Groaning, she replied, "Don't I ever!"

"Well, if they're going to be in London, maybe rather than buying them a physical present, we could treat them to an experience. Maybe a night at the theatre or a posh dinner—or both. Or…" He tailed off, thinking. "Afternoon tea at a nice hotel, a visit to a spa?"

"Hmm, I like your thinking, Char. Though we'll have to make our minds up. I'm pretty sure the present-buying budget of a student and a lowly PR assistant won't stretch to the theatre, a meal, afternoon tea *and* a spa visit."

"You're right there, sis. But they're just ideas. Maybe the afternoon tea would be a good one. Does your place do them? And is your staff discount considerable enough to make it a viable option?"

"Possibly. But I could see about pulling in some favours. It might not work out, but I can certainly give it a go. Besides," she waved a hand dismissively, "we've got ages to figure it out. Christmas isn't for months yet. It just came up because of a conversation Mum and I were having yesterday."

"Let me guess… The one about not seeing you enough?"

"That's the one."

"Yeah, I get it too. Funny, isn't it, how we get on so much

better with our parents when we're not living in their house any longer? And we get on better with each other, too."

Smirking, Fiona said, "Not really. You know what they say… You can choose your friends, but not your family."

"Hey!" Charlie said, mock-punching Fiona's arm. "That's not nice."

"I'm kidding, little bro. Just kidding." Reaching out, she ruffled his hair, making him protest all the more and indignantly brush the mop back into place. "I wouldn't change you guys for anything."

Though you might not feel the same about me when you find out I'm bedding two blokes at once. Literally.

Chapter Twenty-Four

With her tote bag slung over her shoulder, Fiona strode through the back hallways of the hotel, heading for the staff-only exit to the street. She wore regular clothes—her fetish gear stashed in the bag—but she still preferred not to bump into anyone so she didn't have to lie about where she was going.

It had all happened pretty quickly. The previous evening, she'd received a phone call from Logan, letting her know he and James were coming into town for a last-minute meeting on Friday morning and had brought forward some other meetings to make their time in town more productive. They were free on Friday evening, however, and wanted to take her to another fetish event—at a different place, this time, as the event they attended last time wasn't on again for another couple of weeks.

She'd coolly agreed—though inside she was pumping her fists and grinning like a fool at the thought of seeing James and Logan again.

Now she was sneaking out of the building like a kid skipping curfew, ready to slip into the limo she'd been assured was waiting for her right next to the staff entrance.

Taking a deep breath, she pushed at the door, her heart pounding. Anticipation and excitement rushed through her, but she arranged her face into a neutral smile as she stepped outside.

She'd barely closed the door behind her when the driver scurried around the vehicle and opened the back door to let her in. James and Logan were likely inside the car already, but they were so aware of Fiona getting into trouble for being seen with them that they wouldn't help her into the car themselves. She didn't mind, because they were doing it for her benefit—it didn't make a difference to them who they were seen with, after all. The Portmannow Hotel was hardly going to turn guests away for sleeping with the staff, particularly as they subscribed to the ethos that the customer was always right.

Thanking the driver, Fiona slid carefully into the car—a task made much easier by the fact that she was wearing jeans and flat shoes. No danger of tripping up or accidentally flashing her underwear. Not that James and Logan would have minded the latter, she was sure.

"Hi," she said, still keeping a lid on her excitement as she turned to the men, who sat opposite each other on the leather seats running the length of the vehicle. She'd settled onto the shorter seat that went across the width of the limo.

"Hi," they said in unison, then glanced at each other, grinning. The spark, the chemistry between them was hugely apparent in that moment, and Fiona was both turned on by thoughts of them together and feeling slightly left out. A third wheel, as it were.

She shoved the idea to the back of her mind, chastising herself for being stupid. Of course things were going to be different between the two of them than they were with her. They were in love with each other, for heaven's sake, and in a long-term relationship. She was just someone lucky enough to share their bed once in a while, have a bit of fun with them.

When they turned their attention back to her, she wriggled in the seat, the intensity of their twin stares making her self-conscious and feeling not unlike the proverbial deer caught in the headlights. Or, perhaps more accurately, like prey in a showdown with two predators—two strong, virile predators. Damn, she wouldn't even run. She'd give herself over to them willingly any day of the week.

"It's great to see you, sweetheart," Logan said, sliding along the seat so he was closer to her. James did the same on the other side. "And I very much look forward to seeing what treats are in store in that bag of yours."

"Well…" she began, her cheeks heating, "I'm afraid it won't be much of a surprise. It's the schoolgirl outfit. It's the only fetish gear I've got, and since you only called last night, I haven't had a chance to buy anything else. I didn't even know, after last time, whether I'd get the opportunity to wear this again."

Both men grinned widely, making her wriggle again.

"Personally," James said, leaning back in the seat and giving her an appraising look, "I don't see a problem with this. You'd look gorgeous in a bin liner, my darling. You look gorgeous *now*. So if you want to wear a next-to-nothing PVC get-up, you'll hear no complaints from me, whether you've worn it before or not!" Pressing a hand to his denim-covered crotch, he rearranged himself. "In fact, my cock's getting hard just thinking of you dressed up like that, with those sexy pigtails, long socks and geeky glasses."

"I couldn't agree more," Logan added. "Plus, you hardly got chance to show the outfit off last time. So it's almost like starting over, isn't it?"

He didn't mention the fact it had mainly been *his* fault she hadn't got the opportunity to show her outfit off, but he was clearly trying to make amends now, so she decided not to say anything, either.

"Absolutely," she said, nodding. "It's barely been seen—except at our private party, of course." She glanced at the two men, gauging their reaction to her words. As they both continued smiling and sported growing bulges between their legs, she knew she'd had the desired effect—giving them a big fat reminder of the kinky fun they'd got up to the last time she'd dressed that way.

"Of course," Logan purred. "And what a wonderful private party it was." He grinned, his perfect teeth glinting. "James and I are actually going shopping. We need to replace a couple of bits and pieces, so we'd love for you to join us, if you're free tomorrow or Sunday."

Shrugging in what she hoped was a nonchalant fashion, Fiona replied, "Yeah, sure, why not?" Did this mean they wanted her to go to fetish events with them on a more regular basis? She hoped so.

"Great." Logan nodded in satisfaction, and the three of them passed the rest of the journey across town by indulging in more general chit-chat.

It surprised and fascinated Fiona how James and Logan could so easily switch from talking about sex and kink to a vanilla conversation. But then, they'd been in the lifestyle for some time now. It was a part of them, so why wouldn't it be natural? They weren't solely successful businessmen, just like they weren't solely kinksters. They had many facets to their lives and personalities, and she was learning more about them all the time. And the more she learned, the more she liked them. She was being taken along on this amazing ride, without knowing how long it would last. All she could do was make the most of it. If nothing else, she'd come out the other side with a bunch of unforgettable experiences and valuable knowledge.

Really, she had nothing to lose. Except maybe a little bit of face, and she also ran the risk of ending up with a broken heart.

A broken heart? She chastised herself. Her heart had nothing to do with this. This was three people having safe, sexy fun together, and that was the extent of it. James and Logan had each other, *loved* each other—that much was obvious. There was no room for a third person in their relationship—not on a permanent basis, anyway. She was just a pleasant addition for the time being, and as long as they continued to treat her as respectfully as they had so far, she'd stick around until things fizzled out or until someone else caught her eye. Maybe she'd even meet someone at a fetish event. Now that would be interesting…

She'd been so caught up in their conversation that she hadn't been paying the slightest bit of attention to where they were going, so was surprised when the car pulled to a stop outside a nightclub she'd never heard of. Apparently, lots of other people had heard of it, though. The queue was even longer than the one at the place in Vauxhall.

The driver opened the door, and Logan climbed out before leaning back in to offer Fiona his hand. She took it, relishing the heat that trickled through her veins at the skin-to-skin contact. To her confusion, he led her right past the queue and to the front, where he approached one of the security staff. Instead of kicking their arses to the back of the queue, as she'd expected, the guy opened the rope barrier to let the three of them pass. She made a mental note to ask what the hell that had been about when they were alone.

Whipping some cash from his wallet, Logan paid the cashier before Fiona had even found her purse in the voluminous bag. She opened her mouth to protest, but Logan held up a hand to stop her. "My treat. I'm still making up for last time, okay? Now, come on. Let's go and get changed."

It was then she realised James was carrying a couple of smart black holdalls, and she wondered what they'd be wearing this time. The variation on outfits for men didn't seem as wide as for women, which was a shame. She'd quite like to see James—and Logan, for that matter, though it'd probably never happen—in a pair of arseless chaps.

Nice.

"What are you smirking at, Fiona?" Logan asked, having apparently adopted his Dominant persona.

She, on the other hand, hadn't decided who she was going to be tonight. Did she *have* to decide? Did she have to stick with either Dominant or submissive, or could things be fluid? She was still finding her feet, testing her limits and trying to figure out where she fit in. With Logan, she was a submissive—albeit a sassy one—and liked indulging in some light impact play, before being ordered to her knees to suck his engorged cock.

But with James, she enjoyed taunting and teasing his

delicious body until he begged for release. Other times, though, kink and D/s didn't come into it at all. More than once the three of them had simply tumbled into bed and pleasured each other in myriad ways until they passed out with exhaustion. There was no set order to what happened when they were together and no expectations. The only given was that they'd all have a great time.

Tonight would be no exception. So why bother to plan things out, or to steer them in a certain direction? She'd just put on her slutty schoolgirl outfit and go with the flow. James and Logan would look after her, make sure she was safe, so this was the ideal opportunity to dig deeper into the fetish world, to check out what made other people tick, and to maybe uncover a little more of what made *her* tick. It was a win-win situation.

"Just looking forward to the evening," she replied, shrugging. "Where do we get changed?"

"Come on," Logan took her hand again, "I'll show you." He led her to the ladies' changing area, then pointed along the corridor. "We'll be down there. But when you're done, wait right here. We'll come and find you, so please don't go anywhere."

He was asking, not commanding, but she still sensed the earnestness of his tone. "I'll be right here," she replied, smiling.

"Good." Returning her smile, he turned to continue down the corridor.

James followed, but not before giving her backside a hearty squeeze. Gasping, she shot him a narrow-eyed look even as arousal skittered across her skin. "I'll get you for that, James Kenrick," she said quietly, so only he could hear her. "You mark my words."

He leaned in and brushed the lightest of kisses on her cheek, then moved towards her ear and whispered, "I was hoping you'd say that, Mistress."

As he stepped away, she saw the glint in his eyes, and the skittering arousal turned into a full-on rush right between her thighs.

God, an entire Friday night spent with James and Logan… The possibilities were endless.

Chapter Twenty-Five

"Wow!" Fiona said, getting into the limousine, dropping her tote bag to the floor and flopping onto the rear seat. "*That* was amazing."

James and Logan had entered the vehicle behind her and were settled side by side on the left-hand seat. They were close, very close, and Fiona wondered just how horny they were after the evening's activities, whether they were itching to get their hands on each other.

"Which part?" James asked, his luscious lips curving into a sexy grin. "Would that be the part where you sucked Logan's cock for an audience, where I licked your pussy for an audience, where you watched people being spanked, flogged, whipped and caned, or where you saw a gagged, blindfolded, handcuffed man being fucked up the arse with a strap-on?"

"Can I say… all of it?" she gushed. "I'm just learning so much. Being able to watch people is great because I can get an idea whether I might like to try something without actually doing it—"

"You mean you *wouldn't* want to fuck James up the arse with a strap-on?" Logan interrupted, his grin positively devilish.

"I never mentioned that specifically," she stuttered in response, her cheeks heating up. "Why?" She turned her wide-eyed gaze to James. "Would you want me to?"

James still wore the sexy smile. "I wouldn't say no."

"Christ!" she said on a lengthy exhale. "I think I need a drink."

"Of course," Logan said, moving over to the mini-bar,

collecting three glasses and filling them with chilled champagne. "You've earned it. Here you go."

Taking the drink with thanks, Fiona relaxed back into the sumptuous leather seating and supped at the liquid. It was cool, crisp and delicious, and the bubbles soon set off a pleasant buzz within her. It was only her second alcoholic drink of the evening. Logan, in his usual bossy mode, had limited the three of them to a single alcoholic beverage while at the club—and now she enjoyed the second one immensely, closing her eyes as a further mouthful trickled down her throat.

As she began to unwind, memories of what she'd seen and done in the past few hours flashed into her brain, shocking and arousing her all over again. Her eyes were well and truly being opened to the fetish and kink world. Just when she'd got to a point where she thought nothing could surprise her, something came along to prove her wrong. Essentially, the only limit was a person's imagination.

Her own imagination snagged onto Logan's comment. *Would she be interested in using a strap-on with James?* She enjoyed topping him, yes, but could she go full-on Dominatrix and fuck his arse? It wasn't like he wouldn't be able to take it—Logan had screwed him enough times, after all. It'd just be a fake cock, wielded by her, instead of Logan's real one. And she was sure the two of them would teach her what to do, how to do it properly.

Still, with her eyes closed, she imagined herself in the position of the woman she'd seen earlier, pounding a big black dildo into her submissive's upturned bottom. Both of them had clearly been getting off on their actions, big style, and Fiona had been rapt. But did that mean it'd get her off? Maybe there was only one way to find out...

"Fiona, are you all right?" James's voice sliced through her filthy imaginings.

She opened her eyes, met his gaze, and nodded. "I'm fine, thank you. Just, um... decompressing, I suppose. Trying to process everything."

"Fair enough. I think we probably all need to unwind and switch off a bit. How about going the *very* long way back to the hotel?"

"What's that?"

"Dunno, really." He shrugged, then smiled. "I'll leave that up to the driver. We can see the sights of the city all lit up."

"Sounds wonderful."

After scooting to the partition, James pressed the button to lower the screen and speak to the driver. She couldn't hear what they were saying, but soon the partition was back in place and both men were looking at her expectantly. Logan was patting the space they'd left between them on the seat. They wanted her to sit with them. Either that or it was because she'd get a better view of the aforementioned sights from there. Who cared? Sitting between two gorgeous blokes in a limousine, supping on expensive champagne wasn't exactly a hardship, though the latter did seem to be going to her head rather quickly.

Taking the place they'd created for her, she smiled at each of them in turn before settling back into the seat and waiting for the show to begin. She wasn't entirely sure where they were at that moment, just in a maze of nondescript back streets and one-way systems. As they made their way through the dim city roads, she finished off her drink and accepted a top-up from Logan. The three of them sat in a companionable silence, and Fiona suspected they, too, appreciated the opportunity to wind down after an intense evening at the club.

Before long, a familiar sight came into view. *Ah, Oxford Street.* Since she'd been making more of an effort to explore London during her spare time, she was getting a real handle on the city's layout and improving her sense of direction. Now she knew where they were, she'd probably be able to figure out where they were going, and probably even what they'd see on the way.

Or she could just sit back, relax and enjoy herself. That was the whole point, surely?

Yes… Enjoy herself. She could do that. Letting out a happy sigh, she watched the designer and large high street retailers whizz by in a blur, to be replaced by Marble Arch, then impressive buildings and even more impressive hotels. Though, she thought with a sense of pride, not as impressive as The Portmannow. She'd definitely lucked out there.

Hyde Park Corner and Apsley House soon appeared, and a left turn along Constitution Hill provided a view of the side walls of Buckingham Palace, mostly screened by trees, until the space opened out and they could see the building itself. They continued to get a good look at the royal residence as they looped around the memorial to Queen Victoria and headed back up Buckingham Palace

Road.

What followed was a tourist's dream journey—like being on one of the tour buses, but much more comfortable, and with champagne. The Houses of Parliament and Westminster Abbey, then across the river to the London Eye and the South Bank. Tower Bridge and the Tower of London with their strategically-placed lighting were particularly awe-inspiring, drawing gasps and murmurs of appreciation from all three of them. Back across the river, still with excellent views of the Tower, then past a column that was a monument to the Great Fire of London in 1666, followed by St. Paul's Cathedral. Eventually they glided past Trafalgar Square, up towards St. James's Palace—which Fiona felt was massively underrated due to its more famous neighbour—and back into Mayfair.

As the exclusive shops gave way to stately buildings and the hotel grew ever closer, Fiona realised she'd downed the second glass of bubbles without even being aware of it. *Oops. Oh well, no harm done.*

Only when they pulled up to the side door of the hotel and Fiona attempted to get out of the vehicle did she come to the conclusion that actually wasn't true. Almost as soon as she'd got off the seat and reached for her bag, the world began tilting uncomfortably, then spinning. *Shit!*

She was vaguely aware of being gently pulled back into the car and settled onto the rear seat, then of whispered, hasty conversation.

"What the hell—?"

"Get her back to her room—"

"If someone sees her with us—"

"Make sure she's okay—"

"Not eaten properly—"

"What if she's sick?"

Fiona opened her mouth at that last, planning to let them know she wasn't going to be sick. She wasn't that bad. Just a bit tipsy. And tired. So incredibly tired all of a sudden…

God, if she didn't trust the two of them implicitly, she'd wonder if she'd been drugged. But then one of their snatched comments came back to her whirling brain. She *hadn't* eaten properly. She'd been later finishing work than planned, and to ensure she was ready on time, she'd had to rush back to her room straight away and jump into the shower. The only thing she'd eaten since lunchtime was a bag of crisps she'd found in her cupboard, which she'd munched on before putting the finishing touches to her makeup, packing her bag and heading out to meet James and Logan.

That'd be it, then. Not only had she drunk on a practically empty stomach, she'd drunk what was probably some of the finest champagne available. And now she was going to be carted back to her room and miss out on what would no doubt be some totally mind-blowing sex.

As she barely hung on to consciousness, she was aware of the vehicle moving again. "Whatareyoudoing?"

"Shh," a voice said from close by, and a hand stroked her hair. "You'll be all right, sweetheart. We're going to look after you." She thought it was probably James, though she couldn't be sure.

"I'm going to take your hair out of the pigtails, honey, so when we carry you in it'll help cover your face. We don't want your colleagues seeing you, do we? Especially not in this state. All right?"

"'Spose."

Gentle hands carefully pulled at the ties securing her hair, then raked through the strands. It felt nice, so relaxing, that she teetered on the brink of unconsciousness once more.

"Hey," James said softly, patting her cheek. "Stay with us, Fiona. Let us just get you up to our room and get some food and water into your system, and probably some painkillers, then you can sleep all you want, okay?"

"'Kay."

The car drew to a stop once more, and she grumbled as she was helped out of the vehicle, then quickly lifted into strong arms. Her head was tucked into a broad chest, and strands of hair tickled her skin. Somehow, she held on to just enough common sense to resist the temptation to brush her hair away from her face. What had James said? Yeah, that was it—didn't want her colleagues seeing her, especially not in this state.

A giggle escaped, surprising her. The surprise set off more giggles, and she tittered away, her face still pushed into the chest of either James or Logan—she had no idea which—as she was carried up the steps of the hotel and into the lobby.

Through the sudden buzzing in her ears, she heard a wry voice. Logan. "She's all right. Just had too much to drink, that's all. My sister." The arms squeezed her, as though in warning not to open her mouth and expose his blatant lie. "We're going to get her upstairs and get some food and water in her. That'll teach her to drink on an empty stomach."

Hey! How did he...?

"Fuckingknoweverythingsmartarse," she grumbled. Who the hell had he been talking to, anyway? One of the door staff, probably.

Chuckling, Logan continued his journey, and she sensed the movement of the elevator as they were carried up to James and Logan's floor, then, after what felt like the longest ever walk down a corridor, came the unmistakable swish and click of the key card in the lock.

Finally, a muttered "Thank fuck for that," followed by the *whomp* of the closing door and, a few steps later, she was lowered onto a bed.

Ahh... Now I can sleep. Fiona let her eyelids flutter down, sealing off the outside world.

Chapter Twenty-Six

"Ah-ah, no you don't!" Through the thick fog of her mind, Fiona felt herself being gently pulled upright, and pillows piled up behind her back. "Fiona?" James said. "Are you still with us, sweetheart? Can you try to stay awake, just a little bit longer?"

"Don't wanna."

"I'm sure you don't, but we'd really like you to. We want to get you into some more comfortable clothes, get some painkillers into you, plenty of water and some food."

"Wanna sleep."

"You can sleep, just as soon as we've done all that."

"Humph." She folded her arms, her eyelids fluttering again.

"James," Logan said. "I think we should just get on with it. You can see how desperately she wants to fall asleep. I just placed an order with room service for some nice unhealthy food, which should arrive soon. So, in the meantime, let's get her into some pyjamas and a dressing gown. Maybe a black coffee to keep her awake long enough to eat, then plenty of water."

"Yeah, all right. I'll go and make the coffee. You want one?"

"No thanks. I'll keep an eye on her while you're doing that."

"Okay." James left the bedroom, and Fiona, still bleary-eyed, watched him go. Then, with some difficulty, she shifted her focus back onto Logan.

"I'm sorry," she forced out, her tongue feeling thick and furry in her mouth. "You should've just taken me back to my room."

Logan shook his head. "Nope. Not happening. You scared the crap out of us. One minute you were ooh-ing and ahh-ing at the sights along with us, and the next minute you could hardly stand. You're staying right here where we can keep an eye on you, to make sure you're not sick or anything. *No* arguments."

Fiona rolled her eyes. "Okay."

Apparently satisfied, Logan turned to the chest of drawers and pulled out a set of pyjamas. Fiona raised her eyebrows. She'd never seen either Logan or James in nightwear before. They usually wandered around naked or pulled on a pair of boxers or a robe if they were going to answer the door.

Hmm, seems even über-sexy businessmen wear comfy jammies.

Logan closed the drawer, then carried the items over to the bed and placed them down beside her. "You want me to help you?"

"I'm all right, thanks," she said, though she wasn't sure if it was true or not. She hadn't tried to stand since attempting to get out of the limo, so she had no idea whether she'd be able to now. Figuring she didn't have to discover that just yet, she tucked her knees up to her chest and removed her shoes and socks, smiling gratefully as Logan whisked them away and placed them on a chair.

Then she removed her checked shirt, fumbling with the buttons as the alcohol continued to affect her coordination. Biting her bottom lip in the hope it would sharpen her up a bit and stop Logan having to step in and help, she finally got the top off. Now it remained to be seen whether she could get her jeans and knickers off without hitting the deck.

"Come on," Logan said kindly, holding out his hand. "Let me help you. There's no need to be proud."

"Think I'm a bit beyond that, don't you? I've made an utter fool of myself tonight. Didn't bloody eat properly, did I?"

"You've done no such thing. You just made a mistake, that's all. We all do. We're only human. Now stop bringing yourself down and do as you're told. I can still boss you around, even though I'm not going to spank that luscious arse of yours."

"Y-you're not?" Confusion wavered its way to the forefront of her mind.

Logan's expression turned incredulous. "No, I'm bloody well not. You've had too much to drink, sweetheart, and we're going to look after you. So that means there'll be no kinky business and no sex tonight. You know how I feel about sober playmates."

She did. He was always very careful to pay attention to how much alcohol she and James consumed, and he rarely had more than one, himself. Sometimes it bugged her, but she reminded herself he wasn't being overbearing, or a control freak. He was looking out for them, just like he was looking out for her now. She should be grateful he was so considerate and caring.

Taking his hand, she shuffled to the edge of the bed and let her feet dangle off the mattress. She was just sliding towards the carpet, hoping her legs held her up once she got there, when James reappeared with her coffee. He placed it down on the bedside table, then grabbed the pyjama bottoms from the bed, unfolded them and held them up, ready.

She cringed as her feet found the soft fibres of the carpet and locked her knees. Logan never released his hold on her. She wove slightly, causing Logan to grab her around the waist, but her legs remained steady.

"You all right?" Logan said, looking her in the eyes.

"Yeah, I think so." *The world's still a bit fuzzy, mind.*

"Okay. Hold onto me if you need to."

Just to be sure, she took him up on his offer, gripping his muscular shoulders as he knelt down and made short work of undoing her belt and flies, then pulling her jeans down. He helped her to step out of each leg in turn, then did the same with her knickers. Once her mound was bared, she couldn't help the embarrassment that still flooded her body, despite her drunkenness. She'd got used to being naked and in various states of undress in front of the two of them, but this was different. They were getting nothing out of this. They might like what they were seeing, but Logan had said sex was off the agenda.

They still had each other, though. Perhaps as soon as they'd fed and watered her and she'd gone to sleep, they'd head into the other bedroom and fuck each other's brains out? She was so desperate to sleep that she doubted she'd hear them, not even if they were super-noisy and they left the internal doors open.

Disappointment lanced through her, but she forced a smile as Logan collected her jeans and underwear and put them on the chair, too.

James appeared in front of her, brandishing the pyjama bottoms. "Let me help you put these on, sweetheart."

Nodding, she now held onto his shoulders as he knelt in front of her and lifted each of her feet in turn to put them in the trousers, then pulled them up. They were much too big, so James used the ties at the waist to cinch them tightly, then rolled up the legs a little so she didn't trip over them.

"Okay." He patted her outer thighs in a fond, platonic fashion, making her heart sink further. "Sit down and we'll get this T-shirt on you, too. Do you want a robe, or are you going to get under the covers?"

"Under the covers," she said in a small voice. Of course she was going to choose that option. It meant she could pull the duvet over her head to hide herself and her overwhelming mortification. There was no judgment in either of the men's eyes, but it didn't stop her embarrassment at the situation.

Perched on the mattress, she let James put the T-shirt on her, then shuffled back towards the centre of the bed. As she rested against the pillows, she decided not to get into the bed properly yet, as she'd probably need to use the bathroom soon.

James handed her the mug of coffee.

"Thank you. You're both very kind."

"Nonsense. We're just doing what any decent person would do," James replied.

A knock came at the door, and Logan left the bedroom to answer it.

Fiona sipped at the coffee, hoping Logan was right and that it would keep her awake long enough to get herself sorted out. When Logan came back into the room, he brought with him the mouth-watering scent of chips. Her stomach growled, and she clutched it, her cheeks flaming. "I'm sorry." She put her drink down on the bedside table.

Smiling, Logan said, "Don't be sorry, just listen to your stomach and eat as many as you can manage. They're cheesy chips. I hope you like them. If not, let me know and I can order something else. Or if you're still hungry, I can order more."

"No, that's fine. I actually love the chips from here. They're thick cut, twice fried and utterly delicious."

"You don't have to tell me," Logan said, handing her the plate, then grabbing one of the thick strips of hot potato, a string of cheese stretching through the air, growing thinner and thinner before finally breaking. "It's why James and I spend so much time in the gym while we're here. The food is just so damn good that we eat too much of it!"

Glancing between them, her eyebrows raised, Fiona said, "Well, you don't look bad on it, it has to be said. How do you think I feel? I bloody well live here. It's a good job the salads are delicious, too, otherwise I'd be the size of a house!"

James chuckled, also reaching out to grab one of the chips. "Stop being ridiculous and eat up while they're still nice and hot. Then more coffee, water and painkillers, then sleep. All right?"

"Sleep, yes. Great." She fell silent then, except for the occasional contented moan as the unhealthy yet tempting and delicious snack tantalised her taste buds. She polished off the entire portion, then thanked Logan as he took the plate away and handed the coffee back to her.

After downing what was left, she made to get up.

"Whoa," James said. "Where are you going?"

"To the bathroom."

"You going to be okay?"

"Yes. I'm feeling much better already, actually. Less drunk, more utterly exhausted."

"Good. Well, don't lock the door, just in case."

Barely stopping herself from rolling her eyes—he *was* just looking out for her—she nodded and entered the bathroom. After using the toilet, she flushed it, then washed her hands and rinsed her face. The result was a mass of smeared mascara. Cringing, she raided the cabinet, sighing in relief as she found the posh makeup remover and cotton pads that resided in every cabinet in every room.

After removing every scrap of makeup and throwing away the soiled pads, she grimaced at herself in the mirror. It was just as well sex was off the menu tonight—James and Logan would probably take one look at her bare face and run screaming from the room.

Pleased she was at least feeling a little more human, she went back into the bedroom to find Logan placing a pint glass full of water and two white tablets on the bedside table. "Here you go," he said, flashing her an adorable smile. "Take those, then we'll tuck you up in bed."

A minute later, she was settling beneath the thick duvet, her eyes closing almost before her head touched the pillow—in spite of the black coffee. It had served its purpose—making her lucid enough so the men could take care of her. And boy, had they taken care of her. So patiently that she knew she'd have to find a way to pay them back for their kindness.

"Thanks, guys," she mumbled, hoping they heard her through

the duvet.

She was holding onto the last vestiges of consciousness when she felt the mattress dip on either side of her. They were joining her, rather than going into the other room and having some naked horizontal time? Crazy.

They were really taking this looking after her thing seriously. She grinned, secure in the knowledge they couldn't see her face. It was nice, having two gorgeous blokes taking care of her. Really nice. But she shouldn't get used to it. It wouldn't last forever. Things this good never did.

Chapter Twenty-Seven

Fiona woke up, several things hitting her at once—the fact she couldn't see, or breathe particularly well, and she was boiling hot. As she flung the duvet off, she immediately realised her mistake.

Or her stroke of utter genius, depending on which way you looked at it. Once her brain had helpfully supplied a reminder of what had happened the previous evening, telling her why she'd been hiding beneath the duvet, she took in the sights she'd uncovered with her half-asleep duvet-throwing action.

James and Logan had apparently spent the entire night nestled up beside her, and, probably through some sense of propriety, had chosen to don boxer shorts, rather than sleep naked. She'd have preferred naked, but the view as it was wasn't half bad. The underwear in question was tight enough to show off what was underneath. And there was plenty more male flesh on display for her to feast her eyes on.

She was having a damn good time doing just that, raking her gaze up and down the finely muscled bodies, when she had a surprise. Once she reached Logan's face, she found him peering right back at her, a lazy and amused smile on his face. "Good morning, lightweight," he teased.

Instead of caving in to instinct and giving him the finger, she flashed him what she hoped was an apologetic smile. "I'm sorry, Logan. I really didn't mean to get like that last night. I had no idea it was happening. I've well and truly learned my lesson, that's for sure. Thank you so much for looking after me. I appreciate it."

"That's okay," he replied, stretching like a big cat, his long limbs seeming to take over the bed. "It's no problem. It's partially my fault, I suppose, for not making sure you'd eaten something before we went out."

Fiona shook her head vehemently. "No, don't you dare blame yourself. I'm an adult. It's my own stupid fault. And, like I said, I've learned my lesson. No food, no booze. Simple as that."

"Fair enough." He shrugged, then swung his legs around and hopped off the bed. "I'm going to put some coffee on. You want some?"

"Yes, please. I'm just going to use the bathroom. Won't be long."

"Take as long as you like. Well, not too long, otherwise your coffee'll get cold."

He smiled before sauntering out into the main room. She watched him go, his high, taut buttocks bobbing up and down as he walked. God, what she wouldn't give to dig her nails into them as he pounded her pussy.

Shaking her head at the inappropriateness of her thoughts, she too hopped off the bed, and headed for the bathroom. She was surprised to discover all her limbs were in perfect working order and that she didn't have so much as a headache. Clearly the coffee, chips, painkillers and water combination had done the trick. She deserved to feel like shit. Instead, she'd got extremely lucky.

As she used the toilet and freshened up, Fiona decided she'd have her coffee, then get dressed and make her excuses to leave. James and Logan had been incredibly selfless in looking after her, despite her ruining their evening. The last thing she wanted to do was put a dampener on their Saturday, too. It wasn't fair. They deserved some time alone together, to work off some of the sexual frustrations they'd built up in the club. James, especially. At least she and Logan had had an orgasm apiece before the limo had whisked them off into the night. Poor James had to have blue balls.

Raking her fingers through her hair, which had transformed overnight into some kind of blonde bird's nest, she tugged and untangled it until it was vaguely presentable, before leaving the bathroom.

"Morning, gorgeous," came James's voice.

She looked over at the bed. He was settled against the pillows, cradling a mug.

"Good morning." Her cheeks flushed as some of the embarrassment came creeping back. She was fully aware of what a mess she looked, and it didn't help that the two of them, with the exception of a spot of bedhead, could still easily grace the pages of a fashion magazine. Bastards. How was it that men could wake up looking as sexy as they did when they'd gone to sleep?

"Logan's just on the phone, ordering some breakfast. Warm croissants okay?"

Her stomach grumbled in response, and she hoped like hell the sound hadn't carried across the room. "Perfect, thanks. Though I can sort myself out some breakfast back in my room."

"Nonsense. He's ordering it now. And your coffee's just there." He pointed to the bedside table. "Have some before it gets too cold."

"Thanks." She gave him a small smile, grabbed the coffee and settled into the chair next to the one that still held her neatly arranged clothes from the previous evening. "Mmm… This is great."

Logan came back into the room, mug in hand. Standing next to Fiona's chair, he stroked her hair gently with his free hand. "Feeling okay this morning, sweetheart?"

Nodding as she swallowed the mouthful of coffee she'd taken, she then replied, "Surprisingly, yes. You two and your magic combination clearly worked. I'm pretty sure I should be feeling like death warmed up right about now. But, other than a spot of tiredness and a whole lot of embarrassment, I'm good."

Shaking his head, he replied, "There's no need to be embarrassed, Fiona, honestly. You're okay. We're okay. No harm done whatsoever. Breakfast'll be here in a few minutes, by the way."

"Yeah, James said. Thank you. I'll get going once I've eaten, I think."

"There's no rush, sweetheart. James and I have no plans this morning. Stay as long as you like."

No plans? They obviously didn't intend to pounce on each other as soon as her back was turned, then. "No, it's okay. I need to get going. Get showered, clean clothes and whatnot. I might go for a run and clear my head."

Logan glanced at James, then back at Fiona. "That's not a bad idea, actually. It looks like it's going to be a nice day. Would you have any objections if we joined you?"

Objections? No. Confusion? Yes. Why aren't you desperate to see the back of me after last night?

"No, of course not," she replied.

"Great! Cool—we could do that, then get showered and changed and head back out to get the fetish gear I mentioned last night. Then maybe grab some lunch somewhere?"

God, he seemed to be planning out an entire day together. It was obviously what he wanted, though, otherwise he wouldn't be suggesting it. "Sounds good to me. Though are you sure you don't mind, James?" She didn't want James to feel he had to go along with it, just because Logan had said so.

She and Logan looked over at him, still relaxing against the pillows. "Nope, I'm happy with that. The perfect Saturday, if you ask me."

Fiona frowned. "Really? You're easily pleased."

"Why do you say that?"

"Well." She cleared her throat, wondering whether she could say what she really meant. "Wouldn't you prefer to spend some time, you know, alone together? Without me?"

Now it was James's turn to frown. "Um, I'm not sure how I'm supposed to answer that. Obviously I want to spend time with Logan, but not necessarily alone or without you. I enjoy your company, Fiona, and so does Logan."

"What's brought this on, Fiona?" Logan asked, moving her clothes to the floor and sitting down in the chair beside her. "Why do you suddenly think we might want to get rid of you?"

"I-I dunno, really." She took a sip of the coffee, buying herself some time to think, to formulate an answer. She swallowed, then continued, "It's just you two are in a committed relationship, and I'm just…"

"Just what?" Logan said gently, reaching over and taking her hand. She turned to meet his eyes, the intensity in the baby blues almost making her lose her train of thought. "Fiona? Tell us, please."

"Well, I'm a temporary addition, aren't I? From my perspective, I'm the luckiest girl in the bloody world. But I don't understand what you two are getting out of this… arrangement. Before you met me, you were living your lives together, going to fetish events, having lots of sex. You're still doing that, only sometimes I join in. So how exactly do I add anything to your lives? I'm like a third wheel in your relationship."

"Hmm." Logan's tone had hardened, but he didn't release her hand. "You said something similar last night, but I assumed it was the booze talking. I'm sorry you feel that way. What can we do to help?"

"Help? I don't know what you mean. It's the way I feel. How are you supposed to change my feelings?"

Huffing out a breath, Logan let go of her hand, then stood up. He placed his coffee cup on the bedside table and paced up and down a couple of times, running his hands through his hair. "James? Help me out here?"

After putting down his own mug, James got off the bed and hurried across the room, where he knelt down beside Fiona. Logan retook the seat he'd just vacated and pulled in a deep breath, then let it out. "You used the word 'arrangement' not so long ago. To describe this," he pointed between the three of them, "what's happening with us. We've never discussed any kind of arrangement, have we? It all just happened, and we've gone with the flow ever since. And actually, it's something James and I have been talking about. As much as we've enjoyed the time we've spent together, we wonder if it's fair on you."

"What do you mean?" *Christ, are they ditching me? Fucking hell—why couldn't I keep my big mouth shut?*

"Well, as you said, James and I are in a committed relationship—one we're happy with, one that works for us. We know the parameters, what goes, what doesn't. But you… well, you've become, and I apologise wholeheartedly for using this turn of phrase, a bit of a booty call. This… arrangement has become something that happens when we're in town, and although it's fun and amazing and mind-blowing, it's probably putting you in a bit of an awkward situation."

"A little, I suppose," she replied, her brain whirling. What was he getting at? She couldn't make head nor tail of it, so far. "But as long as we continue being discreet, I don't have a problem with it."

"That's not what I meant, sweetheart." He paused. "Can I ask you a personal question?"

"Yes." *The things we've done together, and he's worried about asking a personal question?*

"Are you seeing anyone? Besides us, I mean?"

"No, why?"

"Do you feel like you can? Do you want to?"

"Bloody hell, Logan, what's with the Spanish Inquisition?" *Where the hell is the room service? I could do with being saved by the bell right about now.*

James shuffled so he was in front of her, took her mug and placed it on the nearby table. Taking her hands, he shot Logan a dirty look, before returning his attention to her. "What Logan is *trying* to say, Fiona, and failing miserably, is that we feel like we're being a bit unfair to you. This thing between us has just happened. We haven't discussed it, haven't put any kind of label on it, so you might be confused about it. Understandably."

I wasn't, but I bloody well am now.

"Basically, because we haven't mentioned any kind of exclusivity, you might feel conflicted about seeing other people. We certainly can't stop you, but we'd rather you didn't."

"I'm not," she snapped, pulling her hands from his and shrinking back in the chair. "But I don't see why you have the right to stop me."

"That's exactly what we're trying to say! Apparently I'm doing a shitty job of it, too. Fiona, listen. You asked what Logan and I are getting out of spending time with you. Aside from the wonderful additions and variety to our bedroom activities, we genuinely enjoy simply being with you. We look forward to seeing you, hanging out together. And we'd really like it if you'd consider making it an exclusive and more permanent thing. We understand that your job, your career is here, so seeing each other more often isn't really an option, unfortunately, but we'd like to carry on as we are doing now, on an exclusive basis, and see how things go. We *care* about you, Fiona, very much. You're not a third wheel. You're just one part of a whole. Or at least, we hope you are."

By the time he was done speaking, Fiona was frowning so deeply she probably resembled her chain-smoking grandmother. Then, when her grey matter was done processing, she gaped at him. Turning, she gaped at Logan, who flashed her a hopeful smile. "What do you say, sweetheart? Again, sorry for the rubbish phraseology, but—be our girlfriend?"

After leaping from the chair, knocking James to his backside in the process, she snatched up her tote bag, threw her clothes and shoes into it, and raced for the door, gasping. Her heart raced, and her pulse thundered in her ears. "I need… I need to think. I've got to go, all right? Just let me go!" she added as Logan followed her.

"Well," she heard James say, just before she reached the door into the corridor, "that certainly wasn't the fucking reaction we were hoping for."

Chapter Twenty-Eight

On Monday morning, having gone the long way from her room to the PR & Marketing Suite to steer clear of the public areas of the hotel, Fiona finally arrived at her desk. She was the first to arrive—even Sophia didn't seem to be in yet. But then she was pretty early, having lain awake since long before her alarm was due to go off.

Heaving a sigh of relief at having successfully avoided James and Logan, she put her handbag down and pressed the button to boot up her computer without even checking her phone. It was on silent, and had remained so since Saturday morning when she'd scurried out of their suite, in so much of a hurry that the fact she'd been wearing men's pyjamas hadn't bothered her.

There had been a couple of phone calls since—one from each of them—and a few text messages—all polite, but growing in urgency and desperation. Apparently, they hadn't meant to freak her out and just wanted to talk. But there was no way she was ready for that. What would she even say?

How the hell was it possible to be the girlfriend of two men? As in, at the same time, with everybody knowing about it? A ménage à trois, as it were.

She'd spent the time since their bombshell alternately trying to figure it out and burying her head in the sand. She'd gone for that run, after all, but had headed for St. James's Park rather than Hyde Park, just in case they'd decided to go running too. The last thing she wanted was to bump into them, not while all the weirdness was so raw. She'd needed time and space to think—not that it had helped much.

Now, she was glad to be back at work. She wouldn't have to make a concerted effort to think about something other than James and Logan. Her job would occupy her brain for a good eight hours, at least.

Her computer having booted up, she was just about to click the icon for her emails when her desk phone rang. Jumping so violently that she banged her knees on the underside of the desk, she clutched at her chest and winced as she reached for the handset. "Hello?"

"Hello, Fiona?"

"Speaking."

"Hi. It's Beatrice. I know I'm calling early, but I just saw you walk past my office. I thought I'd catch you before you started work, so I'm not disrupting you too much. I hope that's okay."

Fiona's heart skipped a beat. *Shit.* Beatrice was from the Human Resources Department. Her mouth suddenly dry, Fiona swallowed and forced herself to formulate a response. "Hi, Beatrice. What can I do for you?"

"Could you pop in and see me, please? No need to worry about letting Sophia know where you are. She already knows I want to talk to you."

"Yes, of course. Be with you in a couple of minutes."

"Okay, bye."

"Bye." Fiona's stomach lurched as she put the phone down, and she clapped a hand to her mouth, fearing she was going to be sick. Closing her eyes, she took a handful of deep breaths, willing the panic and nausea to subside. What the hell was going on? Had she not been discreet enough, sneaking to and from James and Logan's various rooms and in and out of the staff entrance? Had someone seen her? One of the security staff, perhaps? They were trained to be as unobtrusive as possible. Maybe there'd been one right there as she had entered their room and she hadn't noticed. *Fuck!* She thought she'd been careful—more than careful, in fact. Bordering on obsessed. She hadn't breathed a word to a single soul about James and Logan, hadn't said anything to even hint she was seeing anyone…

But had someone put two and two together? Noticed she'd missed out on a couple of Friday night get-togethers and not been seen anywhere the following morning? Then there were the flowers… Sophia had tried to dig for information, and got nowhere, and Lisa from Reception had delivered them in the first place. The only reason she hadn't fired off a load of questions was because Sophia had interrupted. Christ, she was really in the shit if a Sherlock Holmes wannabe had been keeping an eye on her.

Standing, she figured she'd better get a move on and get to Beatrice's office. The sooner she went, the sooner this would all be over with. Maybe she could even come back and clear her desk before anyone else arrived, saving her the indignity of having to do it with everyone staring, wondering why she'd been given the boot, but being too polite or scared to ask.

After grabbing her bag and a notebook and pen, more out of habit than actually thinking she'd need them—even her creative writing skills wouldn't get her out of this—she left the department and headed for Human Resources.

The front office there was quiet too, and Fiona passed the empty desks as she crossed to the glass office in the corner. Beatrice, spotting her, stood up and opened the door ready for her. "Morning, Fiona. Thanks for coming so quickly. Please, come on in and take a seat."

Shooting Beatrice a nervous look, she gave a small smile. She didn't seem pissed off, or even the least bit stressed, like she was about to fire someone. But then, she was a professional—she was probably trained not to have feelings about these sorts of things. It was part of her job to conduct uncomfortable meetings about verbal warnings, written warnings, final dismissals and the like. Giving the new girl the boot was no skin off her nose.

"Morning, Beatrice. Thanks." She sat down and placed her bag by her feet, and the notebook and pen on the desk in front of her.

"Would you like a drink?" Beatrice asked. "I probably interrupted you before you even got the chance to make yourself a coffee. I'm sorry."

"N-no, it's okay, thanks. I'm fine." *Not unless you've got a bottle of vodka stashed in your desk. That'd do nicely right about now.*

A tiny line appeared between Beatrice's eyebrows. "Hey, don't look so nervous. I don't bite, you know."

"I…um…" She took a deep breath and made herself look Beatrice in the eye. *Come on, let's get this over with.* "What was it you wanted to see me about?"

The frown remained in place as Beatrice grabbed a folder

that had been sitting on the desk, just off to one side, and placed it directly in front of her. "I've been talking with Sophia about you lately, Fiona…"

Great. Everybody knows! She picked up her pen and gripped it so hard her fingers began to ache.

"About how well you've been doing here, how you've learned so much, progressed. In fact, you've taken to this role like a duck to water. The campaigns you've assisted with and managed have been outstanding. Even the bigwigs have commented. You're quite the rising star, I'm told."

The woman smiled, but Fiona just stared at her. What the hell was she saying? And why was she saying it? Why build someone up, then tear them down? God, she never knew HR folk could be so bloody cruel.

"Honey," Beatrice's voice, firmer now, cut into Fiona's panicked thoughts. "Learn to take a compliment, would you? This is a *good* thing."

"A g-good thing?"

The frown was back. "Are you sure you don't want something caffeinated? It is early on a Monday morning, after all, and you don't seem quite with it yet. I just thought I'd take advantage of you being in the office sooner than planned. I'm a morning person, myself."

"I'm fine, honestly." She gave herself a mental kick up the arse. Clearly, this meeting was not about what she thought it was. Unless Beatrice was the best actress in the world, her body language and the vibes she was giving off were positive ones. "Sorry, I'm just not quite sure what this meeting is about. I'm not used to being unprepared."

"So I've heard." Smiling again, Beatrice continued, "I'll stop beating around the bush. Basically, what I'm saying, honey, is that an opportunity has come up. Right from your interview you showed promise and an interest in climbing the career ladder. You've impressed everyone you've worked with so far, so when this opportunity came up, you were one of the obvious candidates."

Pausing, she took a sip of the water she had by her right hand, then put it back down and focused on the paperwork in front of her. "Some funding has become available for staff training. The various management teams have been putting their cases forward for a few weeks to sort out what funds were assigned where, and now it's all been settled, things are being arranged. There's money in place for you to take some exams—gain some formal PR qualifications. You'd have to start at the bottom, unfortunately, but you'll whizz through the initial course and the exam, then you can move on to the next stage. Before I go on… Is this something you're still interested in?"

Having finally realised she'd got completely the wrong end of the stick as Beatrice had been talking, Fiona now nodded so quickly her brain felt like it was bouncing around in her skull. "Yes, yes, absolutely! I'm definitely, one hundred and ten percent interested, thank you! Please sign me up. When do I start?"

Raising her eyebrows and smirking, Beatrice said, "Well, there are a couple of other things I need to mention to you first…"

"Okay, fantastic." She'd relieved the pen from the death grip now and had it poised over the pad, ready to take notes.

"First, and most importantly, I need to remind you about the clause in your contract with regards to formal qualifications funded by The Portmannow Hotel. Since the money is coming out of the company pot, so to speak, and you'd be taking some time out of your regular working schedule to complete the course, you are legally obligated to remain with the company for at least two years after gaining your qualification. If you wish to leave before those two years are up, you must reimburse the company for the amount of the course. I know it probably sounds harsh, but that's a pretty standard thing across the board."

"Yes, I understand. That's fair enough. You're investing in me, so you want me to stick around for long enough to reap the benefits. Trust me, I get it. But you don't have anything to worry about." Fiona grinned. "This is an amazing place to work. Unless some seriously sexy billionaire suddenly declares undying love for me and proposes, I'm not going anywhere."

Beatrice chuckled. "We do work in close proximity to an awful lot of billionaires. Or millionaires, at the very least." She wrinkled her nose. "But I'm not sure how many of them you'd class as seriously sexy."

"Like I said, you don't have anything to worry about." They exchanged a wry smile of understanding.

"Okay, great. Fantastic. I can see we made the right choice here. And you're absolutely correct in what you say, about investing in you. That's exactly what we're doing, Fiona. Sophia believes in you, and she's really hoping you'll take us up on our offer. It'll be tough, juggling your workload with the course and the eventual exam, but she's confident you'll manage. And she will, of course, provide you with the support you need to make sure you're not overwhelmed. She—*we* want you to succeed."

"I want me to, too."

Sliding a brochure over the desk, Beatrice said, "Here's some information on the course. It's more detailed, and there are web links so you can do further research. Take that away with you and have a good think about it. The academy is taking applications at the moment, so if you could let me know one way or the other by the end of the week, I can get the ball rolling for you."

"Thank you. Though I'm sure it won't take me until the end of the week to let you know. I'm pretty sure my answer is going to be a resounding *yes please*. But I'll be thorough, so I know what I'm letting myself in for."

"I understand. Well, I won't keep you any longer. And I look forward to hearing from you. Just drop me an email, if you like, with your answer. You know where I am if you have any questions, too."

Both women stood. Beatrice moved over to the door and opened it to let Fiona out.

Fiona gathered her things, then paused in the doorway. "Thank you so much for the opportunity, Beatrice. I really do appreciate it."

"Don't thank me." She shrugged. "I'm just the giver of good news. It was Sophia who put you forward. Thank her—and yourself. You've clearly earned it."

"I'll speak to you soon, then. Bye." As she headed through

the door, nodding at the couple of members of staff who'd now arrived ready for their day's work, Fiona's polite smile grew wider and wider with every step she took, until it could grow no more.

Yes! This is it, the opportunity I've been waiting for. I've bloody well done it. The only way is up, baby!

It was a battle to keep walking normally when she wanted to skip and jump like a puppy on Red Bull, but she achieved it, getting all the way out into the corridor. Scurrying into the nearest ladies' toilet, she made absolutely sure it was empty before doing a crazy little victory dance.

Then, rearranging herself into some semblance of normality, she went back to work.

Chapter Twenty-Nine

Fiona's day passed in a flurry of activity. Sophia popped in and out of meetings all day, so all Fiona got was a knowing smile as she passed her desk, which she responded to with a big grin of her own. She was sure Sophia would know it was her way of saying thank you. Maybe she'd have time to actually say the words tomorrow, if Sophia's schedule was less hectic. If not, she'd ping her a quick email, just to express her gratitude—the woman had believed in her from day one, after all. It was important that she knew how much Fiona appreciated it.

She hadn't said anything to anyone else. For one, she wasn't sure if she was supposed to, and she preferred to wait until she was actually signed on to the course. Secondly, it occurred to her there was a chance not everyone would be pleased for her. Perhaps they'd wanted some of that funding to do some courses of their own, and it had been awarded to her, the new girl? Granted, she'd been working there for several months now, but she was still the newest member of the department and she could see why there might be resentment. *Yeah, definitely keep it quiet for now.*

Her tasks for the day complete, she shut down her computer, tidied her desk and left the office, saying goodbye to everyone who was still there on her way out. Still bubbling with excitement over the news, she decided to drop her mum a text message to see if she was around for a chat on the phone a bit later. There was no reason not to tell her family her news, and she was dying to tell *someone.*

As she headed for her accommodation, she pulled her phone from her bag. It was only when she looked at the screen that she remembered it was on silent, and, more importantly, *why* it was on silent.

There were no more missed calls—James and Logan knew she'd be at work—but there were several text messages. The gist being that they were leaving London that evening, and would she *please* at least reply to a text message, even if she didn't want to talk to them on the phone or face to face. They just wanted to know she was all right.

Logan had even risked a little joke.

At least can I have my pyjamas back? They're my favourites. ☺ *xxx*

Unbidden, Fiona smiled. Logan was so often in a serious mood that when he did make jokes, they were all the more amusing. Figuring it was safe now—it had been a couple of hours since the last message—she flipped the switch to put the sound back on. She shook her head at Logan's silly note. She'd already washed and dried the pyjamas in question, so she could sneak up and leave them outside their suite without them knowing.

She navigated to a new message, added her mother as the recipient and began to type.

Halfway through the message, the display changed and the ringtone began playing. Startled, Fiona grabbed more tightly onto the device to stop her dropping it, then grimaced as she saw James's name on the screen. She froze. Should she ignore it and hope he didn't call again? Or should she answer it and find out what he had to say? Her resolve melted a little and she leaned towards the latter. They hadn't actually done anything wrong, other than freak her out. And that reflected more on her than them.

Sighing, she glanced around to make sure no one was close enough to hear her conversation, and answered the phone. "Yes, hello?"

"Fiona! *Finally*."

"Hello, James," she replied coolly.

He sighed. "Don't be like that, sweetheart. We only want to talk to you, to try to sort this out before we go home. We don't know when we'll be in town next, and we really don't want to leave with this… situation hanging in the air between us. Please? Just talk to us, and if after that you still want us to leave you alone, then I promise we will."

"I thought you'd have taken the hint by now."

"Most people probably would have, but Logan and I don't give up that easily. Plus, if I'm honest, we don't know exactly what happened. We'd just like to chat, understand what went wrong. What *we* did wrong."

Now it was her turn to sigh. Running a hand through her hair, she said, "You didn't, James. Do anything wrong, I mean. Okay, where do you want to meet? I'm not coming to your room." She added the last part hastily, thinking neutral territory was best. If she went into their suite, a place designed for relaxation and seduction, who knew what would happen?

Falling into bed with them without actually having a grown-up conversation was unlikely to help the situation in the long run.

And if she succumbed to their not-inconsiderable sexual charms, her post-orgasm addled brain would probably make her agree with everything they said, whether she really meant it or not. No, if this was going to be resolved one way or the other, for good or for bad, it had to be resolved with brains, not bodies—and certainly not hormones.

"That's fine. I'm assuming you don't want us to come to your room, either." It wasn't a question. "How about the bar?"

She shook her head, though she knew he couldn't see her. "No—too public. This is a private conversation, and I don't want to set any tongues wagging." *Especially not after the shock I had this morning, thinking we'd been caught out.* She thought for a moment. "What about the library?" It'd be quiet at this time of day, with people thinking about dinner, heading back to their rooms, freshening up, or just returning from a day on the tourist trail. She was sure they could find a private corner.

"Yeah, all right. Are you free now?"

"I can be. I was just going back to my room." She wanted to slap herself. Why was she being so bitchy?

Fear. You're afraid of what's going to happen next.

"Great." James had either not noticed her tone, or was ignoring it. "We'll go there now."

"Head for the back corner on the right. There probably won't be many people in there, but it's the most private area."

"Gotcha. See you soon." He hung up before she had a chance to say anything else, possibly before she had the chance to change her mind.

Continuing towards the elevator, she stuffed her phone back in her bag for now, resolving to finish the message to her mum later. She'd probably need a dose of normal, everyday conversation after meeting with James and Logan.

Wiping damp palms on the sides of her skirt, Fiona then tugged at the material, straightening it. She ran hasty fingers through her hair, hoping she didn't look too dishevelled after a busy day, because there was nothing she could do about it now.

***

Entering her favourite room in the hotel, she walked slowly, drawing in the scent of the books, knowing it would soothe and calm her. Maybe even give her courage. It didn't matter if she felt brave or not, though. Deep down, she knew this had to happen.

The question was… What would the outcome be? And was she ready for it?

Her heels click-clacking across the floor, she passed the rows of enormous wooden shelving units with their valuable contents. Finally, as she rounded the final row, she saw them. Sitting in her favourite place, no less, and still in their business attire.

Hmm. This could be a good thing. Anyone who does see us— as long as they can't hear our conversation—will most likely draw the conclusion that we're having some kind of business meeting.

She had to work hard to hold her head up as she walked towards them, the temptation to look at her shoes growing greater with every step. But she didn't. She fixed her gaze on a point just behind James's head until she was within a metre or so of the table, which they'd shifted slightly, adding two extra chairs so they could all sit around it. *Like a business meeting.* There was no one in this part of the library other than them, anyway. The only other people she'd seen were over at the computers, right at the other end of the cavernous space.

Both men jumped up, their expressions tentative, and Logan hurried to help her into a chair. "Thank you for coming," he said quietly, his breath fanning through her hair as he pushed the seat forwards under her bottom.

Heat flared between her thighs.

Seriously, hormones? We're in a frigging library, not a bedroom, and all you can think of is sex?

Her next thought was—*having sex in a library would actually be pretty damn amazing. Especially with these two. Multiple orgasms and books at the same time, what could be better?*

Forcing her brain back to the reason they were there, she said, "Okay, I'm here. Let's get on with it."

The men exchanged a glance, then turned their attention back to her. James spoke first. "Well, we're glad to see you're all right, at least. You had us really worried, you know."

Looking first at James's expression, and the hurt in his green eyes, then at Logan, who wore a similar expression, she said, "I'm sorry. I'm fine, thank you. And you?"

"Well," Logan cut in, clearly making an effort to rein in his irritation, and not entirely succeeding, "other than having had a shitty couple of days trying to work out what the fuck we did wrong, we're just fine and dandy, thanks."

James glared at Logan. "Hey. We're trying to sort this out, not make it bloody worse."

Logan held his hands up. "All right, all right. I'm sorry. I'm just being honest, that's all."

James continued, "We're fine, thank you. Now, do you think you could tell us what the hell happened on Saturday? And, more to the point, why?"

It seemed the pleasantries were over. It was time to face the music. Staring at her hands, which she was unconsciously twisting and untwisting on the table, she said, "You freaked me the hell out, okay? We went from what I thought was casual fun and sex to suddenly being all serious and discussing relationship statuses. I wasn't expecting it. You totally blindsided me, and I reacted badly."

"You can say that again," Logan muttered, his brow drawn low.

Ignoring him, James said softly, "And how do you feel now? You're here, so that's a good sign, right?"

The hopeful look on his face made her heart melt, and she smiled. "Yeah, I guess so."

"You seem surprised."

She shrugged. "Honestly? I don't know what the hell is going on in my head. Since I took off on Saturday morning, I haven't figured a damn thing out."

"Can we help, honey? We'd really like to." James reached out and took her hand. When she didn't pull away, he squeezed it gently.

"I don't know. I'm down with same-sex relationships, obviously, but I can't seem to wrap my head around how having three people in a relationship works."

James looked at Logan, then back at her. He gave a wry grin. "Honestly, we don't really know how it works, either. We've only ever had other women play with us on a temporary basis—just as long as the situation suited us all. We've never considered, or wanted, to make anything permanent. Until now."

"Why now?"

Logan interrupted. "We already told you this, Fiona. We *like* you. We like you as a person, like spending time with you. We don't know when, or how it happened, but for us, this has become about much more than just sex. But that's no different to regular two-person relationships—there's not always a defining moment when casual dating, or casual sex, or whatever, becomes something else. We know it's not conventional, but there it is. We're not exactly conventional guys."

"You can say that again," she said, grinning as she parroted his earlier words back to him. "So what you're saying is you haven't got a bloody clue what's going on, either?"

"Pretty much," Logan replied, shrugging. "All we know for sure is we don't want this to end. We're not declaring undying love here, or proposing marriage. We'd just like to continue what we were doing, but make it… more official, I suppose. See where it goes."

"What, tell people?" Her pulse fluttered.

"Relax." James squeezed her hand again. "Nothing like that.

Well, not yet, anyway. I think you're a little hung up on the fact there are three of us. Right, imagine there are just two of us, all right? We somehow skipped the dating, getting-to-know-each-other part and ended up having sex straight away. Then there was the whole kink and fetish club thing." He huffed out a heavy breath and scrubbed his free hand over his hair, fluffing it up. "Fuck, this really is complicated, isn't it? *Anyway,* we can't take that back—and I wouldn't want to—but we'd like to take the next step—acknowledge there's more here than casual sex and move to a more exclusive arrangement. Nothing scarier than that. If it doesn't work out, we go our separate ways. If it does…? Well, I guess we'll have to cross that bridge if and when we get to it. Yes, it's complex, but fuck me, it's fun, isn't it? And our happiness is all that truly matters."

She let his words sink in, mulled them over. He looked earnest, his white teeth trapping that sensual bottom lip…

Snatching her gaze away before the sight distracted her too much, she peered at Logan. He appeared altogether more serious, as usual, but she thought his eyes held a glimmer of hope.

Unable to resist another glance around to make sure there was no one looking or listening, she held out her other hand towards Logan. He took it.

Fiona's heart skipped a beat. Fucking hell, was she really doing this? Closing her eyes momentarily, she shook her head in surprise, then opened her eyes again. "You know what? You're right, James. I've been hung up on the fact there are three of us, hung up on the complexity of the situation. But it's really only me making it complicated. Really, when you think about it, it's simple.

You like each other—well, *love* each other. You like me. I like you. To shamelessly steal your words, James, our happiness is all that truly matters. And you two make me happy. Hopefully I can make you happy, too. Everything else is semantics."

"So," James ventured, "you're agreeing to give it a go?"

"Yes, I am. If you'll still have me?"

Logan squeezed her hand, just hard enough to give a twinge of pain. She looked at him questioningly.

"*Have* you?" he said, his eyes darkening, his voice almost a purr. "I'd like to bend you over this table, flip your skirt up and turn your arse red for what you've put us through these past couple of days, you bloody minx."

The idea thrilled and scared her in equal measure. Arousal began trickling through her body, but she tried her best to tamp it down. "Just as well you two are heading home soon, then. Looks like I've escaped a spanking for the time being, at least." She grinned triumphantly.

What she wasn't expecting was the equally smug grin on Logan's face. She peered at him, getting the sense that something wasn't quite right. "That's what you think, you little brat," Logan shot back at her. "We might have told you a little white lie."

"A-a white lie?"

"Yes. We're not going home tonight. We just said that to force your hand. We're sticking around until the morning."

Fiona's mouth dropped open. *Ohh… fuck!*

Chapter Thirty

James winced. "Any particular reason you've now got my hand in a death grip?"

His words made Fiona aware that she was doing it to both James and Logan, but Logan hadn't mentioned it. Instead, he continued to look at her with that smug expression on his face.

Snatching her hands away, she then surreptitiously wiped her damp palms on her skirt. "S-sorry." She offered no explanation. One wasn't needed.

"So," Logan said, his features now arranged into a look so wicked she half-expected horns to sprout from his head, "will you be joining us in our suite, Fiona? I believe we've got some unfinished business, don't you?"

Emotions rushed through her at a rate of knots—and she couldn't make sense of a single one. *Christ.* She gripped the edge of the table, then increased the pressure until the pain in her fingers and wrists sharpened her mind, allowing her to focus. "Yes," she forced out, meeting Logan's gaze. "I believe we do."

A flicker of surprise crossed his face but was gone so quickly she almost doubted it had ever been there. "Good. Well then, shall we meet you there in… say, no more than half an hour? So we can all get freshened up and change clothes? Though," he added, looking her up and down, "I certainly won't complain if you're still dressed like that. Have I ever told you that business attire is a seriously good look for you?"

"Once or twice," she replied dryly. Standing, she continued, "Well, I'm going to get a move on if I'm to be at your suite in half an hour. See you soon."

***

Twenty-nine minutes later, she knocked on the door to their suite. God, was this making-it-permanent thing even going to be possible? If they wanted to go public, people at the hotel would find out, then her job would be in danger all over again. How could she keep both her job, and James and Logan? Would they consider frequenting another hotel while they were in London?

Her increasingly confusing thoughts were interrupted when the door opened. James stood there, looking mighty fine in a pair of jeans and a tight white T-shirt. He was barefoot. "Come on in, gorgeous," he said, standing back to let her pass, then closing the door behind her.

Heart pounding, she entered what she felt, at that moment in time, was the lion's den. Logan was going to spank her arse. And, given it was intended as a punishment, rather than just for fun, it was going to *hurt*. Sitting down afterwards was going to be an interesting experience.

Just then, Logan appeared in the doorway to their bedroom. He was dressed the same as James, except his T-shirt was black. Fiona stifled a smile. Had that been intentional? White and black? Good and evil? Submissive and Dominant? She doubted it. Just because James was submissive, the most laid-back, and the calmest didn't mean he was an angel. In fact, when it came to beneath-the-sheets action, he was just as passionate, creative and crazy as his lover.

"Good timing," Logan said, his smile as filthy as it had been in the library—possibly filthier.

"Here," she replied, tossing a bundle at him. "Your precious pyjamas. Washed and dried."

After neatly catching the flying garments, he narrowed his eyes. "You know damn well that was a joke. A ploy to get you to bloody well say something."

She shrugged. "Doesn't matter. They're here. I'm here. So what's next?" Bloody hell—why did Logan always bring out the cheekiness in her? She was already set to receive a spanking, so she wasn't doing herself any favours by sassing him.

Or was that why she was doing it? Trying to spur him on to spank her sooner rather than later? She often didn't know why she did certain things around James and Logan, and had given up trying to figure it out. They'd made things simple—focusing on fun and happiness and seeing how things went—so reading too much into things was pointless.

Logan spun on his heel and went back into the bedroom. Fiona and James exchanged a look, but remained where they were. After a beat, Logan called, "In here, you two!"

Fear and arousal rushed through her in equal measure, and she did as Logan had instructed, with James hot on her heels. As she crossed the threshold, she looked around, expecting to see… well… *something*. Something to indicate what Logan had in mind. But there was nothing. He just stood at the end of the bed, peering at them expectantly.

As Fiona and James waited side by side, looking back at him, he broke the silence. "I've had a better idea. As much as I still want to turn that arse of yours red, Fiona, I'm going to wait, just a little while. I think this evening should be a celebration of the three of us, of our new relationship status and of our hopefully very bright future."

Fiona had no idea whether to be excited, aroused or terrified. Logan's facial expression was enigmatic, gave nothing away, and, as a result, made her feel all three of those at once. "Okay…" she said, nodding slowly.

"James?" Logan prompted. "Are you happy to play along for a while?"

"Of course. I look forward to seeing what you have in store, Sir."

"Very good." He shot Fiona a sharp look.

"Yes, Sir," she said quickly, despite knowing Logan was playing her and James off against each other. She'd never be as good a submissive as James. She didn't have it in her. It wasn't the way she was wired, and she was all right with that. The more time she'd spent with the two men, the more she'd come to realise just how well all three of their preferences and personalities complemented each other. Why try to change something that was already perfect?

"On your knees," Logan commanded.

Fiona and James dropped to the soft carpet. She now at least had an inkling of what was going to happen next. And when Logan undid his belt and his fly, then pushed his hand down the front of his jeans, her suspicions were confirmed.

His lips twisted into a lascivious smile. He moved closer to them before manoeuvring his cock from the confines of his clothes. It was hard, and grew harder still as he pumped it a couple of times in his fist.

Fiona's mouth watered at the sight. More saliva still filled her mouth when the scent of him reached her nostrils—clean, masculine and seriously fucking sexy. She licked her lips.

"Eager, aren't we?" Logan said, an eyebrow quirked.

She gulped. "Yes, Sir. Sorry, Sir."

"Don't be sorry, sweetheart. Just suck me." He stepped right in front of her and aimed his swollen dick at her mouth.

She opened her lips and took him in happily, her taste buds tantalised as his shaft filled her mouth. Closing her eyes, she began working him with gusto—licking and sucking at the hot, vital organ, gratified when salty liquid seeped out onto her tongue.

She was just getting into her stride when Logan jerked out, leaving her open-mouthed and blinking in surprise. He then took a step to the side and fed his thick shaft into James's mouth.

Although she was disappointed she hadn't had longer to suck Logan's cock—though there was every chance he'd return to her in a moment—she was more than happy to watch James do it. The sight of the two men together, whether they were simply kissing or touching, tossing each other off, giving each other blow jobs, indulging in their kinks or fucking each other's brains out, seriously got Fiona's juices flowing. There was just something so erotic, so primal about watching them together, and she could still scarcely believe she'd been invited—on a more permanent, exclusive basis, no less—to be a part of it.

As she enjoyed the sight of Logan's thick cock pistoning in and out of James's mouth, bulging and hollowing his cheeks, making Logan moan, her pussy grew wetter and more swollen by the minute.

She was just contemplating whether she'd get away with squeezing her thighs together to get a little light relief when a popping sound alerted her that Logan had snatched his cock from James's mouth the way he had hers. He approached her again, and she parted her lips, taking the saliva-slick shaft as deep as she could, before picking up where she'd left off.

"Oh," Logan said, reaching around to pull the grip from her hair, sending the blonde locks tumbling around her shoulders. "You're both so bloody good." Fisting a hand in her now-loose hair, he held her still and began fucking her mouth.

She'd gone from sucking his cock to being merely a receptacle in the blink of an eye, and her body responded to it. Her nipples pressed against the inside of her bra, and her pussy throbbed and ached, juices seeping into her underwear and threatening to leave a stain on her jeans, too. There was nothing for it, she was going to have to—

"Hey," Logan said, stopping suddenly, his cock still invading her mouth. "Are you trying to get off?"

He didn't wait for an answer. He returned his attentions to James, keeping his eyes on her as James's eager, talented mouth brought him closer to climax. His warning expression told her to behave herself, and by the time he threw his head back and moaned in pleasure, coming between James's lips, her legs ached with the exertion of *not* pressing them together.

Finally, his orgasm apparently having waned, Logan looked back at her while stroking James's face and tucking himself away. "Hmm, looks like you managed to control yourself. Just about. Well done."

"Yes, Sir," she murmured, her mind racing with the possibilities of what would happen next. He'd put his cock away, so did that mean he was going to spank her? If so, would he use his hand, a flogger, a paddle… *a cane?* She really hoped it wasn't the last—she'd managed to avoid it so far, and based on how James had described the agony of it, she hoped to avoid it for a great deal longer—ideally forever.

"Fiona?" Logan said, his tone commanding and querying all at once. "How would you like to fuck James?"

With the strap-on? she wondered, but kept her mouth shut. She didn't want to put ideas in his head. He was already full of them, and she wanted to see what his wicked imagination had come up with, without influencing it in any way. His sexy plans were probably better than anything she could think of, in any case.

"I'd love to, Sir," she said, smiling widely. "If that's what you want."

Chapter Thirty-One

Quirking an eyebrow at her, as if unsure whether her saccharine tone was genuine or put on, Logan said, "Excellent. Stand up, both of you, then take your clothes off."

It was no sensual strip tease, but the action of revealing her body, and watching James bare his, still got her pulse racing. Probably it was the anticipation of what the nudity was *for*. And, with anticipation in mind... What the hell was going on with her spanking? He'd threatened it back in the library, and had seemed good to follow up on it, but now he was orchestrating her and James getting naked and horizontal with no further mention of it.

What was he playing at? Winding her up? Lulling her into a false sense of security?

She grinned to herself. This was one of her favourite things about Logan... She never quite knew what he was going to say or do next.

Now naked, she waited.

His thumbs hooked into his belt loops, Logan circled her and James, making appreciative noises as he considered them. "Good," he drawled as he moved behind them, no doubt eyeing up their buttocks. "*Very* nice."

Oh shit, he's going to do it now!

"Very nice indeed," he repeated, then landed a swift strike on James's arse, followed by hers. They both gasped, and she resisted clenching her buttocks as the pain bloomed across her skin. It'd only make it hurt more when he spanked her again.

Except... he didn't. Continuing his circuit, he paused when

he arrived in front of them. A crooked half-smile twisting his lips, he looked at James's face, then down at his cock. "Well, it's obvious *you're* ready, gorgeous," he said, then stepped forward and grasped James's chin. "You're always ready, aren't you, my horny little fucker?"

With that, he crushed his mouth to James's, possessing him with a passion and ferocity that made a gush of wetness seep from Fiona's core and run down her thighs. Risking a glance down while Logan was otherwise occupied, she saw James was seriously turned on—his cock stiff and thick, angry-looking, his precum so copious that a trickle of it was making its way back down towards his balls.

After several minutes of kissing, in which both men became increasingly vocal, Logan pulled away. James was left gaping and panting, but somehow Logan remained cool and collected, despite the fact his cock tented his jeans. Only that, and his widened pupils and spots of colour on his cheeks gave away his true feelings.

"What about you?" he asked calmly. "Are you horny, girl? Is that sweet pussy of yours slick and ready for James's cock?" Stepping right in front of her, he repeated what he'd done to James—taking hold of her chin and beginning to plunder her mouth. Only, at the same time, he insinuated his free hand between her legs to see just how aroused she was.

He growled into her mouth as he discovered her soaked, molten sex, then deepened the kiss, taking her roughly and ruthlessly until she was dizzy with need. She whimpered.

Breaking their kiss, but keeping his hand busy between her legs, he said, "Yes? What's the problem, girl?" He grazed a fingernail over her clit, grinning wolfishly as she whimpered again.

"Please... Please, Sir."

"Please what? What do you want?"

"I-I want to come, Sir. Please."

"When have you ever known me to deny you an orgasm, girl?"

It was a good point, well made. "N-never, Sir. Thank you."

Turning to James, Logan said, "On the bed, on your back. Rubber up."

The fact that all their decisions were being taken from their hands, that their upcoming fuck was being planned and ordered by Logan could and probably should have taken away from the eroticism. But instead, it added to it. Maybe because she knew what was coming next, and her brain was racing ahead, imagining how it would feel to slide onto James's cock, to have it stretching her walls, stroking her in all the right places...

What she didn't know, of course, was what Logan intended to do while this was taking place. It was a curious mixture of the known and the unknown, and the cocktail was heady.

James had, as always, hurried to do as he was told, and was just securing a condom into position.

"Go on then," Logan said, giving her bottom a playful slap as she turned and clambered onto the bed. "Go and ride him, claim your orgasm. Give him an orgasm."

"Yes, Sir." Quickly, she straddled James's hips, and remained hovering over him. Then she reached for his shaft and held the base to keep it steady while she aimed the swollen crown at her entrance. She met his gaze and smiled as she sank down onto him, taking him in inch by inch until he was buried deep inside her.

"Christ, that feels good," James said, smiling at her.

"Likewise. Now, are you ready? I've been told to ride you, to claim my orgasm. And I'm really fucking desperate for my orgasm, so this could be a bumpy ride."

Gripping her hips, he replied, "Bumpy rides are my favourite kind." His eyes glinted with arousal and mischief.

Wriggling a little to get into a better position, and enjoying the flutters that set off low in her stomach, Fiona then braced her hands on the bed either side of James's chest and began to move. Slow, undulating movements at first. She groaned as James's shaft stroked her insides in all the right places. "God, you feel good."

"You too, sweetheart. You too." Still with his hands on her hips, he guided her movements, subtly urging her to go faster. "Uhhh!"

Ready for it now, Fiona picked up her speed, putting her hands over James's and using only her legs to power her thrusts. Tingles radiated out from her abdomen. She guided James's hands up to her breasts, continuing to rock and bounce on his luscious cock as he squeezed the mounds of flesh.

Already her orgasm was building, and when James began to pinch and roll her aching nipples, she rocketed ever closer, her nerve endings sparking.

Suddenly, a blow landed on her buttocks. Multiple points of contact, sharp stings, but nothing unbearable.

Fuck! Logan was flogging her! And, judging by the gasp

James had just let out, he was getting it, too, probably on his thighs and balls.

Fiona was torn between pausing her bouncing, turning around and seeing what the hell Logan was playing at, and carrying on, riding James even harder and faster, in spite of Logan's sudden flogging.

After a moment or two of indecision, she opted for the latter. Why stop a perfectly good fuck to demand an explanation she probably wouldn't get? And besides, the licks of pain actually added to the experience. The slow build-up a thing of the past, Fiona closed her eyes and let the sensations wash over her as she rode James's cock, driving him into her over and over as Logan continued to wield his implement.

He landed blow after blow on the two of them, the starbursts of pain growing ever closer to agony as he matched his pace and force to theirs. The faster and harder Fiona rode James, the faster and harder Logan swung the flogger. Pleasure mixed with pain until it became impossible to know where one ended and the other began. They blended seamlessly, invisibly, until Fiona was just one big mass of overwhelming sensation. And that sensation soon gave way to her rapidly approaching climax.

She hardly knew what was happening anymore—only that everything felt so damn *good.* Her pussy was being filled and pounded to perfection, delicious shivers rolled over every inch of her, and her clit was fit to burst. So was she. There was just something so perverse about fucking one gorgeous man while being flogged by another. Slipping her hand between their bodies, she sought her aching clit and rubbed it roughly as she continued to fuck James's brains out.

Logan hit her harder, but her veins were so flooded with endorphins that she barely noticed. It just added fuel to the fire. Throwing her head back, she lost herself to pleasure, every last part of her tingling. Then, with an almighty scream, she succumbed to the climax, her heart racing and pulse pounding as her insides contracted around James's shaft, and waves of sheer bliss crashed through her.

James held her hips as she rode out her climax. Moments later, limp and trembling, she opened her eyes and offered him a small smile. Logan had ceased raining blows down on them. "All right?" James asked.

She nodded. "Yes. More than all right. Fuck me, that was intense."

"Fuck you? Well, if you insist." Logan's voice came from close behind, and this time she did turn to see what he was doing.

Now naked, Logan smoothed a condom over his straining shaft. Then, crossing over to the bedside table, he retrieved a bottle of lubricant, before returning to the end of the bed.

Fiona raised her eyebrows. "Are you planning what I think you're planning?"

"Yes. But only if you're up for it."

Just then, James's still-stiff cock twitched inside her, sending a series of tiny aftershocks coursing through her. With a gasp, she said, "Yes, all right. Just…"

"Just what, sweetheart?" His tone was gentle, coaxing.

"Just don't hurt me, all right?"

"I won't. We won't. We'll take good care of you. Remember your safe word. It applies in this case, too. Use it if you want me to stop, all right? Promise?"

She nodded. "I promise."

Thankful that even in the highly charged sexual atmosphere, Logan's priorities still lay with her consent and comfort, she turned back to James. "So," she said, grinning wickedly to hide her nerves. "Where were we?"

James pulled her down so their torsos were pressed together, and murmured, "Better keep it slow while he's lubing you up. It needs to be done properly."

Her response was to kiss him. Tangling her fingers in his soft hair, she sucked, licked and nibbled at his sinful lips and battled with his tongue. They rocked gently together, the sensations different but no less pleasurable than before.

Soon, she felt the dip of the mattress behind her, and heard a squirting sound. Chilly liquid dribbled into her crack, and Logan worked it around the crinkled skin of her arsehole, relaxing her there. Still rocking on James, she heard more squirting. This time, fingertips directly on her hole, pressing gently but insistently.

He stretched her back there, adding more lube until he was apparently satisfied she was ready.

The bed shifted again, and she felt the heat of his body before anything else. She stopped moving on James, and waited. Waited until the blunt head of Logan's cock was positioned against her rear, and did her best to relax as he began pushing inside.

James cradled her face and kissed her harder, likely trying to distract her from any discomfort. But actually, apart from the initial stretch and burn, there was none. He'd prepared her well, and as Logan forged slowly into her, the sensation that overwhelmed her was one of fullness. Complete fullness.

She broke hers and James's kiss and lifted her head. *Wow.* Everything they'd done together, and still it was possible to find something that topped it all. With two cocks inside her, no nerve ending went unstimulated and, as the two men began moving, establishing a rhythm that worked for them all, Fiona, her eyes wide open, stared into James's. A mixture of surprise and satisfaction filled her. She certainly didn't feel like a third wheel now. More like… she was complete.

"Hey," Logan said, leaning down to murmur close to her ear, "this is just the beginning. If this is how it can be, how it has been up until now, imagine what it's going to be like in the future. The three of us together. Fiona—you're amazing. Thank you for agreeing to give this a chance."

James added, "Yes. What he said."

Grinning lazily as they continued to rock together, building up speed, she let herself be carried away on the waves of bliss that lapped at her. As Logan had said, this was just the beginning.

She was very much looking forward to seeing what the future would bring.

Epilogue

Several months later

It was a Saturday morning, and the three of them were lounging around on the plush leather sofas in James and Logan's suite, catching up on the latest news while munching on nachos. They'd had a late night, having visited a fetish event, and were enjoying a companionable silence, broken only by the sounds of the TV and their crunching.

After another disturbing news report full of hatred and violence, Fiona turned away in disgust. "Well, that's my cue to get moving, I think. I'm gonna go for a run. Either of you want to come?"

"Hey," Logan said, catching her wrist and stopping her from getting up. "Wait. Can we, uh, talk to you about something?"

Uh-oh, I'm not sure I like the sound of this.

"Yeah," she said, taking in the awkwardness they both displayed, and wondering how the outcome of a conversation that made them nervous could possibly be good. "Sure. What's up?"

"Oh, nothing's up, sweetheart. This is nothing to worry about. Just, well… Something we need to discuss."

"Spit it out, then," she said, unable to stop her frustration shining through. Despite Logan's words to the contrary, she couldn't help thinking the worst.

Logan was on one side of her, and James got up and sat down on her other side. They each took one of her hands.

Her heart pounded, then skipped a beat altogether.

Apparently unwilling to wait for Logan to 'spit it out' any

longer, James began. "We've been thinking, talking. It's been almost a year since we met—can you believe it?"

Fiona shook her head. No, she couldn't believe it, but knew it to be true.

James continued. "We're so, *so* glad you decided to give this, us, a chance. It's been amazing, hasn't it?"

She smiled, and heat came to her cheeks as her brain was inundated with memories. Amazing was right. In fact, it probably wasn't even a powerful enough word to describe what they'd been experiencing. Three was certainly not a crowd in their case, and the more Fiona had worked past her hang-ups about their unconventional relationship, the better things had become. Having a smart, successful, sexy, kind and loving boyfriend was fantastic, and when you multiplied that by two, it was a magical combination.

"Yes," she finally said, pulling herself out of her reminiscence and answering his question. "It truly has. But," her heart skipped another beat, "why are you talking about it in the past tense?"

Her horror must have been clear on her face, because both men tightened their grips on her hands. "No, no, Fiona!" Logan said, shaking his head and making his curls bounce madly. Not for the first time, he was overdue a haircut, but she loved the mad black mop so much, there was no way she was going to tell him. "It's nothing like that. Quite the opposite, in fact."

"Go on…"

"Well, you remember all those months ago, when we had that conversation in the library here?"

"Yes."

"We discussed our future, or at least part of it. Well… James and I think we have come to that metaphorical bridge. We've come to it, and we'd very much like to cross it—with you."

After swallowing in an attempt to moisten her suddenly arid mouth, she said, "And, uh… What exactly does this metaphorical bridge-crossing involve?"

The men exchanged a glance, then Logan spoke again. "Fiona," he said, his expression serious, "you know we care about you, right?"

"Yeees…" Her uncertainty at where this was going drew the word out to ridiculous proportions. "And I care about you, too. Very much."

A smile flirted with his lips for the briefest second, then was gone again. "Well, that's good… because it's more than that. More than caring about you. I love you, Fiona. I'm *in* love with you."

James piped up. "And so am I. I love you!" The last sentence was said with an excited giggle, and she turned to him, wide-eyed and stunned into silence.

It seemed Logan couldn't handle the silence. Agony laced his voice as he said, "Fiona, say something, please."

Twisting her neck left and right to look at each of them in turn, feeling as though she was watching a tennis match, she replied, "I-I don't know what to say. I really wasn't expecting that."

"You weren't?" Logan said, scornfully. "Are you mad? We're fucking *crazy* about you. And we want you to move in with us."

"Wait—you *what?*" Blinking, she scrabbled to get her thoughts into some kind of order.

Logan sighed, and James cupped her cheek and turned her to face him. His green eyes fixed on hers, he said quietly, "It's really not that surprising, Fiona. Think about it. If there were two of us, this would be the natural next step. So why the hell shouldn't we be the same?"

He was right, and she knew it. Knew it from the very bottom of her heart. The heart that still raced, the heart that loved them, both of them, right back, and fiercely. She'd felt this way for some time, and they deserved to know.

She took a deep breath. They'd said it first, so why was she so nervous? There was no risk—they all loved each other. Life was good. Amazing. *Spectacular.*

"I…" She got to her feet and stepped away from the sofa, then turned so she could see them both at the same time without getting a crick in her neck. "I love you, too. Both of you. Madly!"

Warmth flooded her being as their faces broke into huge smiles. It wasn't conventional, but so what? It was nothing to do with anyone else, and anyone who didn't like it would have to jolly well lump it. They'd agreed long ago their happiness was the only thing that really mattered.

Nodding decisively, she opened her mouth. A thought slammed into her head, strangling the words before they came out. "Shit."

Both men looked at her with concern.

"What is it, sweetheart?" James said.

"I meant what I just said—truly I did. But I can't move in with you. I want to, but I can't."

"Why not?" Logan said, a deep crease appearing between his eyebrows.

"Well." She flopped down onto the sofa behind her, and scraped a hand through her hair. "You know the PR courses I did?" The question was rhetorical, but they nodded anyway. "Well, when they were arranged, I was reminded of a clause in my contract. Basically, because The Portmannow has funded my progression, they understandably want to get their money's worth. So I can't leave the company until two years have elapsed from the completion of my course. My *most recent* course," she added, reminding them all that she'd completed her third only a week previously.

Several seconds passed, and Fiona felt, for some reason, that she had to say something else. "I'm sorry, guys. I really am. Wait for me?" Her voice was tiny by the end, and she hated how meek she sounded. But she couldn't help it—they'd all laid their hearts bare and now she ran the risk of losing it all because of some small print in a fucking contract!

Logan, still frowning, said, "Surely there's an exception to that rule? A company can't keep you trapped somewhere against your will."

Fiona shook her head. "No exceptions. If I leave, I have to pay back the money for the courses—all three of them. I don't have that kind of money."

"Wait," Logan said, "so that's it? If you leave, you just have to pay the money back they shelled out?"

"Yeah. But didn't you hear what I said? I don't have that kind of money!"

"Maybe not, but we do."

"No." She shook her head again. "Absolutely not. I've worked my arse off to get to this stage. I'm not going to walk away now and have it all go to waste. And I'm definitely not going to take money from you to do so."

"Who said anything about walking away and taking our money? We're not looking for a housekeeper, Fiona. We just want you with us, every day, instead of every few weeks. We'd figured you'd get another PR job somewhere in Cambridge or close by. Especially now you've got those qualifications under your belt. You could even consider commuting, if you wanted to. Whatever you want to do, we'll support you. And if that means a *loan* to pay The Portmannow off, then so be it. It's a small price to pay if it means you moving in with us."

"Bloody hell, this is a lot to take in."

"I know, sweetheart," James said, moving over and sitting next to her, "and we're sorry we sprang it on you like this. But we couldn't keep quiet any longer. It's been driving us mad for weeks. It's out in the open now, though, and I couldn't be more delighted. But when it comes to the moving in with us and your job situation, we've no intention of pressuring you. Like Logan said, we'll support you, whatever you decide. Even if you decide *not* to move in with us. We love you, and that's not going to change. Yes, we miss you like crazy every time we're apart, but if that's the decision you make, we'll live with it. We're not going anywhere, all right? The decision is yours, and you make it when you're ready."

Logan piped up, "And nothing's going to change with our job situation. We'll still be in London every few weeks or so. If you move to Cambridge, you can come into London with us. You could stay here as an actual guest, no creeping around, and we can keep attending the various fetish events. I know you're the one who's making the sacrifice here, honey. Trust me, I know. But, ultimately, all we want is for you to be happy. So take a few days, give it some thought and let us know. Okay?"

She nodded, silently implying that she hadn't already made her decision. But she had. Ignoring the part about them paying the course fees, her instinct had been to say yes. They'd been in this kind of limbo for months already, and although it hadn't made her *un*happy, she'd known for a while that the metaphorical bridge was looming. The only thing that could improve on the amazing life they had was to spend more of it together.

Yes, she loved her job, her burgeoning career, and she'd desperately miss her colleagues, her friends, as well as being part of such an amazing team and an iconic company. But what it came down to was—jobs came and went, but a love like this, a love like she, James and Logan had, was rare. And there was no way she was going to let it slip through her fingers. Not a bloody chance.

"Yes," she said, breaking the silence that had fallen.

"Great," Logan said, smiling. "So you'll let us know, then?"

Frowning, she replied, "No, I mean *yes*. Yes! I'll move in with you. Not right away—I'll need to find another job, as I'm not up for the commute, work my notice and so on, but as soon as I can.

I will gratefully take a *loan* from you guys, which I will pay back. And while we're on the subject of finance, we'll need to discuss my contribution to the household—"

Her words were abruptly cut off as James pressed his lips against hers. Startled, she remained motionless for a second or two before responding. She heard Logan's whoop of delight from across the room, then, as she melted into James's embrace, heard Logan again, on the phone this time.

"There's champagne already on ice? Excellent. Great, thank you. We'll be down in half an hour. No, out front is fine. Hey, guys," he continued, interrupting them, "can you put each other down? We've got a limo to catch!"

Fiona and James broke apart and looked at Logan. From the corner of her eye, she could see James's expression wasn't one of surprise. Whatever Logan had planned, he was in on it. "A limo?" she asked. "Where are we going?"

"Going?" Logan said, practically bouncing as he pulled her up off the sofa. "We're going for a quick shower and to get dressed, then we're going for lunch. A celebratory lunch."

"Um, okay… Where to?"

"It's a surprise."

Fiona rolled her eyes good-naturedly. "Okay, but am I going to need a change of clothes? I only have these, and what I wore last night."

"Good point," Logan replied, then dialled out on his phone again. After a second, he said, "Change of plan—make it forty-five minutes. Thank you." He strode over to the door and opened it. "Get a move on then, gorgeous. I want you in your most comfortable smart-casual wear and in front of this hotel in forty-five minutes. If not, I'm coming to your room to give you a hiding."

"And what if I want a hiding?" she shot back, raising her eyebrows provocatively.

With a groan, he said, "Just go. I'll owe you a hiding, all right? Don't be late for this lunch… or what we've got planned afterwards."

After grabbing her stuff, she gave James a peck on the cheek, scurried to the door and kissed Logan on the lips. "Yes, Sir. Forty-five minutes."

Smacking her arse on her way out, he said, "See you then."

She'd just opened the door to her room when her phone bleeped. A text message from James.

For God's sake, act surprised in front of Logan, but I thought I should warn you what we've got planned so you can dress accordingly. Itinerary: lunch at the top of the Shard, a private pod on the London Eye and a boat on the Serpentine. So probably not a skirt ;) I love you, J xx

Almost tripping over a pair of shoes she'd left on the floor in her haste to get into the room, she closed the door before composing a reply.

Wow. Okay, Mum's the word. And trousers it is. See you soon. Love you too, F xx

She pressed send, then hugged the phone to her chest and jigged excitedly on the spot a couple of times, before making a move to get ready. She wanted to be back with her gorgeous guys, and pronto. It looked as though she had yet another amazing day with them ahead, a day of celebration, and hopefully there would be many, many more to come.

***

A note from the author: Thank you so much for reading *Eyes Wide Open*. If you enjoyed it, please do tell your friends, family, colleagues, book clubs, and so on. Also, posting a short review on the retailer site you bought the book from would be incredibly helpful and very much appreciated. There are lots of books out there, which makes word of mouth an author's best friend, and also allows us to keep doing what we love doing—writing.

About the Author

Lucy Felthouse is the award-winning author of erotic romance novels *Stately Pleasures* (named in the top 5 of Cliterati.co.uk's 100 Modern Erotic Classics That You've Never Heard Of, and an Amazon bestseller), *Eyes Wide Open* (winner of the Love Romances Café's Best Ménage Book 2015 award, and an Amazon bestseller), *The Persecution of the Wolves, Hiding in Plain Sight* and *The Heiress's Harem* series. Including novels, short stories and novellas, she has over 170 publications to her name. Find out more about her writing at **http://lucyfelthouse.co.uk**, or on **Twitter (http://www.twitter.com/cw1985)** or **Facebook (http://www.facebook.com/lucyfelthousewriter)**. Subscribe to her newsletter here: **http://www.subscribepage.com/lfnewsletter**

If You Enjoyed Eyes Wide Open

If you enjoyed *Eyes Wide Open*, you may also enjoy the other multiple partner books I've listed below. My full backlist is on **my website (http://lucyfelthouse.co.uk)**.

Stately Pleasures

There are worse things a girl can do to get a boost up the career ladder.

Alice Brown has just landed her dream job as property manager at Davenport Manor, a British stately home. It's only a nine-month contract to cover maternity leave, but it will provide her with the vital experience she needs to progress in her chosen career.

However, her dream job soon threatens to become a nightmare when she discovers her boss, Jeremy Davenport, in a compromising position. Her shock is exacerbated when Jeremy, far from being embarrassed or apologetic about what happened, manipulates the situation until somehow, she's the one in the wrong. He and his best friend, Ethan Hayes, the head of security at Davenport Manor, give her an ultimatum. Faced with the possibility of losing her job and endangering her future prospects, Alice reluctantly agrees to their indecent proposal.

When the dust settles, Alice comes to the conclusion that playing their kinky games isn't such a bad thing, after all. But what happens when she thinks she's falling for both men?

More information and buy links (http://books2read.com/statelypleasures).

The Heiress's Harem Box Set

How does a young woman go from being a long-term singleton, to having four gorgeous guys? Find out in The Heiress's Harem box set.

Contains the complete series, all three books for the price of two—Mia's Men, Mia's Wedding, and Mia's Choice.

Book 1, Mia's Men

Mia's world has fallen apart. Then, just when she thinks it can't possibly get any worse, it does.

Mia Harrington's father just lost his brave battle with cancer. Naturally, she's devastated. With her mother long-since dead, and no siblings, Mia has a great deal of responsibility to shoulder. She's also the sole beneficiary of her father's estate. Or so she thinks.

Unbeknownst to Mia, her father made a change to his will. She can still inherit, but only if she marries a suitable man within twelve months. If she doesn't, her vile cousin will get everything. Determined not to lose her beloved childhood home, she resolves to find someone that fits the bill. What she isn't expecting, however, is for that someone to be into sharing women with his best friend. In the meantime, Mia's friendship with the estate gardener has blossomed into so much more.

She can't possibly plan to marry one man, while also being involved with two others …or can she?

Book 2, Mia's Wedding

Planning a wedding is stressful enough, and that's without a harem of gorgeous men to deal with.

Mia Harrington has had a difficult time of it lately—her father's illness and subsequent death, then finding out she must get married if she is to inherit what's rightfully hers. Fortunately, she's tough and resourceful, and has emerged relatively unscathed from this period, as well as finding herself a suitable husband.

However, things are far from simple. Mia might be planning to marry investment banker Elias Pym, but she's also having a relationship with his best friend, Doctor Alex Cartwright, and is in love with her gardener, Thomas Walker. Add to that broken dates, flashy proposals, a sexy Asian tech billionaire, and a nosey housekeeper, and you've got a situation hectic enough to drive even the most capable person to distraction. Can Mia juggle her men, her job, and the wedding arrangements, or is her happily ever after over before it has even begun?

Book 3, Mia's Choice

But what happens *after* the wedding?

The last few months of Mia Harrington's life have been tumultuous, to say the least. Losing her father, the bombshell in his will, followed by her multiple whirlwind romances and subsequent marriage—it's little wonder she's so thrilled to be spending three weeks in a tropical paradise with her four men. Rest, relaxation and a hefty dose of fun is precisely what they all need.

But the unconventional honeymoon isn't all sea, sun, sand, and scorching sex. Back home in England, they have careers, responsibilities, other things that take up their time. Being in each other's pockets on a tiny island is a challenge—but is it one they can rise to? Will this make or break their relationships? And when being away from it all gives them time to think, what impact will that have on the decisions they make about their futures?

More information and buy links (http://books2read.com/heiressboxset).

Chasing the Chambermaid

Can an exciting new outlook on life help Connie heal her damaged heart?

Connie White is running away from an abusive relationship. Fear and desperation have driven her to Bowdley Hall Hotel in the Scottish Highlands, where, despite an unceremonious start, she appears to have fallen on her feet. The owner, Frances McKenzie, is kind and understanding, and seems happy for Connie to hide out in her hotel for a while.

With a roof over her head and a job as a chambermaid, Connie is in a better situation than she could ever have hoped for. Her workmates seem nice, but she's determined to keep them at arm's length. After all, how can she form connections if she's unwilling to divulge anything about herself?

Her apparent mysteriousness doesn't faze her gorgeous new colleagues Will MacIntyre, Nico Moretti, and Ashley Fox. All three show a keen interest in her, but Connie has absolutely no intention of going there. She hasn't fled one relationship, only to get involved with someone else, no matter how gorgeous. She simply isn't ready for that.

When an epiphany of sorts makes her realise she's living a half-life by keeping herself so cut off from everyone, she finally lets someone in. That someone shows her there can be something between singledom and a full-on relationship. And when casual dating is on the cards, anything is possible…

More information and buy links (http://books2read.com/chasingthechambermaid).

Printed in Great Britain
by Amazon